the LEAVING season

CAT JORDAN

HarperTeen

An Imprint of HarperCollins*Publishers*

HarperTeen is an imprint of HarperCollins Publishers.

The Leaving Season
Copyright © 2016 by Cat Jordan
All rights reserved. Printed in the United States of America.
No part of this book may be used or reproduced in any manner
whatsoever without written permission except in the case of
brief quotations embodied in critical articles and reviews. For
information address HarperCollins Children's Books, a division of
HarperCollins Publishers, 195 Broadway, New York, NY 10007.
www.epicreads.com

Library of Congress Cataloging-in-Publication Data
Jordan, Cat.
The leaving season / Cat Jordan. — First edition.
  pages cm
  Summary: "Middie Daniels is torn between the memory of her
missing boyfriend, Nate, and Nate's brooding best friend Lee"
— Provided by publisher.
  ISBN 978-0-06-235137-1 (hardback)
  [1. Love—Fiction. 2. Missing persons—Fiction.] I. Title.
PZ7.1.J78 Le 2016   2015015558
[Fic]—dc23   CIP
                           AC

Typography by Erin Schell
16 17 18 19 20 PC/RRDH 10 9 8 7 6 5 4 3 2 1

First Edition

For P, who said "I love you" first

the LEAVING season

CHAPTER *one*

Nate called it a shade box.

"A shade is a memory," he once told me. "What's left of a person or place after they're gone."

The box was for cherished objects, keepsakes, curios, the special things you wanted to hold on to and remember forever and ever. Nate had about a dozen of them. All made of wood, a few inlaid with mother-of-pearl, some carved, some sanded so smoothly I could see my reflection in them. He got them from all different places, and each one was special to him.

The one I bought for his trip was the first one I'd ever gotten for him, which is kind of crazy when I think about it.

In all the years we'd been together, I never gave him one. Not for lack of trying; I just never found the right one. But this shade box was perfect and I knew because Nate had picked it out himself.

Last year, almost exactly, we were driving back from Sunset Bay, where we'd spent a weekend at his family's summer house swimming and hiking and beachcombing and, well . . . *not* doing any of those things. The gift shop next to the gas station in Tenmile was the size of a broom closet, and it was filled from floor to ceiling with one or two of *everything*. Nate could have spent an entire weekend in there, picking his way through every shelf.

The only thing he wanted was a rectangular wooden box with hand-carved curlicues and leafy vines and wild animals on top and a gold-plated clasp and hinges. It was about eight inches long and four wide, the size and depth of two really nice paperback books. Inside was lined with the softest black velvet I had ever touched.

Nate loved it. "I feel like whatever I put in there wouldn't just last forever—it would become lucky, you know?" If I could have afforded it, I would have snapped it up then and there.

It was a week later that Nate made his decision to take a year off between high school and college to go with Global Outreach, a nonprofit that provides vaccinations to underprivileged children in Central America. I knew I had to give him the perfect shade box—and fill it with *our* memories—to take with him. Every day for a year I put something inside the box—a note, an object, a memory—representing us.

First date? Check.

First kiss? Check. (Note: *not* the same day).

There were names and dates and places, glass beads and a flat skipping stone, a funky little knot of red and green yarn. I smiled, remembering that bit of fuzzy string. Two Christmases ago, in the five minutes when knitting was cool, I made Nate a sweater. It was an obnoxious red snowflake pattern on a neon green background, and it looked much better in my head than in, well, yarn form. I was so certain it would look fantastic on him. Sadly, when the sweater was complete, it would have fit someone five inches taller than Nate's six-one frame and about twenty pounds heavier.

I was crushed when I saw how it hung on him, but Nate loved it and wore it proudly. "You *wish* my girlfriend made you one of these," he told his basketball teammates with his arm wrapped firmly around my shoulder. "You're all just jealous." He was so convincing and so steadfast about it, I actually felt my cheeks burn with pride.

Before I snapped the lid on the shade box, I placed one last item inside. Beneath the velvet lining was a secret compartment. Nate would have to empty the contents of the box before he could find it—*if* he found it.

I imagined him in Honduras, at the end of his year, relieved to be returning home to me, the box finally empty after three hundred and sixty-five days. He would see the folds in the velvet and stick his finger between them. Curious, he would poke at it until he discovered that there was a false bottom that slid open. He would smile with surprise and then . . . would he cry?

"Oh, Middie, I love you," he would say.

And that's what I wanted. Because I loved him too. Always and forever.

"Middie! Come in, come in!" Nate's mother had to shout over the excited din of the house. "You look so pretty!" She held me at arm's length, her gaze traveling from my French braid to my Grecian sandals. "I love this dress!"

Mrs. Bingham would know: she was as fashionable as they came in our small town of Roseburg, Oregon, where most women considered the L.L.Bean catalog the bible of good taste. For Nate's going-away party, she wore a garnet poplin sundress with pink trim and a soft belt at the waist that showed she still had a figure after four children. She was barefoot, as she often was in the summer, and her toes were painted in the same deep purple-red as her dress. It wasn't hard to see where Nate got his good looks and auburn highlights: his mother was stunning in a simple, uncluttered way.

"Oh, this? Thank you!" In truth, I had agonized over this dress. It was pale blue cotton with appliqué flowers along the skirt and a smocked top. Very classic. It was a relief to hear Nate's mom compliment it. She and Nate had similar taste.

"Come say hello to everyone." She hooked my elbow

around hers and led me from the high-ceilinged foyer of the Colonial to the family room, where all of the Binghams—cousins and kids and babies and aunts and uncles—were gathered. In my ten years of knowing the family, five as *the girlfriend*, I'd had an opportunity to meet every single one of them.

But there was one I hadn't met yet. "This is my great-aunt Pamela from Eugene," Mrs. Bingham said, introducing an elderly woman in khakis and a tangerine knit top straight out of Bean's summer sale catalog. She had hearing aids in both ears.

"Auntie Pam, this is Nate's girlfriend," Mrs. Bingham said a little loudly.

The woman smiled uncertainly. "Hello."

"I'm Meredith Daniels—"

"Middie Daniels," Nate's mom said and then looked at me. "Oops. I'm sorry, sweetie."

"Oh, that's all right." Middie was a nickname I'd had since I was a kid. I was the middle child between my sisters, twenty-year-old Allison and nine-year-old Emma. I didn't mind so much when my family and Nate used the name—even though I'd been trying to be Meredith for a while now.

Aunt Pamela leaned into Nate's mom. "She's the one, isn't she?" she said in a voice loud enough for the rest of the universe to hear. "The one he's going to marry?"

Oh my god. I felt my cheeks burn with embarrassment as every head in the room turned to me. Mrs. Bingham was gracious. "Auntie, there's still a lot of time for that, but we sure do love our Middie!"

Those were the last words I heard as I bolted from the family room straight into the empty-thank-god kitchen. *Oh my god, oh my god.* It was one thing for Nate and me to talk about a future, and quite another to hear about it from his mother and great-great-aunt.

I ran some water in the stainless steel sink, careful not to splash the cold cuts and sandwiches Mrs. Bingham had artfully arranged on a platter on the counter, and rinsed my hands. The cool well water calmed my racing pulse.

What was I so nervous about? I didn't really care about Aunt Pamela's gaffe or Mrs. Bingham calling me Middie or the dress it had taken me a month to pick out.

It was Nate. And it was Nate spending an entire year away from me—not at Lewis & Clark College, which was a three-hour car ride away, but in Central America, in a tiny village with no clean water or internet service—no reliable phones or transit.

It wasn't familiar. It wasn't safe. What if something happened?

"Don't be silly, Middie." I heard Nate's voice in my head, answering the question I'd asked a thousand times. "Global Outreach isn't some fly-by-night organization. And I'm from Oregon. I've spent time in the wilderness. I can handle myself."

I knew that. I did. Still . . .

I opened my purse and felt the shade box inside, wrapped in recycled paper with a bow fashioned from Sunday's comic strips. Being green was important to Nate. He'd appreciate the effort.

Through the window I saw his twin sisters and younger brother playing in the backyard. They were entertaining their cousins—the girls and their swings, their brother and his basketball hoop. I didn't see Nate anywhere, though. I closed my eyes and listened for his voice, imagining where he might be. I knew every nook and cranny of this house, every squeak of the hardwood stairs, every squeal of the hot water pipes. I knew which doors swelled in their frames during the summer heat and which ones needed an extra tug to make them close properly in winter. I knew the boys' bathroom on the second floor always smelled like cat litter, even though the Binghams had no cats, and I knew that the side porch was the worst place to make out because the sound traveled through the whole house.

It was comforting to know these things. It made me feel like I belonged, like I had a special place in this family. Sure, I had my own family—and I loved them too—but Nate's was different, just as Nate himself was different. He was . . . like the shade box in my purse. Perfect.

I felt hands cover my eyes, and I yelped involuntarily. "Nate!" I turned around and leaned my back against the sink as Nate nuzzled his lips along my neck. He wrapped his arms around my waist and pressed his chest to mine.

Oh! How I will miss this when he's gone, I thought as we kissed. Five years ago we'd had our first awkward peck on the lips after ice skating with a group of friends from junior high. Even though we'd graduated far beyond that, kissing Nate made me as nervous now as it did then. I hoped it would be like that for us forever.

When he finally released me, I felt my lips tingling as if I'd been mildly shocked; I ran my finger along them. Nate was a good kisser, but seriously, what was *that*? He saw my confusion and laughed.

"Tingles, huh?" His voice was husky and he lifted one thick black eyebrow at me.

"Um, yeah. . . ." I giggled and felt my cheeks blush.

"Lip balm," he said. "Cassidy and Chelsea gave it to me for my trip. It's cinnamon, but it's supposed to have a million SPF or something like that." He shook his head with a grin.

"That's sweet!"

His smile sagged almost imperceptibly, but I knew him so well, I could see the subtle change. He was thinking about how much he would miss his sisters. "I think they just liked that the tube is purple."

I took his hands in mine, clasping them gently. The pads of his fingers were callused from basketball, his palms rough from working timber with his dad all summer. "They want to take care of their big brother," I said.

He laughed again. "You know they think this is their

chance to get into my room. Chelsea's already planning to redecorate it. There's a *lot* of pink involved."

I rested my head against Nate's chest and listened to the steady thumping of his heart. He was about to leave for a whole year. I wished I could absorb his calm and hold it within me.

A year . . . I could feel my breath about to catch in my throat and tears sting my eyes. *Do not cry, Meredith Daniels! Do not! Not now, not yet.* I fanned my face with my hand and looked at the floor for a moment before meeting his gaze again. "How exactly did you sneak up on me?"

He grinned and pointed to his feet. "New sneakers."

They were lightweight track shoes, blue nylon with bright yellow stripes and green soles.

"Another gift from the twins?"

"Nope. Scotty picked them out. Little brother's got taste."

"Yeah, I do, don't I?" We both turned to the side door, where Nate's eleven-year-old brother was standing. He wore black, red, and white—Trail Blazers' colors—on his oversize jersey and long shorts. He was a mini-Nate, with a tangle of auburn-highlighted hair and the sprinkling of freckles Nate had long since grown out of.

Scotty rolled his eyes when he saw us embrace. "You guys! Don't do that near the food. Geez!" He bounced a basketball on the linoleum floor as punctuation.

"Do what? This?" Nate grabbed me then with both hands and made ostentatious kissing noises.

"Nate! You said you'd shoot hoops with us!" Scotty protested.

"I will, I will."

Scotty's basketball dribbled on the floor, *thump, thump, thump*, echoing Nate's heartbeat.

"Scotty, take that outside, please, and leave Nate alone," Mrs. Bingham said as she swept in with the no-nonsense, take-charge attitude I'd often seen in Nate. She reached for the platter of sandwiches with one hand and lifted it high over our heads. Just before she left the kitchen, Nate called to her.

"Hey, Mom, we're gonna take Rocky for a walk, okay?"

I looked at him. I was not really dressed for a walk in the woods with a dog. He grinned at me.

*Oh, a **walk**.* I bit my smile back and glanced away.

"Fine with me."

"But Nate!" Scotty's voice was on the verge of a whine. "You promised!"

"Scott, what did I just tell you?" his mother said. "Go. Now."

Scotty groaned and stomped his feet as he went back out to the court. Nate smiled and took my hand, whispering, "Let's walk the dog."

My fingers tingled at his touch, no magic balm required.

"Um, guys, hey?" Mrs. Bingham said. "You forget something?"

We both glanced around at the counter and floor. I spotted

my purse near the sink. The shade box! I quickly slipped the strap over my shoulder. "Thanks, Mrs. Bingham."

She smiled slyly and jerked her head toward the side porch, where one elderly mutt was sprawled in a pool of sunlight. "I meant Rocky."

Nate clapped his hands and the dog slowly rose onto shaky legs. "Come on, Rocky! Come on, boy!" My heart always broke a little when I saw Nate try to play with his dog. And Rocky was Nate's, no question about it. They were nearly the same age, Rocky having been rescued when Nate was a little boy, right before Scotty was born. He slept at Nate's feet, greeted him every day after school or practice, and accepted every command from Nate, no matter how hard it was for him to move.

As sentimental as Nate was, I was always surprised he didn't feel the same way I did: sad. "When I look at Rocky, I see the puppy he was," he told me once. "I never see him as an old dog."

Which really tells you everything you need to know about Nate.

No sooner had we stepped outside than we were nearly trampled by the strawberry blond twins. Chelsea and Cassidy jumped off their swings and ran to Nate. He was like a rock god/superhero these days.

"Nate, push us! Push us!" they said in unison.

Nate gripped my hand tighter and whispered. "Just once, okay?"

I pushed down my impatience. After all, they were losing Nate for a year too. It was right to be gracious.

Nate used both hands to push each of the girls as hard as he could, sending them soaring over our heads. They squealed with delight while their cousins begged for the same.

"Nate! Nate! Nate!"

It was like an obstacle course of small children. I gritted my teeth and accepted it. My turn would come—eventually. And as I stood there waiting for it, I felt a cold nose nudge my hand. I glanced down to see Rocky's wide eyes begging for some attention. His white muzzle seemed to smile when I gave it to him.

Finally, after every cousin got a push on the swing, Nate feigned exhaustion and then fell against me. "Come on, let's go before they realize I'm faking."

He grabbed my hand and we ran to the edge of the Binghams' property, where a corral fence separated the woods from the yard. A pair of Douglas firs towered majestically as if they were welcoming us to the forest.

That was one thing about growing up in a lumber town in the Pacific Northwest: we knew our trees. Fir, pine, hemlock—each had its own personality. I always considered the firs to be protective guardians—evergreen sentinels watching over us.

Yeah, I know. Pretty corny.

Nate tugged me farther into the woods to a clearing near the stream that flowed through the mountains past his house and mine. On a summer day like today, the water sparkled like it was made of diamonds. Rocky eagerly lapped at the stream before plopping himself down in a patch of sun.

Nate sat on an old tree stump and pulled me down onto his lap.

"Watch my dress!" I cried as I tumbled. "It's brand-new!"

"For me?"

"Yes, well, for your *party*."

"Aw, you didn't have to do that." He carefully arranged my dress so it didn't touch the forest floor. "You could have worn nothing and I'd be just as happy."

I giggled as he tickled me. "I'll *bet* you would!" I held on to the back of his neck with both hands and stuck my tongue in his ear—*not* romantic at all, just wet and gross. Like that lizard he thought was funny from the Disney movie about Rapunzel.

He immediately recoiled. "Ugh! Do *not* do that again." He wiped his ear with his sleeve.

"How about this instead?" I leaned in again, this time with a gentle kiss. He kissed me back. A kiss that said, *We are alone and I like it that way.*

No kids underfoot. No parents interrupting. No dogs begging—at least not this one, who still lay happily sprawled by the stream. Here in the forest the only sounds were the bubble of the water, the whistling of a few sparrows, the swish of tree branches.

Nate's lips left mine, but he buried his head against my

neck, burrowing under my braid. "Oh, Middie, it hurts to think of being without you."

I exhaled. "Yeah. I'll be so . . . lonely."

"You?" he said. "Nah, you'll have plenty to do while I'm gone." He traced the line of my jaw to my ear with his finger, and then played with my earring, a long dangly heart-shaped pearl with a gold loop.

"Like what?"

"Like . . . I don't know. Applying to college? Graduating? It's your senior year."

"So?"

"So . . . we've got plans. You've gotta make it into Lewis & Clark so we can be together when I get back, remember?"

I smiled. "Yeah. I will."

"When I come back, we'll get started on the rest of our lives together." He took my hand and kissed my fingertips, one by one. "College, engagement, med school, marriage, family . . ."

A shiver ran up my spine when he kissed my pinkie finger for that last one. Family. Our family. His and mine. It felt so far away from where we were and yet, not nearly close enough.

"Sure. Just like that," I said, softly snapping my fingers. He kissed me again and I felt light-headed in his arms. *College, engagement, med school, marriage, family . . .* I thought.

But first, he needed to come back to me.

The shade box was burning a hole in my purse. When we

came up for air, I reached behind me and pulled it out.

"Ta-da!"

He looked surprised. "What's this?"

"You didn't think I would forget to give you a going-away present, did you?"

"Well, no, but . . ."

"Your brother gave you sneakers—"

"He picked them out. He didn't *buy* them."

"And the twins gave you lip balm—"

"I think Cassidy found it in my mom's purse."

"And your parents gave you a big party—"

"They're my *parents*. That's what they do."

"Nate! *I'm* giving you something," I said and firmly pushed the box at him.

He smiled sheepishly. "Okay." He took the package and turned it over in his hands, examining every inch of it.

Grrr . . . Why wouldn't he rip it open? Sometimes he was so maddeningly patient!

He grinned up at me. "You hate that, don't you?"

"What?"

"That it takes me forever to open a present."

"Not really." I tried to shrug, but he knew me so well. "Just open it, okay?"

He carefully slid the bow and ribbon off and then unpeeled the tape with painstaking care. He grinned again. "I might want to reuse it."

"Oh my gosh, I am going to kill you!" I grabbed the paper

from him and balled it up, then tossed it toward Rocky. The dog sniffed once and then went back to sleep.

Seeing what was underneath, Nate inhaled sharply. "Middie . . . the box. You . . . you got me the box?"

I smiled with pride. Folded my hands in my lap. "Yep. I did."

He ran a finger along the woodwork. "But it was so expensive."

"I, um, I saved some money. No big deal." *Gave up Saturday-morning lattes at the Matchbox, took on a few extra babysitting and tutoring gigs . . .* He didn't need to know. "You like it?"

He squeezed me in response. "I love it." He was about to open the clasp when I stopped him.

"No! Not yet. Wait until you get there—to Honduras."

"Why?"

"There's, um . . . stuff inside."

He cocked his head to one side. "Stuff? Nothing that will get me in trouble when I cross the border?"

"Ha, ha." I took the box from him and turned it over in my hands. "It's just some things to remember me—us—by." I held it up in front of him. "Every day you're gone, you can reach inside and take one thing out. For a whole year."

"For a year? I can take one thing out *every single day*?" I nodded and was rewarded with an impressed grin. "That's three hundred and sixty-five things, Middie. In this box."

"Um, yeah, Nate, I think I know how long a year is." I

laughed and handed him the box back. Now he was truly impressed. His eyes widened and he shook his head.

"I can't believe it."

"That I could cram three hundred and sixty-five things inside? Some of them are *really* insanely tiny."

"No. Just . . ." He stopped. "You found three hundred and sixty-five things to remember about us."

I placed my palms on the sides of his face and brought my lips to his. "Try a million. I can think of a million things to remember about us."

We kissed again, the shade box between us, its edges pressing hard against my rib cage. But I barely noticed. For the moment, it was just me and Nate in this vast forest. For all I knew or cared, it was just us in this world.

One of our last kisses, I thought, *for a full year.* I kissed him greedily, swallowing him up with my lips, my hands. Across town, across the country, were other girls like me doing the same thing? It was the leaving season, after all, the dog days of summer, when high school grads went off to college for the first time. Those of us left behind were desperate to hold on, afraid if we let go, we might be forgotten or cease to exist. Or maybe that was just me.

"Middie . . ." I heard him whisper. "I love you."

"I love—"

Bzzz! Bzzz!

"I lo—"

Bzzz!

Nate released me briefly and then fished his phone out of his pants pocket. He held up the screen. "Mom." He silenced the vibration and then quickly texted her.

I leaned back against the tree and rubbed my palm against the whorls of bark. Just then, my phone buzzed in my purse. I reached in and glanced at the screen. *Dad*. I dashed off a text too: *On my way.*

"I guess we've been ignoring the real world," Nate said with a sigh. He helped me to my feet and we each brushed the other free of leaves and twigs.

The real world? I thought. *Can't this be the real world?*

A voice in my head answered, *It will be—soon enough, it will be.*

I took Nate's hand and swung it gently by my side as we walked back to the party. Nate clutched the shade box to his chest with a grin. I couldn't help but grin back; I had made him happy.

I wanted to make him happy for the rest of my life.

CHAPTER *two*

Lockers at our high school were sacred spaces: staff stayed out, allowing us creative freedom to decorate the interiors however we chose, asking only that we didn't leave food overnight and that we cleaned them out at the end of every year. Girls taped up photos of friends and boyfriends, stored love notes and to-do lists, maybe a dried flower from prom, while guys hid a pinup or two behind their football practice or band rehearsal schedules.

I was one of the first at school. I woke up before my alarm in anticipation of meeting Nate for our usual morning run. I was nearly out the door when I remembered Nate left for Honduras yesterday. I even reached for my phone a few times, checking for messages from him. Of course, there were none. My morning felt strangely empty.

With almost an hour to spare before first bell rang, I took my time putting mementos up in my locker: a photo of Nate and me dressed up for last year's Spring Fling, another of us at a poolside party. As I taped each picture to the metal walls, I was reminded of one more outing, one more event, one more party or date or kiss we'd shared. I supposed it was my own shade box.

Just as I was putting the finishing touches on my decorating, I heard my name. Haley Larkin, one of my best friends since grade school, was hurrying toward me, blond braid trailing behind her, canvas book satchel strapped across her chest. "Middie! Middie, we are *seniors*!" She grabbed my hands and twirled us in a circle in the center of the hallway. "Seniors! Whoo-hoo!"

I rolled my eyes, even as I laughed. "You did not just say 'whoo-hoo.'"

"I did. And I'm doing it again. Whoo-hoo! Senior year!" Haley had a contagious smile. Her blue eyes dazzled and shone when she was happy, which was often. She was like a walking positive affirmation, spreading sunshine wherever she went. Except when she was on the softball diamond. Then she crushed everyone in her path. "This is going to be the best first day ever."

"Our *last* first day," I told her when she stopped spinning us. I went back to my locker to get my books for our first class.

"You make it sound so *dire*," she drawled. Her eye caught the photos in my locker, and her smile twitched. "Do you think you can't have any fun without *him*?"

"I think I can get along without my boyfriend for a year."

A year? I gulped, swallowing my anxiety. I could do this. I had Haley and my friends and my classes and family and a million other things to keep me busy. A year would fly by before I knew it, just like Nate said.

"Of course you can! I'll help you!" She tapped a finger against her chin and squinted as if she was thinking hard. "You know . . . there *is* a party on Saturday night."

"Uh-huh." I eyed her warily.

"Dr. Haley thinks a little beer pong is just the treatment you need."

"Well, maybe . . ."

"Really?" Haley's eyes lit up.

Nate and I didn't go out much. We preferred to spend time in his parents' rec room. Haley always understood, even if she wished we'd come along.

"Senior year kickoff party with my best friend!" She clapped with glee. "It'll be amazing!"

Typically, kickoff parties involved gathering around some body of water—either a lake at the edge of town or someone's backyard pool. There were the obligatory kegs, very little food, and lots of making out. Nate and I went to his last year, and it was okay. I couldn't imagine this year's would be much different.

The first bell rang. We had three minutes to get to class.

"Let's do this. Hold it up." Haley lifted her schedule from her satchel.

I grabbed mine from my locker and held it up to hers to compare. "Hmm . . . AP English? Is that it?"

She nodded. "All your classes are for nerds."

I elbowed her with a smirk. "Shut up."

Haley slammed my locker door closed for me. "Senior year, here we come!"

I glanced back at the hallway and saw students quickly filling up the wing: football players and cheerleaders in uniform, lost freshmen desperate for a friendly face, sophomores thrilled to no longer be freshmen. I closed my eyes and smelled someone's breakfast—a fried egg sandwich— sweet coffee in a teacher's travel mug, and a hint of bleach used to clean a locker.

I'd write it all down in a letter to Nate later.

"Middie, come in, please," Mr. Ziegler said, raising his voice a bit over the ring of the last bell. He'd been my guidance counselor since my freshman year, although I rarely needed to see him. Today, however, we had to talk about my college applications.

Mr. Z's cheeks were round and ruddy and he wore glasses perched on the end of his nose. He loved to travel, and his office was filled with souvenirs of his trips from around the world. Every summer he visited a different country, happily crossing one off his list when he returned.

He moved aside a pile of Italian language books for me to sit in a chair opposite him. "How's the new year look?"

I resisted the urge to tell him it had only been one day, and an easy one at that. I rattled off my classes. "AP English, Spanish, and history, Calc 2, Honors Chem."

He nodded, an impressed look on his face. "So, Lewis & Clark, is it?"

"Yes, sir. I've got a campus tour scheduled for November."

"Fine school. Anyplace else?"

I hesitated. "No. Not really."

He leaned forward and I felt his stare. "Why not?"

"Because . . ." *Nate is going there.*

But I couldn't say that. It sounded too . . . Mr. Z wouldn't understand.

"I like it." I'd only visited the campus once before with Nate. It was nice, a lush environment, not much different from our small town. In fact, it kind of *was* our small town, with pretty brick buildings, cafés, green lawns, and a decent football stadium. "I follow their dean on Twitter." I held up my phone as if I needed to remind him what Twitter was.

He frowned. Maybe he did need to be reminded. "That's all well and good, Middie. But it's not a bad idea to have a second choice, or maybe even a third."

My pulse quickened. "You don't think I can get in? Is it my grades?"

"I just want you to consider other options. That's all.

It's a big world out there."

"Oh. Okay, sure." But I didn't need a second choice. I had only one. I picked up my books and started to slide off the chair. "Anything else, Mr. Z?"

He grinned, appreciating his nickname. "No worries. Go do your thing." I could just imagine him thinking, *Do your thing . . . That's what the cool kids say, isn't it?* I smiled to myself as I closed the door to his office.

Hurrying off to my SAT prep class, I felt my phone vibrate in my pocket. A text. *Miss u. Luv u. xo.*

I smiled and felt my cheeks blush. Nate. Somehow he'd gotten a few characters off.

My fingers dashed over the keys: *Miss u more. NM4eva.*

A moment later, it buzzed again. By some miracle had Nate found a Wi-Fi connection in Central America?

Party! Whoo-hoo! the screen read.

Haley. I shook my head with a laugh. I sent one back to her: all exclamation points.

Nate found the community garden two years ago when he was searching for a volunteer gig that would look good on college applications. He wanted something outdoors since he loved spending his free time in fresh air. Naturally, he convinced me—and eventually others—to join him there.

We typically harvested one or two days each week and then spent a day boxing and delivering fresh greens and vegetables to people around town. While I was often nervous visiting private homes, Nate was the picture of confidence. Everyone knew who he was and looked forward to seeing him on their doorsteps.

Today was a harvesting day. When I arrived, I snapped a photo of the vegetables we were going to pick and sent it to Nate.

In the office, I waved to a couple of older, graying volunteers who were finished for the day and washing their hands at a wide stone sink.

One of them called to me over the running water. "You talked to Nate yet?"

"Not yet."

"You tell him all us old ladies said hello, all right?"

"Will do."

They giggled behind their hands like my little sister, Emma, would. Nate would be tickled knowing he had fans back home.

I grabbed a pair of canvas gloves that hung on a nail under a strip of tape with my name on it. Next to them were Nate's. While mine were daintily flowered with purple and pink daisies, his were striped in blue and white. I ran my bare fingers over his gloves, as if I could take a little of him with me, before tying a tool belt around my waist and heading to the garden with a wicker basket.

I really hoped I could talk to him soon.

"No phones at the dinner table," my dad said around a forkful of beets. One of the perks of the community garden was free vegetables, which my parents loved but Emma hated. She'd have preferred that I work at McDonald's and bring them leftover McNuggets instead.

Tonight Mom had roasted the beets with basil and olive oil and served them alongside cold chicken. The night was so warm, we ate on the back patio under the stars, with citronella candles burning to keep the mosquitoes away. The moon was a mere sliver of white, but it shone brightly enough to light up our backyard.

"Dad, you know I'm waiting to talk to Nate." I sighed and sat back in my chair.

My mother's brow creased. "I thought you talked to him yesterday."

I plucked a beet from my plate and popped it in my mouth. The juice left stains of red on my thumb and forefinger. "No. We were supposed to, but . . . it's been weird. He's busy, I guess." I spun my phone on the table, hoping I could jar loose a call. All I got for my efforts was another text from Haley about the party on Friday night.

Emma glanced over my shoulder at the message and opened her mouth as if she wanted to say something. "Yes?" I dared her.

My little sister liked to poke her nose where it didn't belong. She'd tattled on me before, on the rare night when I'd come in a few minutes past curfew.

Her gaze held mine and then flickered away. "It's ringing."

"What?"

She pointed at the table. "Your phone. It's ringing."

"My phone . . . It's ringing!" I had put it on silent. I forgot! I snatched it off the table. "Nate!" His face was on the screen, calling me for a FaceTime chat. I pressed Accept.

My mother waved me away from the patio. "Go inside, please."

With my phone held in front of me, I dashed indoors. On the screen, Nate made a face. "Stop running, Middie! You're making me nauseous!"

I laughed but didn't slow down until I'd gotten upstairs to my bedroom. I collapsed onto my bed and placed my phone on my knees. I wanted to smother the screen with kisses but settled for an air-peck near his lips.

"Where are you? How are you? Is it awful? Are you okay?" My words came out in a rush before I'd even given Nate a chance to say hello. I took a breath and smiled. "Hi."

"Hi." His grin was soft, his eyes tired. A hint of stubble dotted his chin. I wondered how long he'd been awake. The time difference between Oregon and Central America was only an hour. "I'm outside Tegucigalpa," he said. "There are two other Americans with me, and we're training with the doctors now. And learning Spanish."

"But you speak Spanish!"

"It's different here," he said. "Like, I *know* the language, but then when I'm surrounded by it . . ." He rolled his eyes as if he were overwhelmed. "It's not easy." His smile slipped a little, betraying anxiety. *My* Nate? Worried?

"You'll be fine," I told him soothingly. "What about the training? Do you like the doctors?"

"They're amazing!" He went on to tell me about the group of doctors and relief workers who were part of his team, about the other volunteers from the US and Canada. I didn't catch all of it as the connection between our phones started to drop out. While Nate talked, I slowly rose from the bed and walked to the window, hoping to get more bars on my phone.

". . . rainforest . . . ," I heard. And then ". . . gangs . . ."

Gangs? We had talked about some of the dangers. In Central America there was a lot of unrest. Was he seeing signs of it already—before they had even left base camp?

"What? Nate, you're breaking up." His face pixilated on the screen and then righted itself when I leaned out the window and got more range. "Nate?"

"I'm here," he said, waving a hand at me. "Middie?"

"I'm here too." I waved back.

"This is probably the best it's gonna be for a while," he admitted with a frown. "The service is only going to get worse when we leave for the village."

I felt my chest tighten. "What about texts?"

He held his phone out farther from his face and I saw his shoulders shrug. I strained to see behind him, to get a picture of where he was and what he was doing. I couldn't see much but a bulletin board with a map on it and the corner of a metal bunk bed.

His image started to get funky again. *No, no, no!* I leaned farther out the window until my head and arms were free. I filled my lungs with clean late-summer air, as if I could suck it all in for Nate. There was so much I wanted to tell him: the SAT prep classes I was taking, his old-lady fans at the farm, the upcoming party. But it all paled in comparison to what Nate was doing and where he was doing it.

"Middie? I should go. I'm really tired and I have to get up early."

"Oh, sure." But I didn't want him to leave—not yet. "Did you open the box?"

"The box? No, was I supposed to?"

"Get it! Open it! But just take one out, okay? One thing?" I waited while he rummaged in his backpack for the shade box I'd given him. When he came back to the phone, he held it up. "Reach your hand in and close your eyes," I told him.

He did as I instructed, closing his eyes to me. He looked like he was sleeping with a smile on his face. "Can I open my eyes?" He peeled open one eye at me and squeezed the other shut.

"Yes! What do you have?" I watched with delight as he stared down below the screen at something I couldn't see. He grinned in recognition. "What? Which is it?"

He held the fortune cookie paper up to the camera. *The love of your life has always been right in front of you.* "Your fortune," he said. "From our anniversary dinner last year at Kung Pao."

I laughed into my hands, blushing. "Yes! You remembered!"

He rolled his eyes. "Middie, I rem . . . thing." His image was breaking up again. His voice skipped and cracked apart.

"Nate? Nate?"

". . . iddie?"

"I miss you, Nate."

". . . iss . . . oo . . ." *Miss you too,* I filled in the blanks.

"I love you." But it was too late. He was gone and I was staring at the words "Call Failed" across a black screen. *Tomorrow,* I told myself. We would talk again tomorrow night, and I would hear him tell me he loved me too.

On the edge of the windowsill, hands holding tightly to the sides of the wooden frame, I leaned back and found a constellation of stars high in the sky dotting the velvet blackness as if they'd fallen from a giant's kaleidoscope. The brightest of them seemed close enough to touch; I just knew that if I could climb upon a ladder, I could pluck it from among its twinkly friends and hold it in my arms.

And wish upon it forever.

CHAPTER *three*

The barn at the old Dayton Feed wasn't much more than a cavernous structure with rotting wood and only half a roof, but a group of seniors had cleverly turned it into a party scene: strings of lights were crisscrossed along the beams, fresh bales of hay were stacked for convenient make-out corners, and an old carriage housed the kegs. Haley and I arrived when the gathering was in full swing. We recognized just about every person there—every group on campus was represented. And not just the typical jocks, but also the nerds and musicians, the math whizzes, the crafty girls, and the drama geeks.

Haley wrapped her arms around me from behind as we

made our way through the crowd toward the carriage, where the kegs were. "Oh my god, Middie, this is it. This makes it officially senior year. Drink it all in." She cast her gaze around the barn, allowing it to linger on several guys huddled in the center of the barn, quietly talking together. "Hmmm . . . I don't remember Rick McKinnon being so tall."

I found Rick among the group. He wasn't bad-looking; fortunately, the shadows cast by the bare bulbs of the strung lights hid his acne. "Maybe he grew over the summer."

Haley smiled wickedly. "You know what they say about tall guys with big hands."

I snorted a laugh and felt a blush creep into my cheeks. "Hale! Geez."

"What?" She was all innocence. "They wear big gloves." She giggled as she drew two beers from the keg, handing me one. It was half foam, which didn't truly bother me since I, the designated driver, wasn't planning to drink it anyway. Nate and I weren't big partiers. He didn't even like the taste of beer.

Haley turned to me. "So . . . opinion? You think Rick could be Senior Year Boyfriend?"

"Do you want one?" That would be a new experience for her for sure.

"Maybe. I don't know. Isn't that a bucket-list kind of thing? 'Have a steady guy in high school'?" She made air quotes with her fingers, still holding the plastic cup.

I took a small sip from my beer. *Gross.* Maybe I would put

"Drink an entire beer" on my bucket list.

As we watched, two girls with matching French braids and gold hoop earrings approached Rick and his friends. The boys immediately made room in their circle for them.

"Rats!" Haley said with a laugh. "Time to seek out another target." She took a sip of beer and together we watched the room swell. More and more kids were arriving, filling every nook and cranny of the barn. Haley was buzzing with excitement, while I just wanted to shrink into the hay bales and wait for it to be over.

Haley pulled out her phone. "Katrina and Debra should be here by now. I'll text them to see where they're at."

Katrina and Debra wouldn't miss a party if it were held on the moon. They never seemed to have curfew, yet they also managed to deftly skirt trouble.

"Stupid barn is giving me crappy reception," Haley grumbled. "My text isn't going through. Hang on. I'll be back." She slipped into the crowd with her phone held above her head, texting as she walked.

I took a seat on a hay bale to wait. Everyone milled around laughing and yelling, but also *looking*. Glancing out of their periphery or nakedly staring—trying to find *someone*. A person to hook up with tonight or maybe a hookup that would lead to something more.

I had found my guy, and I knew I was lucky. I didn't want to be doing *this*: wandering the crowd, wondering who was around the corner.

My mother didn't understand why Nate and I were, quote, "so serious at your age." But what was the alternative? This? Was *this* supposed to be better?

Nate and I weren't boring or predictable; we were solid. Comforting. And I wanted that for Haley too.

"Oh great, *you're* here?" I heard someone say. I looked up from my beer foam as Lee Ryan approached. He was Nate's best friend, but we'd never gotten along much; he was kind of a slacker, known to smoke weed and skip school. He was so *unlike* Nate, which really tripped me up: How could someone as disciplined and responsible as my boyfriend hang out with a guy who wasn't much more than a surfer dude—without the surf?

Like Nate, Lee was tall but he slouched in a way that made it seem like he wanted to look smaller. He wore a faded brown T-shirt and jeans that hung off his hips, Converse low-tops with dirty laces. His sandy hair was shaggy, the style overgrown, and his high cheekbones emphasized his scrawniness. He might have been cute—even Haley's Senior Year Boyfriend material—if he tried a little harder. But in his appearance, as in all things, Lee just didn't seem to care.

He had a beer in each hand. I held up my own. "I already have one."

"Who said this was for you?" He chugged one cup until it was empty and let out a soft belch.

"Nice."

"You're welcome."

"What are you doing here?"

"Such a friendly greeting, Yoko, thanks," he said.

I felt my face grow warm. I hated being called Yoko, as if I'd somehow prevented Nate and Lee from being besties. As if I had broken up the band.

But that wasn't true. Nate designated time for each of us. They did their thing—whatever that was—and Nate and I did ours.

"This is a party for seniors," I pointed out, "and you already graduated."

He put one foot up on the hay bale beside me and bent forward. I smelled yeasty beer on his breath. He wagged a finger at me. "Did I, Meredith? Does anyone ever *truly* graduate from high school?"

"Uh, yeah, you did. And you were so wasted you didn't even stand up when they called your name at graduation." Nate had had to shake him to get him to the podium to accept his diploma.

"Wasted?" He cocked his head to one side and considered me. "I'm pretty sure I was just napping, but you may be right." His smile was lopsided and lazy. "So, what's new with our Nate?"

Our Nate. I bristled. "He's good. Talked to him last night."

Lee's hazel eyes lit up. "So did I! He's in Tegucigalpa."

That startled me. Which it shouldn't have, I realized. After all, *best friends talk*.

"We did FaceTime," I told him.

"So did we. I told him he needed to shave."

For some reason, this irritated me even more. Not that I had any proprietary hold on Nate, but neither did Lee. And I was the one who had to kiss that face.

"It was crazy, huh? Not hearing from him for so long?" Lee asked.

I felt my mouth tighten to a line. Lee held my gaze, and I saw a twinkle of delight crease the corners of his eyes. Was he trying to tease me—or bait me? I took a deliberate sip of my beer and made a face. I couldn't help it. It was disgusting. Lee laughed.

"Gotta love a cheap keg," he said. He chugged some too and then flung the rest of the watery stuff on the ground, where it was soaked up by bits of straw. "You seniors really know how to party."

"Not up to your standards?"

"Nope." He pushed his foot off the bale just as Haley emerged from the crowd with Katrina and Debra, giggling and sloshing beer in their cups as they tried to drink and walk at the same time.

"Whoo-hoo! Seniors!" Haley called out.

Lee raised one sandy-blond eyebrow in their direction. "Wanna introduce me?"

"Not really."

Lee's eyes widened in surprise and so did mine. That came out a lot harsher than I had intended.

He waved me away with his empty cup. "No worries. I'm not looking anyway."

As in *I've got a girlfriend*? Now *that* was surprising. I stopped myself before I could say anything rude. But it didn't matter. Lee read the unspoken thought on my face and his gaze hardened.

"See ya around, Yoko," he spat before he left. I was relieved to see his lanky figure disappear into the crowd. He wasn't supposed to be here anyway.

"Too bad *you're* not the one in Tegucigalpa," I said to myself.

Over the next couple of days, I called Nate a few times to wish him luck on his first day of work, but each time I received the CALL FAILED message. His mom had the same result when she tried contacting him, but as she reminded me, the village was remote and cell coverage spotty. We would certainly hear from him within a few days.

Fortunately, it was delivery day at Roseburg Community Farms, and the farm's manager, Abby, gave me plenty of work to keep my mind occupied. Long wooden tables were set up in the back of the office, where we filled orders for the local deliveries, ranging from small businesses like a senior group home to individuals and families around town.

When I arrived, the produce was already on the tables and Abby was handing out the list of orders to be filled. A few older ladies and one man were seated in chairs around the tables. I couldn't help but notice I was the only youth volunteer. I supposed without Nate, there wasn't much incentive for other volunteers our age to come.

The lone man glanced up at me, his hands filled with heads of romaine lettuce. "Nate not with you today?" He pushed a pair of black-rimmed glasses higher up his nose with the back of one hand and came away with a smudge of dirt on his chin.

The woman beside him scowled and wiped the dirt off for him. "Nate's away now. You knew that, Harry. We had a party, remember? The cake?"

Harry nodded. "Oh yes, the cake. It was good cake."

After a few minutes of catch-up chatter, we settled into a quiet rhythm and the only sounds in the back office were the soft scraping of the cardboard boxes sliding along the table, the crinkle of paper bags as they were folded and stapled shut, the occasional punctuation of "Roseburg Farms!" as Abby answered the phone in the front.

"...she's in there," I heard Abby say. Feet shuffled across the concrete floor and we all glanced up from our work at the interloper who was disturbing our meditative silence.

"Hey, what's up, old people?" Lee said. His eyes scanned the room, ignoring the scornful looks from the so-called old people he'd just insulted. I cringed when I saw how quickly he'd turned the room against him. "Middie! Hey, Middie, it's me!" he shouted, waving.

He was deliberately aggravating. The room was all of

about four hundred square feet, but he was flapping his hands around like he was calling to me from across the Grand Canyon. I wanted to sink straight into the floor.

Reaching for a handful of potatoes, I avoided meeting Lee's gaze. "What are you doing here?"

"You ask that same question every time I see you." His gaze took in the room and he waved at each of the volunteers, who glared at him in return. I shoved the potatoes into a box. Why *was* he here? Just to annoy me? Or was he actually a new volunteer? My heart sank at the thought.

He leaned over my shoulder and began rearranging the vegetables in the box.

I pushed his hands away. "Don't touch my potatoes."

Lee grinned exaggeratedly. "That's not what the other girls say."

I felt my cheeks blush despite myself. "Seriously, Lee—"

"Chill, it's no big deal."

I continued to work but peeked sideways at him when he wasn't looking. He was wearing a black T-shirt with the words *Mötley Crew* over a silk-screened image of a pirate playing a guitar. His blue jeans had holes in the knees and frayed hems, and his low-tops were decorated with green and blue Sharpie.

"You're staring at me," he said coyly as he waved his fingers in front of my face.

I felt the eyes of Harry and the others on me. "Please. If you're going to stand there, make yourself useful."

"Whatever you want, Yoko."

I pressed my lips into a line. "Do *not* call me that." Then I grabbed a pen and pad of paper with the words *From our farm to your table—Roseburg Farms* written in scarlet script at the top. "Write down what's in each box very clearly and then tape it to the side."

His head lolled lazily toward me, and he jerked his chin at the box. "I can't see inside. Tilt it. No, more this way. A little more." He shrugged. "Still can't see."

I sighed. He was exasperating. I scooted closer to him and showed him the contents of the box. He licked the tip of the pen and began writing.

"Dear Veggie Lover—"

"Don't write that!"

"Dear Vegetable Lover?"

"Just list the items in the box." I held up a tomato. "One tomato."

"Is that with one *e* or two?" I grabbed the pen from his hand and he grabbed it back. "I'm helping!"

"No, you're not." I dropped my voice to a whisper. "You're being a pain."

"In your ass?"

I felt my lips start to twitch into a smile. *Stop that, Middie!* I turned my head so he couldn't see me blush. "I think you should go."

There was a long pause. "Fine." He stood up and waved to the group. "Bye, peeps! That means 'people,' in case you don't know." He turned in a circle. "How do I get out of here again?"

Ugh. "Come on." I led the way from the back room through the office and into the parking lot. Once we were out in the sun, Lee stopped and glanced around, shading his eyes.

"Now, where did I park . . . ?"

Oh my god. "There are five cars in this lot. One of them is—"

Lee snapped his fingers. "Oh, that's right, I don't have a car. I have a motorcycle." He pointed at the space between a Honda and a Toyota.

"That's not a motorcycle," I told him when I saw where he was pointing. "That's a *scooter*. It has a *kickstand*. And it's about a hundred years old."

His ride was a slate-blue Vespa with a leather seat that could fit, at best, one and a half riders. It had a pair of round mirrors jutting out above the handlebars, attached by chrome rods, with a single headlight in the center. A chrome handle wound around the seat for that half person to hold on to.

"Looks pretty motorcyle-y to me. It has a motor and two wheels . . . with which to cycle."

He swung his leg over the seat as if he were mounting a huge Harley. With one foot braced against the splashguard, he turned the key in the ignition and the engine gently *putt-putt*ed before catching.

He revved the engine, which sounded less like a dangerous beast and more like a swarm of angry hornets. He flipped up the kickstand with his heel. "Well, take it easy."

That's it? I grabbed the handlebars before he could turn the scooter around. "Why did you come here today, anyway?"

He stopped and squinted as the cloud cover shifted, revealing the sharp circle of sun against a pale blue skyscape. "Oh yeah. You talked to Nate?"

I shook my head. "No reception. You?"

"Nope. I sent him an email. He might get it if he can find a landline."

"I'm sure he's just between towers," I said, echoing Mrs. Bingham's optimism.

"Yeah. See ya round," he called out over the buzz.

Shielding my eyes with my hand, I watched Lee pull out of the lot and away from the farm, sweeping the dirt road in a lazy S-shaped pattern.

Helmet, I thought with a start. He wasn't wearing a helmet.

Then I stifled a laugh.

Big, tough no-helmet guy—riding off on his puny little scooter.

My little sister, Emma, at nine, was at the tail end of her Brownie career. More than anything, she wanted to be *older.* And crucial to her growing up was *me* moving out. Not for the room of her own, which she had now, but for the solitude of being an only child. I couldn't imagine what that was like. Allison had it for a little while before I arrived, and Emma would have it soon, but me? I am the middle child. I have always been surrounded by others.

"You'll miss me when I'm gone," I liked to tell Emma whenever she pounded on the bathroom door.

"No, I won't! I'll watch all the cartoons I want and eat candy on your bed!"

She *would* miss me, though, just as I missed Allison. Sure, we chatted online and she came home for visits each semester from Willamette University, but it wasn't the same without her around. *I* was the older sister now, the one Emma had to look up to. And it wasn't easy, especially when it came to projects for her Brownie troop.

"You're not doing it right!" Emma fumed as I attempted to iron a patch onto her Brownie sash.

"It's fine." I pressed the tip of the iron against the patch, finished the edging, and held it up in front of me. "Look, it's perfect."

Emma inspected it more closely. "Not perfect. But . . . okay."

The ironing was something I'd happily taken over when Allison left. I was afraid Emma would burn herself or her bedspread if she did it on her own. And besides, there was something soothing about pressing all the wrinkles out— making a sheet or a cotton shirt crisp and perfect.

While I ironed, Emma told me all about her next

Brownie task, which would get her a leadership patch. I wasn't so sure Emma wanted to be a leader as much as she wanted to gussy up her sash.

"I have to write a story," she told me as she carefully hung the sash near her beloved Brownie uniform.

I shut the iron off to let it cool and settled in among the pillows on Emma's twin bed. I stretched my legs in front of me while Emma arranged and rearranged the items in her closet. "To be a leader, a Brownie has to inspire others," she said with a proud tilt of her chin. If it hadn't been for the flowered headband on top of her shimmering blond hair, I'd have thought she was already a teenager the way she carried herself. "I need a story that makes other people inspired."

"Like . . . ," I prompted her. "What have other Girl Scouts done?"

"*Brownies*, Middie. We are Brownies. Not Girl Scouts."

I made a rolling gesture with my hand. "Whatever, Emma. Just tell me."

She flopped onto the twin bed next to me and stretched her legs out as I had. The lace-edged pillows engulfed her tiny head and muffled her voice. "My friend Cynthia's story was about her uncle who was in a war."

"That's good." While she gave me the rundown on all of her friends' inspirational tales, my gaze wandered the room. Not long ago we had shared it: our twin beds side by side, a single lamp on a table between them. We'd had one alarm clock too, which meant Emma rose at the same time as I did. We'd even shared Allison's old vanity and its rickety ladder-backed chair. Now all of this was Emma's alone. My room, which once belonged to Allison as well, was on the other side of the house, its windows facing the street. Here, we had a view of the garage and a backyard surrounded by trees.

"You know, I have to write a story too," I told Emma when she stopped to breathe. "For college applications they have these—"

"Don't use Nate!" she said, her eyes wide. "He's mine!"

"He's . . . what?"

"He's my story." Emma sat up and swung her legs over the side of the bed. "He's all smart and always helping people and he's my friend even if he is your boyfriend and I can use him as an inspiration to other people because maybe other people will want to volunteer and help the misfortunate and maybe I will too because of him!" She finished with a gasp for air.

"Unfortunate. The people are 'unfortunate' not 'misfortunate.'"

"Whatever." She mimicked my get-on-with-it gesture, which was a little annoying coming from a nine-year-old.

"I'm not *using* Nate," I said. "I have to write a story about *me*."

"You? You're not inspiring."

"Well, thank you very much. Do they give out badges for being rude?"

"I don't think so." She glanced up at the ceiling in thought. I could see the wheels turning in her head: *Can I get a badge for being rude?*

"So as I was saying, I have to write an essay about myself for my college applications."

Specifically, the Lewis & Clark application requested an essay that told them something that defined me, an event or experience that had made an impression on my life. I had absolutely no idea what I would write about.

My sister gave me a begrudging nod. "All right, as long as it isn't about Nate."

I shook my head. "Don't worry, it won't be." Emma had always known Nate, I realized. We'd been friends and then dated for ten years of my life but *all* of hers.

Back in my room, I turned on my laptop and carried it with me to the bed. As soon as the Wi-Fi connected, a message popped up from Allison. She was online and wanted to chat. I opened a window and typed a greeting. **Hey, Ali!**

Almost instantly, I received a reply: **u up?**

Duh. **Yes.**

Can u look in my closet for a skirt?

I grinned. **You mean MY closet**

topshop, black mini

I'm busy

Go Now

"Fine, I'm going," I said to my computer as I hauled my butt to the closet. Despite having left for college two years ago, Allison maintained an extensive wardrobe in *my* room, taking with her only one season's worth of clothing at a time. It wouldn't be so bad if we were the same size, but she was quite a bit taller than me.

I fanned a hand through her side of the closet, searching for a black miniskirt that had wide, flat pleats and a hidden side zipper. I knew exactly the one she was talking about because I'd tried it on when she was gone.

My phone rang before I'd had a chance to look for more than five seconds. I snatched it from my dresser. "What?"

"Are you in front of my closet?" Allison's voice greeted me.

"Stop calling it that. And yes, I am." I poked my head in farther, inhaling the scent of cedar that lined the walls of the closet.

"Do you see it?"

"Oh my god, give me a chance to look!" I put the phone back on the dresser and pressed Speakerphone. I could hear my sister breathing on the other end of the line. "Why do you need to know if it's here? It's not like I'm going to mail it to you."

"Why not?"

I laughed. "You live two and a half hours away."

"You're going to drive it up here, then?"

"Ha! No."

"Then get thee to the post office, sister-friend."

"Can't you wait till you come home?"

"Nope. Hot date."

I raised an eyebrow. "Really? Who?"

"Whom."

"No. It's 'who.' Just because you're in college—"

"He's no one. Just a guy."

I stepped deeper into the closet and called out over my shoulder. "A guy you *have* to put on an awesome black skirt for." I was up to my neck in Allison's clothes, but I still couldn't find the skirt she wanted. "Even if I do find it, you're not gonna get it till next week."

"Overnight it."

I had to laugh. "Is this guy worth an expensive FedEx delivery?"

A long pause and then I heard her sigh. "You're probably right. Forget it."

I grabbed my cell and took her off speaker. "Wait! I was just kidding. You sure?"

"My skinny jeans are pretty hot," she joked. "They'll have to do it for him."

I laughed and pulled a chair up to the window. I cracked it open to feel a cool breeze on my face. Climbing through the closet had made me sweaty.

"You know, Al, I've never been on a date," I told her. It was weird to say it out loud, but it was true.

My sister snorted. "You've been on plenty of dates."

"Not really. Not like you. I knew Nate for five years before we got together. It wasn't ever *him asking me out* and *me getting all nervous*. Is it fun?"

"It sucks! You gotta worry if the guy likes you, if he has another girlfriend, if he *wants* a girlfriend, if he just wants a booty call—"

"A booty call? You? No way."

"I could be a booty call," she joked. Her voice was haughty. "When it works out, yeah, it's, I don't know . . . exciting." She paused. "Anyway, you don't have to worry about it."

"Yeah, I guess you're right." But I did have something to worry about—and that something was gnawing at my brain. "Hey, what'd you write for your application essay to Willamette?"

I tapped the screen of my laptop and opened the application. Every field had been filled in—my name and address and so on. But the space for the essay was a big fat blank. "I can't think of anything to write."

"Hmmm . . . I can't remember. It must have been good, though. I mean, I got into three colleges."

"Gee, thanks." I flopped back on the bed and rolled onto my side. On the other end of the line, I heard voices calling to my sister.

"Oh, hey. I gotta go, Mid. Talk later?"

"Sure, okay." I was always reluctant to let Allison go. It so often seemed like she was on the verge of sharing something really important. I clicked off the phone and returned to my computer, paging through my bookmarks until I found one of my favorite websites, a vintage clothing reseller. I loved the looks of the dresses on these pages even though they were styles and textures I'd never worn before: soft and flowing with layers of chiffon over silk, lace over cotton, lovingly embroidered with flowered appliqués and trails of beads.

These dresses were completely impractical and I loved looking at them. I imagined myself at my wedding with Nate, dressed in a diaphanous cream-colored gown with a beaded bodice and velvet trim, pulled in tight at the waist, with loose, flowing sleeves. I'd even bookmarked a photo of one I especially liked, but I'd never shown it to anyone, not even Nate.

I glanced at the time on my phone. It was just about ten where Nate was. I dialed, fingers crossed the call would go through. After three failed attempts, each one crushing my optimism a little more, I texted him instead.

Miss u, love u, NM4eva.

CHAPTER *four*

In the morning, my phone was still in my hand and my body twisted around it, as if I were protecting it in my sleep. I stared at the screen. *Miss u, love u, NM4eva.* I sat up quickly, my heart leaping to life. But it didn't take long for me to realize that was my message to Nate. It hadn't been answered.

I felt a stiffness in my shoulder and back from sleeping in a pretzel shape and a mild ache in my neck. This day was not off to the most promising start.

It didn't get any better.

At school, it seemed like every teacher had agreed *this* would be the day to give out massive amounts of work. After ten days of classes, we were slammed with homework assignments and a killer midterm exam schedule. I didn't foresee a break until almost Thanksgiving.

Haley felt the pinch too. In last-period AP English, our only class together, she slid into the desk beside me and dropped her head on it with a *thunk*. "Oh my god, Middie. I'm swamped. Literally swamped."

"Well, not literally."

She turned her head to the side and stared up at me, one cheek smooshed into her nose. "Yes, literally. There is a swamp of homework around me. Math, history, chemistry. It's more than a swamp. It's a sea. An ocean of work."

I chuckled at her hyperbole even as I reached across the aisle to gently shake her shoulder. "We'll be okay."

"Promise?"

"Promise."

She smiled and pulled herself up off the desk; strands of blond hair clung to her eyelashes, and she blinked them away. "Maybe a little extracurricular activity will help." She dug her cell phone out of the pocket of her jeans. "Check it out."

I peeked at the screen as she opened an evite with a photo of an inflatable bounce house. "A kids' party?"

"No, no. That's what it *looks* like, but watch. . . ." She tapped the screen with her finger and the bounce house magically transformed into a backyard pool. "Ta-da! Katrina's. Saturday. Her parents are going to a wedding or something." Haley put her finger to her lips and then mine, swearing us both to secrecy. "Very hush."

"She sent an evite, Hale," I said with a laugh. "How hush can it be?"

"Hmmm . . . good point." She paged the screen again. "I'm sending you the link." After a moment, my phone vibrated in my purse. Haley smiled slyly. "You're supposed to have that turned off."

"It is off. Kind of." I put my hand over my bag. "Just in case. You know." Nate could call or text at any moment and even if I couldn't answer it, I wanted to know the message was there, to *feel* it.

We were interrupted by a sudden commotion in the hallway outside the room. Haley and I glanced up at the door, expecting to see Ms. Templeton shooing in the stragglers before the bell rang, but instead there was a crowd of students hanging around the door.

Haley clucked her tongue when we saw everyone staring at their phones. "Templeton's not gonna like that," she said. She waved at a girl standing closest to the door, who was mesmerized by her phone. "Hey, Corey! What's going on?"

Corey Sanchez turned and froze in place. Her fingers gripped the phone more tightly, and she forced a smile through her braces. "Um, nothing."

"Nothing?" Haley, who had to know everything that was going on, jumped up from her desk and headed straight for the center of the group. She poked her chin over Corey's shoulder, keeping her back to me. The girls whispered to each other furiously, but I couldn't hear a word.

What on earth could be so intriguing? I wondered. Curious, I started to stand, but the ringing bell pushed me back into my seat. I glanced around me. With Haley gone, I was alone in the room. No teacher, no classmates, and everyone still milling about in the hall. Maybe this was a senior ditch and no one told me?

I pulled my phone out too and scrolled through my emails. The only thing that was unread was the evite Haley had just forwarded to me.

"Middie, hey, don't do that!" Haley called to me, her voice on edge. She hurried toward me and snatched my phone from my hand. "What if Templeton came in? That witch would send you straight to admin, and then where would you be? Your parents would get called and probably it would go on your permanent record, and college, well, you know, forget college." Her fingers fumbled around the sides of the phone and tapped the screen as if she'd never seen one before in her life.

"What are you doing?"

"You don't really need to have this on," she said hurriedly, keeping the cell out of my reach. "I mean, there are studies that say you could get cancer from the battery being on all the time. Damn it, where is the button that shuts this thing off?"

"Haley, keep it on. What are you doing, Haley . . . Haley?" I lunged for the phone, but it was like a game of keep-away with her. "Don't shut it off. Nate might call."

I leaned, she dodged. I dove, she weaved. But I was agile too. I faked a move and then plucked it out of her grasp. "Come on, Hale, you know I'm waiting—"

And she grabbed it back. "No! He's not going to call, Middie."

"What? Of course he is."

Haley's face turned red, and she looked like she might cry.

"Haley?" I put my arm around her shoulder. "What's going . . ."

"Oh my god, Middie! Are you okay?" Katrina burst through the door with her phone held in front of her. Some students from the hallway poured in behind her.

"Me? Yeah, why?"

I was surrounded by classmates. Katrina and Debra and Corey, among the girls, and a dozen more who weren't in my classes but whom I recognized. And then, in a blink, it seemed, there was Ms. Templeton in her teacher attire—a simple blouse and matching skirt. Her tight black curls fell over her tortoiseshell frames. Her hand fell gently onto my shoulders. "Meredith, I think you should come with—"

But it was too late.

I had already seen the screen of Katrina's phone.

Video from a news channel. Words in white block letters in a crawl under a reporter's face.

ATTACK ON HONDURAN VILLAGE.

AID WORKERS MISSING.

ALL FEARED DEAD.

A wall of shock and fear and anger hit me. It washed over me, knocking me back into my seat.

I sucked in a breath. *No. No. No.*

"That's not Nate," I choked out. "It's not him. He's—"

"Honey. Come with me," Ms. Templeton repeated, more softly this time.

I allowed myself to be helped up from the desk, felt a hand at each elbow guiding me from the classroom and into the hallway, felt a palm pat my shoulder and rub my back and touch my hair. Voices called to me, voices of friends, classmates, acquaintances. Teachers, staff, students shrank as I walked the gauntlet of bodies pressed tightly against the lockers.

"—so sorry, Middie—"

"—be all right, I'm sure—"

"—here for you, okay?"

Mr. Z's office door opened. "Come in" was murmured by someone. Mr. Z? Ms. Templeton? I wasn't sure.

A corduroy-covered sofa magically appeared, having been liberated from beneath piles of papers and books and trinkets by my guidance counselor. The door closed on the clamor in the hallway, on the voices of my friends, who called my name.

The principal sat on the small couch beside me, a woman named Ms. McMahon who was new to the school. She wore her hair in a chin-length bob and favored black and gray. Her frightened eyes mirrored my own. "We're calling your mom now," she said softly. "You can wait here until she comes."

I felt my chin nod.

On the right side of the office a television was showing the same footage I had seen on Katrina's phone. Principal McMahon flicked through the channels. CNN, Fox, MSNBC. Every news outlet was showing the same images of a destroyed village: trees down, buildings on fire, bodies littering the ground.

67 KILLED IN VILLAGE ATTACK.

SPLINTER GROUP OF LOCAL MILITARY SUSPECTED.

VILLAGERS AND MEDICAL VOLUNTEERS KILLED WHILE FLEEING.

No! The tiny hairs on my arms rose up and my skin went cold. I shut my eyes and felt tears fall down my cheeks and drip off my chin. This couldn't be. It couldn't. It was a terrible, horrible nightmare.

It was nerves and anxiety over school and personal essays and Nate being gone and somehow Emma's inspirational Brownie troop story got mixed up in my dreams and . . .

. . . *this is not real. Not real. This is a mistake. This is someone else's village, not Nate's.*

I felt my throat tighten and my breath choke—every ounce of air was gone from my lungs and I couldn't inhale, couldn't stop my heart from thumping against my ribs.

"We shouldn't have this on." Mr. Z shut off the television. "Everything's going to be okay," he said.

Is he serious?

"We don't know anything for sure yet." Mr. Z spoke carefully, like some kind of hostage negotiator. "Meredith, talk to me."

"Talk?" I choked out the word. I could barely form a sentence in my brain, let alone hold a conversation with another human being. What the hell would I talk about?

My phone buzzed in my purse: Haley. I tapped the screen to send it to voice mail. Then it buzzed again. Katrina. And again. Debra. Each time I glanced at the ID in vain. Finally, Ms. McMahon took the phone from me and shut it off completely.

"No!" I cried, grabbing it from her and turning it back on. *"He might call!"*

Our eyes met and I had to glance away. Because in them, I saw the truth as Ms. McMahon saw it. Nate wouldn't ever call. Ever.

My skin was clammy and moist. The air was stale and everyone was too close. Too close. I could feel Ms. McMahon's leg against mine on the too-small couch. I clutched my purse and phone tightly and lurched from the sofa to the door. "I have to go."

"But your mother isn't here yet—"

"I'll wait outside." I flung open the door and ran straight into Ms. Templeton, who was consoling Haley.

She reached for me, but I couldn't spare her more than a glance.

I tore down the hallway and burst through the doors.

"Meredith!" I heard. I turned and spotted the Vespa. Lee waved at me and I ran, away from school, away from everything. I sat on the back of the scooter, tucked my purse between my knees, and grabbed the chrome handle that wrapped around the back of the leather seat. Lee motored away from the curb.

CHAPTER *five*

I was grateful for the wind on my cheeks, for the cool air that numbed my skin. As the school receded in the distance, I saw my friends spill out of the doors and wrap their arms around one another, consoling themselves. My eyes stung with tears, and I turned forward to let the wind whisk them away, temporarily at least.

We pulled into a driveway and Lee wordlessly took my phone from my purse, tapped the keys, and then handed it back to me. He shrugged. "In case you need it."

I stopped short when I saw where we were: Nate's house.

"You should probably be here, don't you think." It wasn't a question. He was right. This was where I should be: with Nate's family. *My* family.

I nodded and slowly dismounted the bike. "You coming in?"

"Not my thing." He was on his scooter and gone before I could thank him for the lift.

For the rescue.

For *not* saying, *It'll be okay.*

I stared at the front of the house, willing my feet to move forward. I knew I had to go inside and see Nate's family, to console them, to be consoled by them. But I couldn't! I looked at that house and remembered the thousands of times Nate and I had made out on the creaky porch swing. I heard the sounds of Nate's footsteps on the front stairs as he ran down to greet me at the door. I smelled the hot buttered popcorn and melted Junior Mints he liked on movie nights with his family.

My fingers trembled as I sent my mother a text, telling her where I was. They fumbled on the keys so badly that autocorrect couldn't even hazard a guess, translating the message into "Agnats hiss" instead of "At Nate's house." I pressed Send anyway and stood at the end of the driveway to wait. I couldn't go inside alone. I couldn't.

A few minutes later, my father's car pulled up and my mother and sister jumped out. They hugged me between them, and my father wrapped his arm around my shoulder. Emma, in her precious Brownie outfit and freshly ironed sash, tugged on my hand. Her eyes were red-rimmed and puffy. I scooped her up in my arms and her legs wrapped around my waist. I held her tightly all the way inside the house.

The Binghams were assembled in the front living room, much as they had been on my last visit for Nate's going-away party. Could that truly have been just a couple of weeks ago? My brain couldn't reconcile that—it simply wasn't possible. But there was Nate's great-aunt Pamela in another classic knit shell and matching twill pants set from L.L.Bean. She sat in the same chair as when I'd met her.

I carried Emma in with me, finding a place for her on the couch where she could sit with my father, who quietly introduced himself to Aunt Pamela and the others in the room. I braced for what must surely come next: Nate's parents.

"Be strong, sweetie," my mother said in my ear. "I'm with you."

We entered the kitchen together, hands clasped, and were stunned by the frenzy of activity, a sharp contrast to the gloom of the front parlor. Mr. and Mrs. Bingham dashed from counter to counter to window to door, constantly in motion but never bumping into each other, almost as if their movements were choreographed. I recognized Nate's older cousins and aunts and uncles, each on a cell phone, all talking at once. There were two televisions in here and three computer screens, all set to different news channels. Nate's cousin Brad, a freshman at our high school, was manning the media, constantly changing the stations in search of updates.

"No, there isn't any reason to suspect terrorism," Mr. Bingham was saying into his cell. "We've heard nothing about motive."

"—not going to give up, not this soon," Mrs. Bingham said into hers. "The reports are sketchy at best. . . ."

She spotted us both and leaned over a table to embrace us with her arm and elbow. "Lillian, thank you." She kissed my cheek. "Middie, sweetheart."

Perhaps the only sign that something was amiss was her untucked blouse and her lack of makeup, save for a dash of lip gloss. Otherwise, she was the same army general that I knew so well.

"I'll be in touch. Yes, thank you, Reverend." Nate's mother clicked off her cell, and she came over to hug us more thoroughly. "Oh my goodness, Middie, you're shaking." She held my hands in hers and rubbed them together as if she were warming me up. "We have plenty of coffee if you want a cup."

"Caroline, why don't you take a seat," my mother said, "and I'll bring *you* some coffee." She got a shush and a wave in return.

"Not at all," Mrs. Bingham said. But her voice cracked as if even she could not believe she was playing the good hostess at a time like this. She quickly composed herself. "Brad, honey, would you pour coffee for Middie and Lillian?"

Nate's cousin seemed reluctant to leave his computers, but he did as he was asked, bringing us two mugs of black coffee before quickly retreating when we thanked him.

My mother handed me hers and shooed me away. "Would you find some cream and sugar for mine, sweetie?"

I knew she was sending me off while she spoke to Mrs. Bingham, but I looked for the cream and sugar anyway, finding it on the counter closest to the sink. While I stirred some of each in, I glanced out the window at the twins on their swings. Nate's brother sat on the ground, staring up at the basketball hoop with a ball balanced on his knees. I had a feeling the girls were ignorant of the real reason everyone was at the house, but Scotty was old enough. Fresh tears sprang to my eyes as I imagined Nate's parents delivering the bad news, but I wiped them off with a napkin before I turned away from the window.

I carried the coffee back to my mother, who was attentive to Mrs. Bingham's every word.

"—not exactly the most reputable government we're dealing with down there," she was saying with disdain. "Who knows the level of corruption in that country? Am I right, Tom?" she called over her shoulder to her husband, who nodded.

"You're right, Car."

"No group has claimed the attack, right, Tom?"

Mr. Bingham gave her a nod and a thumbs-up. "Right, Car."

"We haven't seen his body, Lil," Mrs. Bingham went on. "No one has seen the *actual* bodies."

My mother nibbled her fingernail. "But the photos—"

"Those could be anyone! That village could be any-where!" Her voice quavered as it rose. She seemed to sense she was sounding a bit hysterical, and she took a deep breath, exhaling through pursed lips. "All I mean to say is, we're not giving up hope, not yet." She saw me and pulled me in to her. "You wouldn't give up either, would you?"

"Never," my mother said firmly.

"That's why Tom and I are going to Honduras ourselves."

My mother's face creased with worry. "Are you sure that's safe?"

Mrs. Bingham nodded and reached for her husband's hand. "It's what we have to do."

The room suddenly quieted and, for a moment, we heard the little girls outside giggling and squealing, cheer-fully caught up in their swings. Inside the kitchen, we all managed a smile, and then a CNN reporter returned after a commercial break to update everyone on the attack.

Nate's mom slipped into her husband's arms while my mom hugged me closer.

I envied those little girls; I would never be that inno-cent again.

For seventeen years of my life, death had been a stranger to me. I'd never known anyone who'd died. One set of grandpar-ents was still living, while the other pair had died before I was born. A few students at my school had lost their older broth-ers or sisters overseas, but they weren't people I was close to, so while I mourned *for* them, I couldn't mourn *with* them.

Nate's death, on the other hand, felt like my own. From the moment I'd heard the news at school, I couldn't think, could hardly speak. While I was at the Binghams', I was surrounded by activity. There was food to cook, dishes to wash, and coffee to brew. I shot hoops with Emma and Scotty and pushed the twins on the swings like Nate used to. I didn't cry. Especially not in front of the kids.

But at home, I could not stop weeping. Leaving the hub of noise and optimism of the Bingham house meant returning to my empty bedroom, where there would be no FaceTime call, no text messages, no emails. Nothing.

And the more time that went by without them, the more likely it seemed that there would never be one again.

The shock of that realization was overwhelming. Fortunately, Haley arrived on my doorstep with Katrina and Debra and an offer to spend the night.

In my room, Katrina sat on one side of me on the bed, leaning her elbow on my pillow while Haley and Debra sprawled on the floor. "I don't think I'll ever stop crying," I said. Debra climbed onto the bed and passed me a fresh box of tissues.

"You will. You have us. And we will always be here for you," she said, settling herself in on the other side of me.

"I've never even been to a funeral," I said. *Oh god, what was I saying? How could I even think such a thing?*

I felt Debra's hand brush my hair away from my face.

"You and Nate were the perfect couple," she said. "We were all jealous of you."

"Debra!" Katrina snapped.

"It's okay." I tilted my chin. I loved Nate; I *wanted* to hear about us, especially the good things.

"We figured you guys would get married someday and live happily ever after."

The girls were silent and I could feel their sorrow. The loss of Nate hit all of them at the same time, and they all suddenly stopped breathing.

"So did I," I said.

Debra smiled at her lap and then up at me. "We kind of assumed we would be your bridesmaids."

"You did, huh? A little presumptuous, aren't you?" I asked with a hint of a smile. I had indeed imagined all three of them as my bridesmaids, with Emma as flower girl and Allison my maid of honor.

"But you wouldn't have made us wear ugly bridesmaids' dresses, would you?" Haley asked from the floor.

I shook my head. "Never."

"Not like my sister! Remember her wedding last summer and that hideous dress she put me in?" Katrina became animated. "Yellow. Yellow like the sun." She made a face. "And me with my red hair. I looked like I was a corncob on fire."

"Oh my god! I remember that!" Debra cried.

The girls laughed as they recalled all the horrible

bridesmaids' dresses they'd seen or worn. It broke some of the tension in the room—for them.

I smiled along with them, but I couldn't shake the image of Nate and me walking down the aisle. The plans we'd had, the future we'd envisioned for ourselves, the life we'd expected to lead for years to come. I pulled out my laptop and found the beautiful vintage dress I'd bookmarked. I must have been staring at it for a while, because the chatter stopped and Haley's face appeared over the top of the screen.

"What is that?" she asked me.

"A . . . dress," I said, leaving out the *wedding* part. But the girls knew anyway.

I was about to delete the bookmark when Haley stopped me. "Don't get rid of it. Not yet," she said. "It's a memory—"

A shade, I thought, remembering Nate's boxes.

I was too tired to disagree, so I simply closed my laptop; not long after, we went to sleep. Well, they did, but I couldn't. Every time I closed my eyes, I saw the images from CNN. The burning buildings . . . the bodies.

My friends had done everything they could to shield me from more updates, but the pictures in my head had been planted from the very first moment, and I couldn't shake them. I cried softly to myself and in the dark saw a head stir; Haley and the girls were sleeping on the floor under comforters and tucked inside sleeping bags.

I held my breath and my sniffles and waited for whoever it was to fall back asleep. After a while, I heard a gentle snore and knew I alone was still awake.

I carefully slipped out from under the sheets and eased my way past the girls on the floor. On my desk was a photo of Nate and me from a pool party last year, a picture I'd considered putting into his box but nixed because of its size.

I crawled back into bed with the photo and crushed it to my chest. I didn't need to see it to know what it looked like. We were tanned from working at the farm and fit from our morning runs. He'd liked my bathing suit: boy shorts in light blue and a tank top trimmed with white stripes. A little boring to me, but *he* liked it, so I wore it whenever we went swimming.

As I tried once more to close my eyes, my phone buzzed on the bed. A text message?

I snatched up the phone and slid my finger across the screen.

breathe

What . . .

I stared at the screen. . . . Lee? And then I recalled him putting his number in my phone.

I waited for another word, another something, anything.

breathe

Was it that simple? I took a deep breath and felt a hiccup in my chest, then slowly exhaled. I remembered the ride on Lee's Vespa, the wind wiping away my tears.

And I breathed.

CHAPTER *six*

More than a week passed before I felt like I could come up for air. I did what I could to help Nate's parents leave, visiting with the twins and Scotty while their grandparents got settled in. No one knew how long Mr. and Mrs. Bingham would be gone.

But eventually I had to find normal again. And that meant school.

"Are you sure you want to go, sweetie?" my mother asked. Emma wanted me to stay home and watch cartoons with her.

Honestly, I wasn't sure I wanted to do *anything*, but what was my alternative—staying home forever? I felt restless:

my legs and elbows and fingers were trembling and spastic after many sleepless nights.

Besides, the people who knew Nate, who knew me, were at school. We needed one another. School would be my refuge.

"All right, but if it's too much, come home." She offered me the car, with a reminder to fill up the tank and get Emma from Brownies, and kissed me gently.

At the front door of the high school, I stood outside for a long time and watched students enter. They were still in shock: Nate was one of their own, beloved by all. No one wanted to believe he was gone. Groups of girls huddled together as they went through the doors, merged with one or more groups just like them, and collectively moved inside as a single unit. A few boys shuffled in next, tall and lanky like Nate, athletes like Nate, but solitary in their grief. They bobbed their chins at each other, unspoken words of encouragement and sympathy in those subtle nods.

I urged my feet to walk up the steps to the front door, but I didn't step all the way in. I kept one foot outside and my hand braced on the metal frame.

Movement and color caught my eye and I turned to glance down the hallway toward the door to the gym. A group of girls wearing school colors was draping red and black and white crepe paper across the glass trophy case.

Nate is in there, I thought. His trophies, his awards, his team photos. They were honoring him with their colors, paying tribute with what they could: crepe ribbons and construction-paper cutouts. *He's not dead!* I wanted to shout. *His parents are going to pick him up!*

My heart started to race and my hands shook. I felt my temples pound, and the heat in the building, the humidity, was stifling and sudden.

This was a mistake. I shouldn't have come. I wasn't ready.

I stepped backward, nearly stumbling over the threshold until I was outside again and the door had swung closed. I pulled my cell out to text my mother, to tell her I was coming home, when I saw Lee's message:

breathe

I held the phone up to my face, my lips to the word.

breathe

I closed my eyes and inhaled deeply through my nose, holding my breath until it was ready to burst from my lungs, and then slowly, slowly, slowly I exhaled and opened my eyes.

I turned away from the school and walked back to my car.

When Nate's father came back on his own a few days later, I felt a heavy pit in my stomach. There were rumors the Binghams had fought about returning home so soon, but Mr. Bingham insisted his wife just wanted to be thorough. However, it was looking unlikely Nate would be found alive. Rescue workers had been doing their best, but the location and the possibility of further violence hindered their efforts.

I was terrified about returning to school, but I had to do it. In the time I'd been away from classes, homework was piling up, and students and staff were returning to their regular schedules. My parents were good about keeping the television off, but at school, kids were on their phones in every one of my classes. When they saw me coming, they'd turn them off or mute the sound, but I could tell what they were watching by their furtive glances.

Haley stuck to my side for most of my first day back, and thankfully no one asked the dreaded *Are you okay, Middie?*

At the end of the day, I was exhausted. I felt like I'd been sleepwalking with my eyes open and holding my breath. After the last bell rang, I asked Haley if she wanted a lift home, but she shook her head.

"Is it field hockey practice?"

"Um. No." She shifted her weight from foot to foot and her gaze found someone beyond me. I turned and saw Katrina and Debra waiting outside the auditorium. "It's the planning committee for the memorial. For Nate."

My heart began to hammer in my chest. "So soon? It's only been a few days."

"Nearly two weeks, Middie."

I sucked in a breath. The façade of my "normal" day immediately fell away, and I felt weak in the knees.

Of course there would be a memorial. Mr. Bingham was back, and he didn't have Nate, which meant . . .

Haley touched my arm. "I don't have to go."

I thought a moment. "Can I come?"

"Are you sure?"

No, no way was I sure. But this was for Nate.

The auditorium was filled with students; everyone wanted to be part of Nate's memorial. There was a solemn friendliness in the air when we walked in. At the front of the room, Mr. Z was writing a list of people who were planning to speak at the memorial. I saw Ms. Templeton's name there and Principal McMahon's. He asked for a show of hands of who would like to say something. About two dozen students responded and he started writing their names down.

It all felt so *final*. While I knew Mrs. Bingham was probably wrong about Nate still being alive, holding a memorial for him so quickly felt like we were giving up all hope.

Nate's cousin Brad was up at the board with Mr. Z. He looked exhausted. "I'm gonna tell a story about Nate teaching me how to fish when we were kids," he said quietly. He glanced sideways at the guidance counselor. "He was a good teacher." Murmurs of assent rippled through the room.

"That's terrific," Mr. Z told Brad with an encouraging grin. "Anyone else?" He looked at me. And then *everyone* looked at me. My face flushed at the attention, for no good reason at all. "Middie? Would you like to speak at the service?"

Immediately, my friends and Nate's friends chattered words of support. Haley put her arm around my shoulder and squeezed. "You can do it, Mid. You'll be great."

Me? Great? My hand went to the photo of Nate and me

from the pool party; I'd tucked it into my purse so I could steal a glimpse of it whenever I needed to. I felt safe knowing I had that picture with me.

"I . . ." *I love Nate. I loved him. I don't want to let him go.* I heard the words in my head, but I couldn't force them out. "I . . ." And suddenly the room began to spin around me. I tried to hold it together as best I could, but I could feel my whole body trembling, my grief bubbling under the surface of my skin, ready to explode at any moment.

I hit the road and drove. It was selfish, this desire to get away, but I couldn't help it. Everything I saw in our small town reminded me of Nate. That Taco Bell was where we'd hang out after football games on Friday nights. That alley behind the library was where we'd park until our breath fogged up the windows. That movie theater was where we'd cuddle in the back row during the scariest parts of horror movies.

Roseburg was crowded with memories of Nate. I kept driving—and driving—past most of what I knew, all of what I'd grown up with. I was far from town when the car stopped moving. Oh, it slowed down first, but I didn't even realize it until it simply stopped.

I eased it to the shoulder and stared at the red lights on the dash as if they were alien hieroglyphs. *What are you telling me, car?*

Out of gas. That was what it was telling me. I had a vague recollection of my mother saying I needed to fill the tank, but when was that? Today or yesterday or a week ago? I leaned my head against the steering wheel and laughed softly to myself. I couldn't even do *this* right. I couldn't escape without messing it all up.

I tried starting it again, but it was done. I called my parents—neither answered their cells. I managed to get Haley for a minute. But she didn't own a car, so she was no help. 911 was not exactly appropriate. I stared at my phone, hoping it would reveal a number for a mechanic. Instead it gave me a last option.

Lee pulled up about fifteen minutes later on his Vespa with an empty gas can and we sped off without a word. The closest town was a tiny place called Lookingglass. It was so small it had only one gas station, which was closed when we arrived. A handwritten sign on the door said "Back in 10."

Lee tapped his finger against the sign and cocked an eye at me. "But when was it put up? One minute ago or nine?"

I burst into tears. They spilled down my cheeks and chin, and I let them. I didn't care if Lee saw me crying, if people in passing cars knew I was weeping, if the whole town of Lookingglass could tell I was falling apart.

Lee's mouth opened and he started toward me and then stopped. "Hey, Middie. Hey. It's only a few minutes."

But I couldn't stop. I cried fat, ugly tears. My face, no doubt, turned blotchy and red and puffy and hideous.

Lee didn't pat my shoulder or tell me *There, there* or ask me *Are you okay?* He just stood and waited for me to finish.

Finally spent from sobbing, I wiped my nose with the back of my hand.

Lee chewed the corner of his lip and then jerked his chin at me. "You got some snot right there."

I brushed my nose again with my hand and looked at him. "Did I get it?"

"Little bit more." I used the sleeve of my shirt this time, and Lee bobbed his head. "Got it. Want an Icee?"

I stared at him. *An Icee?* My car was back on the side of the road without gas and Nate was gone and he wanted to get an Icee?

It was so absurd that I just muttered, "Yeah, okay."

We left his scooter and the empty gas can at the station and stepped across the street to a convenience store. While Lee ran in to get the slushies, I waited outside, looking around. I couldn't get over how quiet it was. Not that Roseburg was all hustle and bustle, but this town was a mere blip on the map. From where I was sitting, I could see a few houses with large yards and older cars, a bait shop with a motorboat parked in front of it, and a grocery store. Thankfully, there was nothing here to remind me of Nate. Nothing at all.

Lee appeared a few minutes later with a pair of Icees for us. He waved over his shoulder at a girl in the window: from here she looked pretty, with short blond hair and a round face. She smiled as she waved back at him.

"Your girlfriend?"

"That's Liza," Lee said, stabbing a straw into the plastic top of the drink and handing it to me. "Hope you like blue."

"She's cute," I said as I sucked up a mouthful of sugary ice. After a few long sips, my drink was half-gone. "Thank you."

Lee shrugged and dug a hand into the pocket of his jeans. He peeled open the wrapper of a Snickers bar and held it out. "You want—"

"Yes." I snatched it out of his hand before he could finish and took a gigantic bite.

Lee's mouth was open. "What I meant to say was, you want to hold that for me while I put my change away?"

I glanced down at the candy bar, midchew. It looked like a bear had gotten at it. "I'm sorry." I started to hand it back, but Lee shook his head.

"That's okay. I don't really like chocolate." Clearly a lie. But whatever.

I finished the bar in a few quiet bites and then leaned back against the bench with a sigh. "Thanks for picking me up. How did you get to me so quickly?"

Lee sucked down some slushie. "Out here already. I was working."

"Working?"

"Are you . . . surprised?"

"I-I'm not . . . I just . . ." I *was* surprised, actually, nearly as shocked as I'd been when he'd told me he had a girlfriend. From all that I knew of Lee Ryan, from everything I'd heard from my friends and from Nate, he was a loner with barely passing grades and no ambition. His habit of calling me "Yoko" did not endear him to me at all, although his kindness today certainly did.

"I work at a charter thing up the street," he said, gesturing with his slushie cup. "I organize nature tours for people."

"You . . . do?"

He ignored my remark and instead shaded his eyes as he looked across the street at the gas station. "Still closed."

"That's a long ten minutes."

Lee shrugged. Then he held my gaze for a long moment. "What are *you* doing this far from home? Running away to join the circus?"

I nodded quite solemnly. "I am."

Lee grinned mischievously. "I was a lion tamer for a while."

I played along. "Really? What happened?"

"I tamed him. The act was over," he said with a perfectly straight face. "What about you? What's your gig?"

"Um, magic act," I said.

He wagged a finger at me. "Watch out for those rabbits. They really don't like living in top hats."

"Got it." I saluted him with the candy bar wrapper.

"So if the circus thing doesn't work out, you gonna go back or . . ."

I took a deep breath and looked out over the horizon. The sun was beginning to fade, and the sky was turning orange. "They're planning a memorial for Nate."

Lee's neck stiffened, but that was the only sign I could tell he was bothered by what I'd said. "And . . . ?"

"And . . . it's too soon, you know? It *just* happened. I mean, god, can't we wait a little bit and see if, you know, if . . ." My voice trailed off. Did I sound like Mrs. Bingham? Was I holding out false hope like she was?

"You can't stop people from doing what they want to," he said. "If they want to do a service or some shit like that, well, whatever." He shrugged again, but it felt like forced bravado. "You gonna go?"

I nodded. "Yeah."

"What are you gonna say?"

I held my hands open helplessly. "I don't know. I have nothing to say."

"You're the only one who *does* have something to say. And me, I guess. Since I was his best friend."

And there's not a person in the world who understands that, I wanted to say but wisely did not. "Well, what would *you* say?" I turned to face him on the bench, hugging one knee to my chest. "Go ahead. You're at the park under the gazebo—"

He made a face. "That's a dumb place. Nate would hate that."

"And Mr. Z calls you up—"

"Who's that?"

"Guidance counselor. And you say . . ." I gestured to him with a flourish. "Go on." I dug into my bag and found a pen and a scrap of paper.

"What are you doing?" he asked brusquely.

"Taking notes."

He snorted his disapproval. "Are you kidding? Don't do that. Don't *plan* it like that. Nate deserves better."

"Excuse me?" I snapped.

"Speak from your heart. *Your* heart. Not mine."

My heart? The one that was about to crack wide open and bleed all over this paper? I put my pen down. "Really? Let's see you do it."

Lee took a loud slurp of Icee and then turned to mirror me on the bench. He belched softly and wiped his mouth. I could see his lips and tongue were dark blue, and I wondered if mine were too. "I loved Nate. He was not only the best friend I *ever* had, he was the brother I *never* had. He always thought of me before himself. He laughed at my stupid jokes. He made me feel more important than I was. He made me a better person." The sun shifted just then and a shaft of light cut across Lee's face, making his eyes shimmer and accenting his sharp cheekbones with shadow. "Nate kept me sane when all around me was shit."

The silence in the small town seemed to intensify in the absence of Lee's voice. Not far away, a pair of dogs barked and whined and their owner shouted cheerfully. I watched Lee, who seemed to have withdrawn into himself with these words, as if he were pulling a protective shell around him.

Profound? No. Heartfelt? Absolutely. I felt the depth of

his love for Nate in those few words. They were the truth. Nate *was* his best friend.

"I got your text." I wanted to let him know I cared, but he didn't look at me. "It meant a lot to me that you sent it." I waited. Lee's gaze was on his sneaker, on his finger tracing the lines of green marker he'd drawn. "It was really—"

"Station's open," he said abruptly and hopped up from the bench. And like that, he was gone, loping awkwardly across the street. I tossed the Icee cup and the candy wrapper into the trash and followed him.

"You really saved my ass," I told him.

"Nah. You'd have made it to the circus eventually."

I grinned and felt immediately guilty for it.

"Remember," he said very seriously. "Always feed the rabbits in your hat." With that, he was off, back toward Lookingglass, his job, and his girlfriend.

I arrived home as the sun was setting, late for dinner, late to help with Emma or the cooking or even setting the table. The meat was dry and the salad warm, but neither of my parents complained, which made my apology sound even more desperate and my running-out-of-gas excuse lame.

"It's okay, Middie," my mother said as she scooped mashed sweet potatoes onto my plate. "You've got a lot on your mind."

Even Emma was sweet. "I ironed my uniform myself," she said proudly. And then she asked, "Why are your lips all blue?"

I ran a finger along my mouth as if I could rub off the color. I remembered the Icee and the candy bar and my sidesaddle ride on Lee's Vespa. And I remembered his words: *I loved Nate.*

"A friend of mine gave me a slushie."

She smiled. "The blue kind's the best."

"Yeah, it is." My heart ached a tiny bit less. It must have been the slushie.

CHAPTER *seven*

My sister Allison arrived home the night before the memorial, surprising me at breakfast the next morning. She wrapped me in a hug when she saw me. "I'll be right by your side for the funeral."

"It's not a funeral," I corrected her. "It's a memorial, a candlelight vigil." I still didn't know what I would say.

Speak from your heart, Lee had said. But what was in my heart?

All day I paged through photos on my phone for inspiration. I clutched the pool party photo of us for so long the edges warped with my sweat. By the time my parents drove us to the town center, my thoughts were elusive and vague.

I prayed the right words would come to me when my name was called.

A small crowd was gathered around the white-canopied gazebo on the green in front of the town hall. A couple of girls on the cheerleading squad were handing out candles with small paper cones to catch the melting wax. We stood off to one side as the group swelled. It didn't take long for the green to be filled with people, young and old, from all areas of Nate's life, but I didn't see Lee.

Just as the sun began to set, Reverend Platt from Nate's church stepped up to the gazebo. A large man who looked like an ex-boxer, he held no microphone but even without one, his booming voice carried across the green, welcoming everyone. He nodded to the girls with the cones, a signal for them to light their candles and walk among the crowd, passing the flame from one person to another. Soon there was a blanket of flickering lights, as if the stars had tumbled from the heavens and landed on the town green.

"Friends," the reverend said. "We are here to honor one of the finest young men this town has ever produced." His grin was genial, despite the sad occasion. "Everyone in Roseburg knew Nate Bingham. He touched so many lives."

I heard a few sniffles and some whispers around us as the pastor went on. He reminded us that this was a celebration of who Nate was and what he had done with his brief life, not a time to mourn.

I saw Mr. Bingham standing at the back of the gazebo

with the twins and Scotty. He looked resigned to the memorial and to being in front of all of these people. I felt sorry for him being all alone up there—first Nate was gone and now his wife. My mother had told me earlier that Mrs. Bingham had refused to come back from Honduras for the service. She wasn't ready to even consider the possibility her son could be dead until all efforts to find him had been exhausted. When I'd told Mom I agreed with Mrs. Bingham, she'd shaken her head sadly and replied, "A memorial is for *others*. They need to be given permission to move on."

Others, I thought. But not me. Not yet.

A few moments later, Mr. Z brought a blowup of Nate's yearbook photo on an easel. I heard a collective gasp from the crowd. This memorial suddenly became very real.

One by one, Mr. Z called the names of people who wanted to share memories of Nate. Some were poignant and sweet, while others were funny: Brad Bingham's story of Nate teaching him how to fish was far more hilarious than he'd let on at the meeting. Before I knew it, my name was called, and there was a smattering of encouragement from my friends and family. I felt my heart leap to my throat.

The words I'd written down earlier in the day utterly escaped me. My gaze swept the green as I tried desperately to think of something to tell these people about my boyfriend. *He was the love of my life,* I wanted to say. *He was my soul mate. He was the first boy I ever kissed.*

The only boy I ever kissed.

I opened my mouth to say something, anything. Nothing came out but a jumbled mess. "Nate . . . my . . ."

Speak from your heart. Lee's words had been effortless. He'd expressed his sorrow so completely, so easily. How could I not? Did I not love Nate enough?

I glanced over my shoulder at the photo of Nate and heard my breath catch. He was gone. He was really and truly gone. I reached into my purse, and my fingers gripped the edge of the photo. It soothed me but only briefly.

"Nate . . . made me a better person. He made me more important than I was." They were Lee's words, but they were echoes of my own thoughts too.

And I stopped. That was all I could say, all that I had in me. I stood and swayed, feeling my knees getting weak underneath me. As my father helped me down from the gazebo, I couldn't help but think that I'd been a disappointment. I hadn't honored Nate. I hadn't done what others had. They'd spoken from *their* hearts. They'd revealed *their* personal stories. But I—who'd known him the best—had nothing to say. Nothing that was *mine*.

At home I went straight up to my bedroom, flinging off Allison's black dress and heels as I went. I emptied my purse on my desk and found the photo of Nate and me. I stared hard at my image. *Why couldn't you find something to say? Why didn't you tell them all how you felt?*

When I turned on my phone, I saw four text messages

from Haley appear, but I didn't have the energy to read or respond to them.

And then, as I was holding the phone, another one came in: *who is this?*

I glanced at the number. It was from Lee. Huh?

I quickly texted him back: *it's Meredith*

I don't know any Meredith

Shaking my head, I typed again: *Middie*

Yoko? Why r u texting me?

Me? I wasn't . . . ! My fingers tapped the tiny keys. *U textd me*

And then I added, *im not yoko*

No response. I waited, staring at the screen.

Nothing.

Nothing? What the hell? I finished dressing, washed my face, and tied back my hair—and then, nearly half an hour later, a new text came in:

Why did u use my words

My mouth opened. *Why* . . . I stammered an answer in my head. *I—I—I didn't mean to* . . . and just as I realized what his comment meant, the phone rang and I snatched it up. "You were there," I said to Lee. "You were at the service."

"No, I wasn't."

"Yes, you were. Or else you wouldn't know what I said."

"So you did use my words."

"So you did attend the service."

Silence.

"Why didn't you come up?"

"Not my thing."

"But why—"

"Meredith, stop talking."

I was so shocked by the request, which came so matter-of-factly, that I stopped. Not for the first time did I wonder why Nate and Lee were such close friends. Nate was kind and sweet and would never tell me or anyone else to shut up. I crawled across my bed and lay down, resting my head between two pillows.

Lee's voice was slightly muffled. "You got home okay."

"Yeah."

"I'm glad. You . . ." He said something else, but I couldn't hear it.

"What's that?"

"Nothing," he said quickly. "Good night."

Good night? What? "Wait. . . ."

"What?"

"You were his best friend. Tell me—tell me what you did together."

There was a pause.

"We liked hanging out. He liked doing shit with me." Lee's tone was clipped. "Couldn't you say the same thing?"

"Yeah."

His voice softened. "Then why didn't you?"

"I . . . I don't know." I laughed once, embarrassed. "Your words were better than mine."

"We loved Nate. Nate loved us. For different reasons," he said. "He was a pretty funny guy, you know?"

"Funny?" I'd never thought of my boyfriend as *funny* necessarily. He smiled and laughed, but usually other people were telling the jokes.

"He'd call me up in the middle of the night," Lee said with a chuckle. "Just wanting to drive somewhere. Stop someplace random for a burger or whatever. He liked to be . . . What word did he use? Oh yeah. Spontaneous."

Spontaneous? Nate was a careful planner of all things: class schedules, workout routines, life.

"We had some good times, Nate and me," Lee said quietly. "I'll miss him."

He ended the call without another word.

I'll miss him too, I thought as tears filled my eyes. I wondered if Lee cried too. I scrolled through my messages and found his very first one to me:

breathe

I turned over onto my back and stared up at the ceiling. And did as recommended.

CHAPTER *eight*

The house was emptier, my room more lonely after Allison
went back to school a few days after the memorial service,
and I wasn't surprised at all when I was unable to sleep.
Before dawn arrived, I tossed on my running shoes, something I hadn't done in weeks, set the coffee pot to brew for
my parents, and headed out into the crisp morning air. The
sun was still an hour from rising, so the fog that typically
burned off had not yet evaporated. I grabbed a thin jacket
from the front hall closet before I set off to keep the breeze
from chilling my chest and neck and strapped my iPod to my
left biceps. I pressed SHUFFLE as I popped the buds into my
ears. I didn't want to have to choose which songs were on

my run list; I wanted it to be . . . spontaneous.

As I reached the end of the driveway, "Dog Days Are Over" by Florence + the Machine was playing, immediately followed by Neon Trees' "Everybody Talks." I passed Haley's house when Led Zeppelin was on and circled the town green as I heard Michael Jackson. For a long stretch of dirt road, I listened to a violin concerto by Bach, which almost made me cry, but then LMFAO's "Sexy and I Know It" kicked in and I grinned. I sang along with Blondie and Rihanna, songs I didn't realize I knew by heart.

With every song, I took a new turn in the road and before I knew it, I had traveled far past my typical run with Nate. I heard one more song, "Hey Jude" by The Beatles, and then I was at the creek. The one that ran through the woods behind Nate's house. How had I gotten so far off my path?

I felt sweat pooling under my arms and tickling the hair at the back of my neck. After I unzipped my jacket and tied it around my waist, I knelt by the stream and splashed freezing-cold water on my face. The shock of it made me gasp, but it felt good. I was suddenly exhausted. I'd run on fumes, having not had any breakfast or even orange juice, and was ready to collapse. I leaned my back against a tree and slid down carefully until my butt hit the tree stump below.

From this angle, I could *just* see his house, which meant that this was *our* tree. A month ago Nate had sat here with me on his lap, not a care in the world. My finger traced a lazy pattern on the side of the stump. Funny that we'd been together for so long, living in a town filled with trees, and we never once carved our initials into one. Were we so much a part of the digital age that declaring our love like that was too analog for us? I smiled, thinking of how Nate the environmentalist might cry, *Carve a tree? That would damage it forever!*

My gaze found the side porch at the Bingham house where we studied and the old-fashioned swing where we would curl up as night fell. On those nights, Nate and I would simply melt into each other and ignore the prying eyes of his sisters, who were determined to catch us kissing. I felt my cheeks flush, thinking about the many, *many* times they had succeeded.

I tilted my head back against the gnarled bark of the tree and felt the world spin around me. I had run too far without water and was probably dehydrated. Nate would have reminded me to drink water; he would have brought it on the hottest mornings. I missed that. I missed his sweaty hand pulling me along for the last quarter mile. I missed his salty kiss when we finally finished.

I heard a rustle in the leaves and saw two figures coming toward me. They looked exactly like Nate walking Rocky, and even though I knew it was akin to a mirage, my hands gripped the stump I was sitting on and I tried to push myself up. God, I was tired. My eyes blinked a few times, bringing Nate's image into and out of focus. I wanted so badly to see Nate that my mind was eager to play a trick on me.

"Come on, boy!" It sounded so much like Nate calling

to his dog, but I knew it couldn't be. It was only my sleep-deprived, dehydrated brain being cruel.

He's not there. It's not real.

"That's it, Rocky! Come on!"

Oh, Nate, I thought wistfully as he loped toward me through the woods, dog at his heels. His hands were dug deep into the pockets of his jeans and he elbowed aside bushes and stepped over fallen branches as he came toward me. He was so handsome: the sun filtering through the leaves gave his chiseled features a golden glow and highlighted his hair. As he came closer, I caught a glimpse of a brooding grin, a look I hadn't seen before—it was sexy.

Ha! Sexy. I must have been *very* dehydrated to imagine . . .

"Hey, Middie."

Oh. Shit.

I gasped as the guy I'd imagined became very real. And very someone else.

"Lee. Hey."

What the hell? I felt my blush spread down my neck, and I had to quickly look away from him. I jumped up to go, but my head swam and I began to sway.

"Meredith?" He reached for me and I clutched at his arms, falling forward over his shoulder. He caught me with one hand at my waist and the other on my back. My face was pressed against his neck for a brief second, and I breathed in his scent. Sharp, soapy. Nothing like Nate's spicy aftershave.

No. Nothing like Nate at all.

I pushed Lee back and put some distance between us just as Rocky swished his tail around my legs. I bent down to rub his face between my hands and let him place a sloppy kiss on my cheek. "Hey, boy, you going for a walk today?" I needed to pull myself together. I was just tired, not crazy.

Lee knelt down too and scratched Rocky's neck. "Watch for his ears," he said. "His ears are really sensitive." Lee's face was so close, just a few inches from mine.

"Are you really telling me how to pet a dog I've known since he was a puppy?" I stood up again, but slowly this time so I didn't faint. "What are you doing here anyway?" I crossed my arms over my chest and took a few steps away from the tree. Lee stayed on his knees with the dog, gently stroking the back of his neck as if he hadn't heard a word I'd said.

"I'm walking Rocky, what does it look like?" His words were abrupt but his tone sweet. He crooned softly into Rocky's ear. "We're walkin', yes, indeed, we're talkin', 'bout you and me . . ."

"Does Mr. Bingham know?" I was irritated by his presence, annoyed by his *knowledge*. He wasn't supposed to know so much, to be so much a part of Nate's life. That was *me*. Not him.

Lee finally glanced up at me over his shoulder and fell back onto the log. "Rocky and I go way back," he said as if that explained things. "I helped Nate train him. I took him to the vet when he swallowed a plastic bone."

"He was Nate's dog."

"Yup, he was. And now . . . well, I just want to make sure Rocky's getting enough attention." Lee cocked his head to one side. "Nate's dad has a lot on his plate, you know?"

He was right. Why did he have to be right?

I reached a hand down to poor Rocky and combed his fur with my fingers. "Yeah. Okay."

"I got my Vespa, if you want a lift back," Lee said. He mimed revving the engine with invisible handlebars.

"I'm good." But I did still feel a little woozy. "Maybe I should sit for a bit longer."

Lee moved aside, and I took his place on the stump. Rocky plopped himself down on top of our feet so we couldn't move without disturbing him.

"You might be right about telling Mr. Bingham," Lee admitted. "He probably should know I walk him every day."

"Yeah, they might wonder why Rocky's always exhausted."

"He's old. He's always exhausted." But he said it with affection.

"How'd you get in? You have a key?"

Lee held a finger to his lips. "There's a door that doesn't close all the way."

I felt myself grin. "The one next to the cellar. Yeah, I know." Lee looked surprised. "What, you think you're the only one who knows the secrets of the Bingham house?"

Lee's eyes widened. "You know about the bodies?"

"What . . . ?"

He held his finger to his lips once more. "Shhh . . . let's never speak of this again."

I laughed in spite of myself. And then I remembered something. "There was a body once—"

"Shhh!"

"But it was a gerbil."

Lee nodded. "Scotty's gerbil, Harry Potter."

Nate's little brother had tried to cover up the animal's death from his parents by simply pretending it was alive. One day Mrs. Bingham, with the assistance of the twins, decided to clean the cage. The girls' screams echoed for miles.

We both fell silent, content to listen to the rush of the water over rocks in the creek bed, a crisp birdsong high in the trees, and the hiccupy snore of the old dog at our feet.

"What'd you mean the other day," I said quietly, "about the shit in your life?" It sounded more abrupt than I'd intended. Lee seemed to bring out bluntness in me.

"Take your pick. You wanna hear about the school shit? The father shit? The mother shit?" He picked up a small stone and chucked it into the water. It plopped with a teensy splash. "I have many different shit flavors."

"Uh, school?"

He shrugged. "Crappy grades. No money. Ergo, no college." He aimed another rock at the water, and it skimmed the surface of the creek before sinking. "Next."

I hesitated. I wasn't sure why I wanted to know about Lee's life. Maybe it would help me understand what Nate saw in him a little better. "Your dad?"

"He's a contractor. Overseas. Don't see him much."

"Oh. Um, you ever get to visit him?"

He grunted. "Uh, yeah, no. Iraq. Awesome, right? Next."

And just like that, I felt the wall go up again. It was like a layer of steel and stone between us; it surrounded him, protected him. He'd told me to ask. Was I not supposed to take him up on it? Was I not supposed to know? Sometimes it seemed like talking to Lee was walking in on a conversation that had been going on for a long time before I arrived, as if he simply expected me to know stuff. But how could I when Nate had never talked to me about him?

"I said, next," Lee huffed at me. "What else?"

I felt a chill run up my spine. I'd hit the edge of something, and I was afraid to go further. I swallowed and shook my head. "I should probably go now. I'm sure I'm late for school."

"School? Nate *died*, for god's sake. Give yourself a fucking break."

The harshness of his words hit me as hard as if I'd been smacked in the face. I smacked back. "I can't. It's . . . important."

"Why?"

"Uh, so I can get *good* grades and *go* to college?"

Lee waved a hand at me. "Whatever." This "whatever" was dismissive, no doubt about that.

I dislodged my shoes from under Rocky and stood carefully, walking my hands up the tree until I was sure I could stand without collapsing.

Lee rose as well and stamped the ground next to the old dog to get him up. "Come on, ya old bag o' bones," he mumbled.

I bent at the edge of the stream to get a sip of water before the run home. I tried holding my ponytail out of my face to splash water into my mouth, but it was impossible to get more than a tiny sip while using one hand—and impossible to not get wet as I was doing so.

If Nate had been here, he'd have brought water, I thought again, or reminded me to bring a bottle.

But he wasn't here. The weight of that loss nearly made me weep. Would every tiny thing make me think of Nate? For the rest of my life?

I felt Lee come up behind me and kneel next to the stream. "I'll hold your hair."

"What—"

"Just—I'll hold your hair, okay? Use both hands." With his shoulder pressed to mine, he lifted my ponytail from my neck, making it easier for me to scoop water with two hands.

After gulping down as much as I could, I pulled my head and hair away from him and wiped my mouth with the sleeve of my jacket. "Thanks."

Lee stood without another word and walked away with Rocky trotting by his side.

"I'll see you around," I said to him.

He lifted his hand but didn't turn around. "I'll call you when you need me."

Huh? "How will you . . . ?"

But he was already disappearing among the trees.

God. He was so strange. Maybe I would never truly know what Nate saw in him.

I stretched my legs on the stump, readying myself for the run home. I popped the buds in my ears and started my iPod—and then stopped. No music for the run home, I decided. I wanted to listen to the trees and the birds and the leaves falling on the road.

And maybe I wouldn't go to school. Not today. Maybe today I would give myself a break.

CHAPTER *nine*

Never in my life had I skipped school. Never. But no one in admin batted an eye when I came in the next day. Principal McMahon gently shooed me out of her office.

"You can take some more time if you want."

I shook my head and left, relieved but also a bit bewildered. *That's it? Not even a slap on the wrist or a wag of her finger?*

My friends noticed, naturally, but they too didn't seem to care. At lunch I joined Haley, who was saving me a seat at our table in the back of the cafeteria, one of the small round ones out of the way of salad bar traffic but close enough to keep tabs on everyone's comings and goings.

I slid my tray down beside her. I had circled the salad

bar a half dozen times before settling on a banana and a bottled water. I felt Haley's eyes on my lunch. She opened her mouth and then quickly closed it again. Her tray contained her usual carb-fueled, protein-packed meal, along with two cartons of skim milk—an athlete's lunch.

"I'm sorry I didn't call you after the service—"

She placed a hand on my arm and her eyes smiled warmly. "No worries."

A minute later, Katrina and Debra arrived, eagerly taking seats at the table.

"Middie, you were so perfect at the memorial," Katrina said as she arranged her salad and soda in front of her.

"And that dress," Debra added. "Where'd you get that? Twenty-One?"

"Huh? No, that's Allison's."

"Oh. Did *she* get it at Twenty-One?"

"Debra, Middie doesn't want to talk about clothing," Haley said.

Oh yes, she does, I thought. I wanted to talk about clothes and lunch and whether it was better to be taking history with Mr. Quinn before or after he'd had his second latte. I wanted a break—or a *fucking* break, as Lee so eloquently put it.

"You know, I heard that Nate's mom is in total denial," Debra said.

"You'd feel the same if it were your son," Haley said.

"Yeah, I guess." Debra shrugged. "But she didn't even come home for the funeral."

"It wasn't a funeral," I told them, a little too fiercely. "Mrs. Bingham will be back. She's just . . . making sure there's, you know, no chance he's . . ." My voice petered out. *No chance he's still alive . . .* Maybe I wasn't ready to say it either.

My friends nodded sympathetically.

"Well, I thought what you said at the service was just right," Katrina said to me. "It was short and sweet and really . . . just really *perfect*." She tossed her salad with a plastic spoon and fork. A slippery tomato flew off her plate and skittered away, landing in the center of the table. All of our eyes followed it as it rolled to a stop, leaving a snail trail of Italian dressing. Haley plucked it off the table and tossed it back at Katrina.

"I'm kind of glad you didn't tell a story about Nate," Katrina said as she wiped the tomato off with her napkin and returned it to her salad. "TMI, you know?"

"What do you mean?" Debra asked her. "I like stories."

"Yeah, but it's better to be mysterious," Katrina said. "Nate and Middie were, like, the best couple—"

"Oh yeah, you would have been voted Best Couple if you and Nate were in the same class," Debra interrupted.

"And you don't want to spoil the image, you know." Katrina spun a limp leaf of romaine around her fork as she talked. "I want to remember them at the prom and at homecoming and holding hands in the hall . . ."

I could feel my heart sink as Katrina went on. Each time

she mentioned a party or dance or event Nate and I had attended, I had a flash of an image in my mind. A snapshot of us together, smiling, happy, perfect.

"What inspired you, Middie?" Katrina wanted to know.

"Excuse me?" I looked up to find my friends smiling sweetly at me.

"The service. What you said. What inspired you?"

"Oh, um, they weren't really my words," I demurred. "I, um, someone else suggested them."

Haley smiled. "Was it Allison? She's so cool."

"Uh-uh." I shook my head. "Lee? Ryan?"

"Lee Ryan . . . you mean . . ."

"Nate's friend. His best friend," I clarified. Katrina and Debra had blank looks on their faces. Since Nate was in the class ahead of us, they didn't really know his friends very well. But Haley did. Her eyebrows lifted in surprise.

"When were you talking to Lee?"

"Oh, um, remember when I ran out of gas? And I called you?"

Haley nodded. "Lee helped you?"

"Yeah. He gave me a lift to get some gas." I could feel Haley's cluck of disapproval, even if she didn't actually make the sound, and I hastened to add, "He was the only person who had a car."

Vespa. Whatever.

"He's really . . . nice." Well, "nice" might not have been the best word to describe Lee, but it was the simplest.

"I think I remember him," Debra said. "Tall, kind of gawky."

"Stoner," Katrina said, as if she suddenly remembered Lee. "Oh my god, he was so wasted at his own graduation!"

Napping, I thought. He was only napping, he'd said.

"Did he play basketball or something?" Debra wanted to know.

"No . . . ," I heard myself say. "But he and Nate were best friends."

"I don't get that at all," Haley said. "They were *so* different."

"Well, he came and helped me. When no one else could."

"I get it." Haley sounded chastened, as if I were blaming her.

"And he's got a girlfriend," I added. "She's pretty."

"So he's not a total loser," Katrina said with a light laugh.

"Listen, I'm glad he was nice," Haley said. "But we can help you too, you know?"

"She's right," Katrina said. "You need anything at all, you just call us, okay? Any time of day or night. We're here for you." She and Debra both reached for me, but because of the size of the table, their arms couldn't really reach mine. All that touched were the slightest tips of our fingers.

"And next time you want to play hooky, call me," Haley said, grinning. "You don't need to get Allison to come all the way from college."

I laughed. "Oh, I didn't hang with—" I stopped. The girls all looked at me quizzically. "I mean, right, you're right. I won't call Allison."

I watched Haley, waited for her to say something to me, to ask another question about my day off and who I really spent it with, but she turned instead to Debra. "Do you have anything but fashion on your mind?"

Debra made a face. "Do you have anything but sports on your mind?"

Haley paused and held her gaze. "Yeah. Boys!" When she cracked up, the rest of us did too. I didn't realize I'd been holding my breath until I felt my shoulders relax. As the talk turned to boys and music and television, I quietly slipped away from the table, but Haley jumped up to follow. I tensed, wondering if she was going to say something else about my day of hooky, to flat-out ask me who I'd spent the day with, but she merely leaned into me and whispered, "You okay, Middie?"

I almost growled at her—did everyone have to ask that question ten times a day? But I knew she was only asking because she was concerned. "Yeah, yeah, I'm good. Just have to get ready for class, that's all."

"Well, like I said, we're one hundred percent here for you. All of us."

"I know. Thank you." I loved Haley, truly. She was an amazing friend with only my best interest at heart. It wasn't her fault she could only come up with trite phrases like *We're here for you*; after all, she couldn't understand.

"I totally understand," she said solemnly. "This is a

rough time, but we're gonna get through it together, okay?"

I let her hug me and told her how much I appreciated her friendship and then slid out of her grasp as politely as I could. Aside from Nate's family, there was only one person who truly understood what I was going through: Lee.

I'll call you when you need me.

But he didn't call that night, not even when I sent him a text: *call me?*

In fact, two more days passed and I heard nothing from him, no call or text. Was I wrong about Lee? Did I put my trust in him too quickly? My gut wanted to say no, but my heart sank a little as the days went by.

Three in the morning had to be the loneliest time of the night when your only companion was the wild thought in your brain. Crazy thoughts, thoughts like, *Was Nate sleeping when they attacked the village? Was he frightened or calm? How many people did he try to save?*

Silly things too. *What was he wearing? Did he have time to put on his shoes? Did he have bad breath or bed head or sleep drool on his chin?*

My gaze flitted from my textbook to my phone about twenty times before I realized that I'd been staring at the same page of chemistry homework for half an hour.

3:05. Density equals mass over volume.

3:09. Molarity. Wave relation. Atomic structure.

My eyes began to close as my lashes grew heavier, my

arms and legs sank into the mattress, light flickered behind my eyelids—

—and the phone on my bedside table suddenly rattled, waking me with a start. My heart skipped a beat as my semi-conscious mind thought, *Nate!* But of course it wasn't.

It was Lee. I resisted picking it up. He hadn't responded to my text, so why should I answer his call?

The muted phone buzzed and shook. I pulled the comforter over my head like a turtle retreating into its shell. It finally stopped ringing and then buzzed with a text.

Sighing, I reached a hand up and swiped the phone from the bedside table, curling up with it under the blanket. I tapped the screen and read the illuminated text. He wanted to know where I was.

Home. Bed. Asleep. Go away, I typed and sent.

A second later, the phone rang in my hand. "What?" I asked him.

"You're not asleep."

"I was studying."

"Studying what?"

What did he care? "Chemistry."

"Waste of time. No one uses chemistry in real life."

I could feel my temperature rise. I threw off the covers and savored the cool air against my skin. "What do you want, Lee?"

"What do *you* want?"

"Huh?"

"You texted me. Why?"

"That was two days ago."

"So? What do you want?"

He can be so bullheaded, I thought and then reminded myself, *He's not Nate.* He wasn't Nate's brother or his dog or even his shadow. He was a loner whose only friend was dead.

I swallowed hard. *Whose only friend was dead.* Oh god. Heartless. I was heartless. I softened my tone. "I have to go. I need to finish studying."

Lee cleared his throat, and his voice sounded phlegmy and thick. "Come outside."

"What? Now?"

"Yes. Now."

"It's after three. I'm not going anywhere." I pulled the comforter back up and snuggled under it. There was no chance of me leaving this bed tonight, not until I'd gotten at least three hours of sleep. I turned over and readjusted the comforter. I was oh-so-cozy.

But oh-so-curious.

"Why do you want me to come outside? I don't smoke, you know," I added.

"Who said I wanted you to smoke anything?" He sighed as if he was disappointed in the world. Or at least me. "Maybe I have something you want to see."

"Doubt it." I threaded a fraying nylon edge of my comforter through my fingers. "Just tell me."

"I can't. I have to show you."

"Lee—"

"It's something Nate would want you to see."

I inhaled sharply and half sat up. "Don't say that."

"What? Why not?"

"Because you can't know what Nate would want and what he wouldn't want," I heard myself blurt out. I could feel tears sting my eyes and I blinked hard against them.

"And you can?"

"Yes, I can."

He let the silence happen for a while.

Damn. I was doing it again. Assuming things. Being selfish with Nate's memory. "Fine, whatever," I said. "Give me ten minutes."

"Five. I'm waiting outside."

I peered through the window and saw Lee standing in the middle of the yard. I tapped on the glass and pointed at him. "You look like a stalker!" I whispered into the phone. He slowly swiveled his head up toward me on the second floor; moonlight danced across his face. "Go wait down the street. I'll be there in a minute."

I watched as he strode across the front lawn. Even his walk was different from Nate's—slow and loose. Did I really confuse him with Nate the other day? How was that even possible?

Five minutes more and I was creeping down the back staircase of our house. Past the driveway, about halfway down the block, Lee leaned against his scooter. I shivered in the brisk air and crossed my arms over my chest as I approached him. He was wearing a lightweight Windbreaker and his hands were bare. "Okay, where is it?"

In answer, he hopped on his scooter and waved me on.

"Excuse me? No. You didn't say anything about *going anywhere*."

"What I have to show you isn't here. Get on. Or walk." He shrugged.

"It's three in the morning!"

Lee started the engine. "Hold on to my waist."

I glanced back over my shoulder at the house, dark and sleepy, all buttoned up for the night. I had come this far; I supposed I could go a little farther. Rather than sitting side-saddle like I'd done before, this time I swung a leg over the back of the seat; the leather instantly chilled my jeans. I held on to the bottom of it with both hands, but as Lee revved up, it was hard to stay upright.

He leaned back against me and said again over his shoulder, "Hold on to my waist."

Since it was the only way to avoid falling off, I did as he suggested, pressing my fingers into his sides and holding on with just my nails. He was soft beneath his jacket, and so thin I could feel his ribs.

The wind was bracing, but as long as I kept my face turned and hidden behind Lee's back, I didn't feel its sharp sting against my cheeks.

As we tooled along smoothly, I marveled at the road, so

quiet and still. Not a soul stirred. It seemed like Lee and I were the only people alive in Roseburg. I tilted my head up toward the sky. Stars were sprinkled across the cloudless night like a necklace of sparkly jewels around the half-moon. I closed my eyes and took a deep breath; brittle, frosted air filled my lungs. I held it for as long as I could and then finally exhaled, releasing pent-up tension through the small O of my lips.

We bounced along the path, with Lee carefully dodging water-filled ruts and tree roots. At last we came to a small cabin, as dark and closed up as the house I'd just left. Lee parked the scooter behind a garage nearly the same size as the cabin and led me to a side door. "Watch your step."

We went from dark to absolute pitch-black inside the garage and I kept my hand at the back of Lee's waist, grabbing his jacket for a lifeline. I sensed we were next to something bulky like a boat or a car, and when Lee snapped the light switch, I gasped at the sight.

A Mustang convertible, circa 1960-something. It was dark blue with a creamy white-colored ragtop, stained in a few places but otherwise in good condition. A convertible in the Pacific Northwest was a luxury item: we had some great summer weather in Roseburg, but we had lots of rain for the rest of the year.

"You like it?" he asked me.

I was speechless. I loved it. How could I not? It was the very essence of cool. I felt my chin nod.

"It's Nate's."

I whipped my head around. "What?"

"Yeah. Well, I mean, it's Nate's and mine. We put it together. Kind of. It's not done, or maybe it is. I guess it is. Yeah, I think so." The words tumbled out of his mouth in short bursts. Lee shoved his hands into his Windbreaker pockets and shrugged, as if doing so would stop him from rambling.

I walked around the car, desperate to touch it, to embrace it—it was a piece of Nate right here in front of me! I ran my fingertips along the sharp edges of the hood, feeling the slickness of the new paint job. Even under the single bare bulb of the garage, I could tell Lee had recently touched it up. I peered through the passenger window.

"She's a '66, V-8. Manual transmission," Lee said.

I nodded, soaking it all in. A car. Nate's car.

"Get in."

"Can I?" But even as I said that, I was opening the door eagerly and scooting my butt onto the leather-covered bench seat, a single long front seat rather than the side-by-side buckets of other models. The interior smelled musty and a little damp with a mask of pine. Hanging from the rearview mirror was a trio of tree-shaped air fresheners. I played with the knot of string that held them, batting them gently to release a little more of their scent.

Lee slid into the driver's side, shutting the door and the world out with a soft *thud*. Again, it felt like we were the only two people alive. I couldn't hear anything but my own heartbeat thumping in my chest.

"Wood trim," Lee said, nodding toward the dashboard panel and steering wheel, which were covered in a shiny light brown. "Original radio."

"No iPod hookup?" I said with a laugh. "I love the color. Pretty blue."

"It's called Nightmist Dark Blue," Lee corrected me. "The interior is Palomino."

While Lee recited more details about the car, its engine, its options and add-ons, I sank back with my head on the padded headrest. "Why?" I asked him when he stopped to take a breath. "How can this be Nate's?"

"And mine." I heard Lee sigh, and when I glanced over at him, I saw he had leaned back like I had, with one hand on the wheel and the other on the floor-mounted gearshift, as if he were driving in his sleep. He smiled slyly. "Nate thought it would be cool to have a convertible."

"That's so . . . impractical!" I laughed. "Where would he put all his basketball gear? His sweats and sneakers—"

"And his fishing equipment! And his gardening tools!" Lee laughed too, an honest-to-goodness chuckle, perhaps the first I'd ever heard from him.

"Maybe there was a small part of Nate that just wanted to look cool," I said.

"Nah. Nate was always cool."

I stared at Lee for a long moment: his smile was soft; his hazel eyes shimmered under the harsh light of the garage.

His expression was unguarded and shockingly open. I felt like I could ask him anything and he would be honest. But what did I want to ask? What did I really want to know about Nate and Lee's friendship? Maybe it was better for Lee to keep his secrets to himself.

"He never told me he was doing this. I feel a little—" Would it be okay to say it? "Pissed."

"What? I'm sure you didn't say 'pissed.' You must have meant 'pleased.'" Lee's lips crinkled into a smile.

"Well, maybe not *this time*." I felt myself smile back.

"It was supposed to be a surprise." He turned to take in the backseat, the roof, the dash and floor, as if he were remembering the two of them working together on them. "Most of this was his idea. He found it online and convinced me to help him fix it up." He laughed again, this time to himself. "It was a piece of crap when we got it. No top. The exhaust manifold was cracked. But it was really cheap." He flung his arm over the back of the seat. "Look at it now. It might even work!"

"Really? Can we try it?" I immediately pictured the car on the open road, speeding through the night with the top down. The wind was blowing my hair, swirling it around my face, and the radio was playing full blast. Something sunny, something warm, something old. The Beach Boys. "California Girls."

"Sure, why not?"

I clapped my hands, giddy with excitement. "This is amazing."

"I don't know about amazing, but maybe it'll be cool." He pulled out a set of keys, started to put them in the ignition, and then stopped, handing them to me. "You want to do the honors?"

"You mean you haven't driven it yet?"

"I started it a few times. But no, no driving yet." He shook his head. "Go ahead. Put the key in."

The ring lay heavy in my hand, a thick brass circle on which hung a silver-plated Mustang key with the pony insignia on one side and the Ford logo on the other. I turned it over a few times, feeling the notches scrape against my skin. Finally, I leaned across the seat and inserted it into the ignition.

"Here we go!" I said cheerfully. It was almost like a dream. Nate's car was a convertible? It was another crazy, wild thought. Maybe *this* was a dream. Maybe I was still in bed, asleep with my chemistry book over my face.

"Go on." Lee grinned proudly.

But it wouldn't turn. I tried a couple more times, but the key wouldn't budge. I glanced up at Lee, who seemed confused as well. "Maybe the wheel is locked," he suggested. "Here, let me try it." He bent forward before I had a chance to sit back and his long torso curved over the wheel, nearly engulfing me. Suddenly I felt his breath against my cheek, his lips brushing my hair. I held my breath and couldn't move.

The air in the car filled with an electricity I'd never felt before. Tension was a tangible thing, a third passenger in the

Mustang, the force between us magnetic. My heart pulsed in the back of my throat and I felt like I was drowning, unable to draw a deep breath.

I expected Lee to pull away, to murmur an apology for crowding my space, but he said nothing. His hand rested on mine and his palm sent a wave of warmth all the way up my arm. I felt his long, thin fingers caress mine, the tips of them rubbing the edges of my nails as if he were gently filing them.

"Lee . . ."

"Hmmm?" He turned to look at me without sitting up and our faces were inches away from each other, our lips a whisper apart. His gaze held mine without blinking. Those inscrutable hazel eyes were asking me . . . something . . . what? What did he want from me?

"The key." I heard my voice crack. "Your hand is—"

And in a flash, his hand released mine and he sat back, his face flushed. "Sorry," he said to the window.

I scooted away from him and turned my head toward the passenger window. My breath fogged up the glass, and I traced a heart through it with my finger, then quickly wiped it away. *What am I doing?*

For a long minute, we were turned from each other, and then I heard him try to start the car again. The ignition clicked a couple of times as Lee cursed quietly. "Come on," he urged the engine. "Come on."

Finally, he gave up. "Damn it." He leaned his forehead against the steering wheel. "Sorry. Fuck. Sorry."

"Hey, it's okay. It's just, you know, just a car."

"No. No, it's not." He banged his hand against the side of the ignition, as if he could force it to work without the key. "We worked on this for months. It should run. It should at least turn over." He slammed his hand again. "Damn it!"

I glanced around the car, marveling at it as he had just a few minutes ago. "Hey, it's pretty amazing that you even managed to do this."

"What do you mean?"

"Well, I had no idea you could do this."

"Fix cars?"

"Well, anything, really." I thought blunt was okay with Lee until I saw the look on his face. The wall was back up, his eyes shaded and hooded. "Oh, I, Lee, I—"

"Forget it."

"I didn't mean—"

"What the hell *did* you mean, Yoko?"

I cringed. We were back to that, were we? I guess I deserved it. "I just meant, well, you know your reputation." *Stoner. Pothead. Lazy. Loser.*

"Are you serious? Who cares about a reputation?"

"Not you."

"Right. Not me. Not Nate. He *never* cared about that shit."

The words hung in the air and the car suddenly seemed insanely small and claustrophobic. I needed to leave, to go home and forget this whole crazy adventure. What was I doing here? In this car? With Lee . . . ?

I fumbled with the door. I shoved my shoulder against the window and felt it give way. Slipping out as quickly as I could, I ran from the garage, kicking up rocks and dry twigs with my boots.

The moon shone a path down the driveway, past the cabin, out to the dirt road. My mind raced angrily with a million thoughts, a million emotions.

How dare you manipulate me? I was going to say when his scooter pulled up next to me.

How dare you ruin Nate's memory for me? I was going to say when he insisted I let him drive me home.

How dare you . . .

But he never did. He never followed me. And I ran all the way home with tears clinging to my lashes.

CHAPTER ten

What *was* that?

It was impossible to sleep with my heart thumping against my rib cage. My face was flushed and sweaty, and I tossed and turned for the rest of the night. I wasn't surprised when my chemistry test was a major bust the next morning. I probably even got *Your name here* wrong.

I managed to put Lee and my nighttime adventure out of my mind for the weekend, and by the time Monday morning rolled around, I'd even convinced myself it could not have happened the way I thought it had. I must have imagined the tension I'd felt between us. In light of day, I felt more than a little guilty for treating Lee so badly. My loss was his loss too.

The Monday holiday meant we didn't have classes, but Haley had field hockey practice anyway and Emma had an all-day Scouting activity. With nothing to do, I realized it was a perfect time to drive out to Lookingglass and apologize.

At the convenience store I was greeted by Liza, Lee's girlfriend. She was dressed in a deep purple short-sleeved T-shirt and pink denim shorts that showed off her curves, and her hair was pinned back in plastic pink and purple clips. Even the earrings dotting her lobes were pink and purple.

"Hi! What can I getcha?"

"Oh, um, two Icees?"

"What flavor?"

"Blue?"

Her eyes lit up. "The best!" While the machine whirred and spat out the bright blue slush, Liza rang me up. "That's six twenty-six."

I handed over the cash and waited for my drinks to be ready. "So, um, Liza?"

She returned some change and glanced up at me under long blond lashes. "Huh? Do I know you?"

"Oh, uh, no, not really." I watched as she finished up with the Icees, swirling the tops into sharp peaks. "I know your boyfriend?"

"What?" she called over the sound of the machine.

"Lee? I know Lee."

"Oh!" Liza's face flushed as pink as her hair clips. She glanced away as if she was embarrassed. "He's cute, huh?"

Yes, my brain answered much too quickly. "He works around here, right?"

"Oh yeah! Right up the street." She pointed behind her through the window. "You going over there now?" She handed me the slushies. "Tell him I said hi, okay?"

"Oh, uh, sure." I thanked her for the drinks and the directions and left the store. A sort of relief flooded me: that was his girlfriend, I told myself. Lee had a girlfriend. There could not have been anything between us last night, thank god. It was me, I concluded. It was all me and my misinterpretation. We were both on edge, both stressed because of Nate's death, nothing more.

Whew. With that settled in my mind, it was time to move on.

I spotted Lee's Vespa on the street outside the "charter thing." It was a tiny stand-alone building designed to look like a quaint cabin. Inside, there were several revolving racks filled with glossy brochures for rafting and hiking trips, and advertisements for local inns and restaurants.

I was checking out a flyer for a place that had every fish taco imaginable for less than a buck when Lee came in through a back door. The look of surprise on his face was priceless. "What are you doing here?" he asked, narrowing his gaze. He hated me. I'd said some very unkind things last night, but I was here to set them right.

Unkind? You were rude and a little cruel. Yeah, I was. In light of day, I recalled the harsh tone of my voice from last night, and it made me wince.

"You need something?" he asked me as he leaned against the back door. He kept his distance, calling to me from the other side of the small room.

"I need a fish taco," I said, holding up the flyer. "Cheap." Nope, not even a twitch of a smile on his face. I turned to the drinks on the counter. "Icee? I got your favorite flavor."

"Blue."

"The best." I added, "That's what your girlfriend says."

One eyebrow lifted. "You saw Liza?"

"She says hi." His gaze dropped to the slushies. "You two fighting or something?"

"What? Who? Me and Liza?" He took a cup and spun it in his hands. "So what are you doing here, Yoko?"

I held out a straw, but he didn't take it, so I plopped one into the center of each slushie instead. "I . . . um . . . I'm running off to join the circus," I said.

"Uh-huh."

"Yup. Got a new trick for my magic act."

That was enough to interest him—slightly. "Oh yeah?"

"Yeah, I'm gonna make the foot in my mouth disappear." I sipped my Icee too fast and my head spun from the brain freeze. I massaged my temple with my finger.

He said nothing but slowly and deliberately took a long sip from his drink. A moment later, he squeezed his eyes shut and placed a finger to his temple as I had. "Whoa . . ."

We stared at each other in silence as we recovered from

the brain freeze. His bright eyes were brooding, his look inscrutable. Did I need to go on? Did he understand I was here to apologize?

"Lee, I—"

"Let's go outside. Warm up a bit."

I followed him out as he flipped a sign on the door that said "Back in 10." I wondered if every business in this town had one of those signs. We walked toward the back of the building to a picnic table under the shade of a large elm tree, taking seats on the table itself, rather than the benches. Only the slightest hint of autumn was in the air, despite being three weeks into the season.

Lee swirled his Icee around in the cup before taking a careful sip. "It's stupid to drink it fast, but I do it all the time. You'd think I'd've learned by now."

"We all do stupid things," I said with a laugh. I felt his eyes sneak a peek at me and I turned, fastening my gaze on him before he could look away. "Lee, last night, when I said . . . I didn't mean to make it sound like I thought you were, um . . ."

"A loser? A pothead?" he suggested.

"Well . . ."

"So you *don't* think I'm a loser pothead?"

"No, no, I don't, and I'm sorry—"

He held up his straw. "Don't apologize. Not to me. Is that why you came out here today?"

I nodded. "Did you think I just wanted a blue Icee?"

"They are pretty tasty." He smiled, revealing bluish lips and tongue. "Or maybe you wanted to do a waterfall walk."

"What's that?"

"This tourist thing. People want to walk under a waterfall, you know? Stand under it." He rolled his eyes. "Tourists."

I tried to imagine it. It sounded dangerous. "Don't they slip and fall?"

"They're standing," he said as if I were a slow child. "Underwater."

"So . . . they drown?"

"You're crazy. No one drowns."

"I would drown. Or slip. And then drown."

Lee laughed and shook his head. He poked his straw around the bottom of his cup with occasional glances up at me. "I'll take you on one sometime. You won't drown."

"Um, yeah, okay." I felt relief surge through me: he didn't hate me! "What about Liza?"

"What about her?"

"She okay with you hanging out with other girls?" I gently teased him.

"Yeah, Liza's cool."

"That's good. I don't want to be Yoko again."

His laugh was low, hearty. "That's when a girl breaks up two guys. Not a guy and a girl."

"Oh yeah, oh, right," I said, blushing. I should have known that.

"Don't worry. You couldn't possibly break up me and Liza," he went on.

"She's really special, huh?" I leaned back on my hands and watched Lee from the side.

He sucked blue Icee from his straw and then turned to me with a crooked smile. His profile was partly in silhouette from the leaves of the tree. "Let me tell you something, Meredith Daniels. My girl is clever and funny and beautiful. I had a crush on her for years before I got the courage to talk to her."

Light and shadows danced on his face and I no longer saw the strangely awkward, goofy guy I'd always assumed him to be. There was so much more to Lee Ryan than I'd ever thought, so much I didn't think I would ever know.

I wondered if Nate had talked about me like that. Had he told his friends he thought I was clever or funny? Had he ever pined for me like Lee did for Liza? "That's nice, Lee. I'm glad for you."

"Yeah, well, when she finds out about the real me, I'm sure she'll dump me." He winked at me. "Don't tell her, okay?"

I zipped my lips shut. "She won't hear it from me."

"Nice blue lips," he said.

"Nice blue tongue."

"Mine is purple," he said, sticking it out and going cross-eyed as he tried to stare at it.

"How can it be purple when you were drinking blue?" I started to laugh.

"I thought you were studying chemistry," he said. "Don't

you know red plus blue equals purple?"

"Uh, that is *not* chemistry."

"Of course it is."

"It's art. Like, painting or something. It's not chemistry."

"See?" Lee shook a finger in my face. "I told you no one uses chemistry!"

I cracked up and then he did too, both of us collapsing backward onto the picnic table. We were both laughing so hard we didn't see Liza approach us. She was just stubbing out a cigarette on the bottom of her shoe when she called out Lee's name.

"Oh, hey, Liza!" Lee said, instantly sobering. We both scrambled up and hopped off the table.

Her smile twinkled merrily as she gazed at him. She looked so happy to see him—it was as if I didn't even exist. She stuffed her hands in the back pockets of her shorts. "You still on a ten?"

Lee glanced at me and then into his cup. "Nah, I'm done. You need something?"

"Yeah," she said. "I want to get some brochures for the store."

"Oh, okay. Back door's open. I'll be in in a sec."

Liza went in, leaving Lee and me alone. "Thanks for the Icee."

"No worries. I owed you from last time. Oh!" I reached for my purse and took out my wallet. "How much was the gas for my car?"

"Save it. You're gonna need it when you finally run away."

I cocked my head to one side. "Huh?"

"To the circus. You know, your magic act."

I felt myself smile. "You just watch! I'm gonna be huge someday."

He rolled his eyes. "Yeah, right. Call me when that happens." He slipped inside, back to his girlfriend and his brochures and his waterfall walks for tourists.

Part of me didn't want to leave the cool shade of the trees, the peaceful solitude of this town. I envied the tourists who would come here seeking an afternoon hike through nature. And I wondered what it would be like to have Lee as a guide.

I took my time getting into the car, starting it up, putting on my seat belt and—

"Oh, shit!" The dashboard clock lit up with the engine. "Emma!" I forgot to pick her up!

By the time I rushed breathlessly into the house, Mom was in the kitchen preparing dinner, wearing a flowered apron and matching pot holders on both hands.

"It's okay, sweetheart. One of Emma's friends dropped her off." She smiled at me before placing a kiss on the side of my head. "You look exhausted."

I waited for the other shoe to drop, waited for a remark about my responsibilities as a sister and daughter and if I was going to be allowed to have the car then—

"Why don't you get washed up for dinner and help me set the table?"

"But . . . that's it?"

She turned me around and gently urged me toward the stairs. "Your dad and I know this is a lot for you to deal with."

I resigned myself to being shooed from the kitchen and went up to my room, passing Emma's along the way. She was on her bed, books spread in front of her, earbuds in her ears. I fell onto my own bed and let the pillow cave around my head.

Middie, you're tired. Middie, you're sad. Middie, go home.

When I looked at my friends, my teachers, my parents, all I saw was pity in their eyes. Their sympathy was too much—too trite, too saccharine. I knew they cared about me, about Nate, but they didn't know what to do or say much beyond *It'll be okay*.

Only Lee treated me like a regular human being, not like a fragile glass figurine that would shatter into a million pieces if someone said the wrong thing.

I pulled out my cell and texted him before I changed my mind: *waterfall walk*.

Seconds later, he responded: *when*

tomorrow

To get to Devil's Rock Falls, we had to leave the Vespa behind and hike.

"Devil's Rock?" I faux-shuddered as I followed Lee through the woods, glad I'd worn jeans and boots instead of shorts and sneakers.

"That's just some shit I made up," Lee said. "Scares the pants off the tourists."

"But you told *me*. Does that make me a tourist?"

He glanced at me over his shoulder. "Nah. You've still got your pants on." I was about to respond when he grinned. "Kidding. Geez, Daniels, lighten up,"

He turned onto a small path, leading me through a narrow passageway, and we emerged under the cliff in a dark recessed cave behind the water. It fell in sheets in front of us, splashing into the pool a few feet away. The sound of the water was like an intense storm, heavy and thundering, and it echoed all around us, deafening me to anything other than my pulse pounding in my head.

Without saying a word, Lee took my hand and led me out of the cave and closer to the water. A thin fence ran the length of the ledge, the smallest separation between rock and water. The rock ledge was slippery, but I felt Lee's fingers grip mine so tightly, I knew I wouldn't fall in and drown.

We were inches from the waterfall when Lee loosened his hand from my grasp and I balanced there on my own. It was incredible. The water was powerful and intimidating; the sound of it crashing around me was isolating, nearly terrifying, and yet . . . I felt calm, serene, the eye in the center of the storm. I could hear nothing, not even my own thoughts. I felt nothing, no fear, no anxiety, no sorrow.

I closed my eyes and allowed myself to breathe in and out, to appreciate the beauty of the world that surrounded me. I smiled, trying to picture myself from the outside: Meredith Daniels standing under a waterfall in a forest far from home, with no worries in her head, no cares at all? That was crazy.

We stood there for a little while longer—ten minutes or half an hour, I had no way of knowing—and finally, Lee led us back through the cave and to the side of the waterfall pool. I leaned back against a tree and glanced up at the falls. Had I really stood under all that water?

"How did you find this place?" I asked him after we'd taken a moment to relax and refresh with bottled water. "It's so far away from everything."

"I got lost." Lee tipped his head back and poured the last drops of water into his mouth. "I was about thirteen. Ran away one night."

"You got lost? At night?" My mind raced, thinking of all the things that could have gone wrong for Lee. I shook my head from side to side. "It's so risky."

Lee laughed as he crawled to the edge of the waterfall pool. "Some of the best things happen when I take a risk." He splashed some water over his face and then flicked some at me with his fingers. "Haven't you ever done something completely new and different?" When I gestured to the waterfall, he added, "Aside from today."

Risk was not part of my vocabulary. I panicked at the thought of being unprepared, of doing something wrong. "I don't like to do things I can't do," I said, finally. I heard the words and started laughing. "That sounds lame, doesn't it?"

Lee laughed. "Yeah, it does. Look, at some point, you don't know things. So you can't do them. And then you do them and then you know how." He stopped and tilted his head to one side, as if he were thinking about what he'd just said too. "Whatever."

"But what if I mess up?"

"You're gonna mess up the first time. Maybe even the second. Or third."

I groaned. Loudly.

"So *what*? Who *cares*?" Lee plunged his reusable bottle into the pool and filled it with clear, cool water—and then poured it over his hair. "I live to fail!" He shook his head like he was Nate's dog Rocky shaking water off his fur after a dip in the creek. "Failing is all I've ever wanted to do."

"You're kind of insane," I said.

"Insane in a good way?"

"There is no good kind of insane."

"Eh. Who cares what you think? You're just a dumb girl," he said, teasing me.

I pretended to take offense. "You don't care what *I* think?"

"Nope. Don't give a shit." Lee ran his fingers through his wet hair, combing it down and away from his face. Pearls of water dripped down the side of his nose and he wiped them off with his sleeve. "Why do you care so much what other people think, anyway? No one's perfect."

Nate was perfect, I thought. Lee caught my eye and his

smile slipped as he read my mind.

"Not even Nate," he said. "I tried to get him out here once a couple years ago." Lee rolled his water bottle in his hands; the rubber covering was torn in places and his fingernails picked at those spots that were coming apart.

"He didn't want to come?"

"I think he was doing something with you that day."

"Oh. I'm sorry."

Lee frowned at me. "What are you sorry for? You're always apologizing for shit that's not your fault. Nate could have come if he wanted. He didn't want to."

"You could have asked him another time."

"Nope." Lee pressed his lips together into a line. This was obviously not up for discussion. I could tell by the set of his jaw and the firm way he held on to his water bottle that if you said no to Lee, you didn't get a second chance to say yes.

He flopped onto his back and stared up at the sky. The clouds were thin as wisps, translucent and slightly gray. I rolled onto my side and looked up too. "Why'd you run away?"

"Hmmm?"

"When you were thirteen, you said you ran away. . . . Why?" In the time I waited for Lee to respond, the clouds passed beyond the trees and the sky turned clear blue.

"I didn't like home," he said simply.

"Why not?"

"Do you like your home?"

"Yes—"

"I don't like mine." He laughed sharply then and turned his head to look at me; leaves of wet grass tangled in his eyelashes and he blinked a few times. "You know, I was only half-right about Nate not being perfect."

I sat up. "What do you mean?"

"*He* wasn't, but his family is," he said with a wistful sigh. "Even that old dog of his. A perfect family." He brushed the grass out of his face and mock-frowned at me. "And don't tell me they're not."

I smiled at Lee and shook my head. "Nope. They're perfect."

He turned away and stared at the sky again. "I always wanted Nate's room," he said. "When we were kids, he got these glow-in-the-dark stickers of stars and planets and his dad put them on the ceiling for him. I loved sleepovers at his house 'cause those stars were the coolest things ever."

"Yeah, they were cool."

Lee lifted an eyebrow my way. "You saw them?"

"Yeah, I saw them."

"You know you can only see them in the dark. When the lights are off. And the door is closed."

I giggled. "Yeah, I saw them."

"Well, well, aren't you the tart?" he teased, but his gaze was sharply inquisitive.

I felt my cheeks grow warm and I knew I was blushing, but I wasn't about to divulge anything. Not to Lee. "I had a good time today," I said. "Thanks."

"Way to change the subject."

"You can say you're welcome."

"Give me your phone," he said, snapping his fingers. "Come on, give it here."

I was digging in my backpack even as I asked, "Why?"

"You gotta commemorate your first trip to the falls," he said. He took my phone and tapped the screen a few times. "Get over here and lean in."

"Why don't *you* sit up?"

"Because I have the phone. Now do it."

"Please."

"Please—now do it."

I scooted down on the grass, laying next to him so my face would be in the picture with his. He held his arm out in front of us and yelled, "Cheese!"

We looked like idiots and I told him so.

"Speak for yourself. I look dashing."

"And insane."

"Dashing and insane. The best ones are."

I teased him back. "Is that what your girlfriend thinks?"

"I hope so." He laughed and it sounded like the cackle of a wild man.

I took my phone back from him and stared at the picture. Just behind our silly faces, I could make out a part of the waterfall. I tried to imagine Nate here, standing beneath the wall of water or hiking to the top. Would he have liked this place? Would he have been proud of me for doing this, for trying something new?

At the end of the day, I made Lee drop me off at the community garden, where Abby had a huge list of chores for me. In spite of the hours I spent hiking, I felt refreshed, as if I'd just awoken from a long nap.

It was the waterfall. It must have been.

CHAPTER *eleven*

Later in the week, Emma knocked on my door, wrinkled notebook paper in hand, pen tucked behind her ear. "Middie, can you read my essay?"

Her story about Nate, I remembered, the one that would help her get her next badge from Brownies. While I read the paper, she wandered my bedroom, touching everything she saw: makeup on the vanity, books on my shelves, clothes in my closet. I allowed her free rein for just about everything, but when she got to my phone, I put the brakes on. "Nope. Not yours."

She didn't turn the phone on, but she also didn't put it down. "It's not fair. Everyone else has one. Why can't I?"

Out of the corner of my eye, I saw her pretend to chat on the phone, turning her head this way and that, admiring herself in the mirror. I tried not to laugh, but it was pretty cute.

Nate Bingham is my sister's boyfriend, I read. *He is very smart and very tall and very good-looking.*

My breath hiccuped and Emma turned sharply to me. "Is it bad? Did I write it wrong?"

"Um . . . you used 'very' three times."

"Well, yeah, 'cause it's important. Very, very, very."

"Uh-huh." I kept my eyes on the page. *Nate is really, really helpful to other people, and he always gives me a present when he sees me.*

"Um, Emma?"

"Hmmm?" She glanced in the mirror at me. "I probably didn't spell everything right. I get confused sometimes."

"Um, were you confused about present tense and past tense?" I asked carefully.

Her expression was quizzical. "Huh?"

"You know what present tense is, right? 'I am.' 'She is.' 'He is,'" I said, holding tightly to her essay.

"Oh yeah, I know that."

"So . . ." How was I going to put this delicately? "You wrote 'Nate is.' Instead of 'Nate was.'" When she didn't react, I added, "You know Nate's not coming back, right?"

I half expected her to roll her eyes at me but instead she said, quietly, "I know what 'dead' means."

I tried not to look startled. "Okay . . . so why did you write it in the present tense?"

Emma tapped a finger at the side of her head; the nail, bitten and chewed to a nub, was covered in purple ink. "Because he's alive for me up here."

"Emma!" Mom called up the stairs. "You left your science project down here."

"My volcano!" Emma's mouth formed a little O and she dashed out of my room, dropping my phone on the bed almost as an afterthought. I turned back to her essay, almost afraid to read what she'd written, but it turned out to be a very sweet story about Nate showing her how to tie knots for—what else?—a Brownie badge. My sister had a one-track mind. No doubt that would change once she finally got a cell phone.

I kept reading, making mental notes about spelling and punctuation errors, but then I got to the last line and I gasped: *Nate was going to be a awesome doctor but he died and now I am inspired to be a doctor too.*

Tears clouded my eyes as I stared at Emma's heart in my hands. I carefully placed her paper on my nightstand, right next to my computer. I tabbed open the application to Lewis & Clark. The *incomplete* application.

Tell us about an experience that defines who you are.

Emma had done that. She had told the story of Nate's importance in her life; his death not only inspired her, it defined her. My nine-going-on-thirty-year-old sister. Part of me wondered if I could crib it for my own essay—without the knot-tying lesson, of course.

I picked up the pen Emma had left behind and tapped it against the screen as I tried a few sentences in my mind.

The death of Nate Bingham had a tremendous influence on my small town of Roseburg. I shook that one away. It was too cold, too impersonal.

Nate Bingham was beloved in my small town. He had friends in every part of the community, in the high school, and . . . Ugh. Boring.

Nate Bingham was the love of my life and his death crushed my world.

No! I shoved the thought out of my brain as fast as I could. I couldn't write that. I couldn't. Although true, it was *too* intimate, too revealing. The pen in my hand trembled and I felt a wave of panic grip my chest as I thought about Nate.

Unlike my sister, I didn't find inspiration in his death. I found terror and sorrow and abandonment. How could I write about an experience that defined me when I had no idea who I was? I half wished I *could* use my sister's story. It would be so easy to say, *This is who I am now; this is who I will be.* But I didn't know.

Was I the girlfriend Nate left behind? Was I the sister Emma and Allison wanted me to be? Was I the daughter my parents expected? As I'd told Lee, I was no risk-taker. I was neither adventurous nor spontaneous, two qualities he insisted Nate had possessed, which made me wonder: Had I been keeping Nate from doing things he wanted to do?

I reached for my cell and tapped the screen until I got Lee's number. He answered on the first ring. "Yo. 'Sup?"

"What else didn't Nate do with you?"

"Huh?"

"He didn't climb the waterfall because of me."

"Well, no, he was busy—"

"What else didn't he do?"

There was a long pause on the other end of the phone. "I dunno. Stuff. Why?"

"I want to do it." I stood and walked to the window and stared up at the sky. No stars tonight, just a half-moon covered in clouds. "Stuff you wanted to do with him." I paced the small bedroom; where before it had been cozy, now it felt cluttered. I wanted to get out and do things. I wanted to be inspired. "I want to try things I've never tried before," I told Lee. "I can be spontaneous too."

"Telling me you're spontaneous is not being spontaneous."

"You know what I mean!"

"Calm down, Yoko, I get it."

"And stop calling me that. I don't want to be Yoko anymore." I stopped, took a breath. "Look, you'll think of something, won't you?"

"Yeah, yeah, I'll think of something." He ended the call abruptly and I fell onto my bed, feeling suddenly wiped out.

A moment later, my phone buzzed with a text from Lee: *tomorrow tree fort*

"Tree fort? What the . . . ?"

And then another: *make sandwiches*

I started to text him back when a third came in: *I like pbj*

What do you do in a tree house? At night? In the rain?

"You brought the sandwiches, right?" Lee asked me when I'd climbed to the top of the tree in our neighbor's yard. The fort had been forgotten when the last son went to college, but it was still (mostly) intact. Hidden away by thick foliage that had grown over the wooden supports, the fort's floor was sturdy and sound, but there were some holes in its roof.

Which we didn't realize until the first drops of rain fell.

I passed him a sandwich wrapped in Saran even as I searched my backpack for something to put over my head. "What's wrong?" he asked when he caught a look of concern on my face. "You live in Oregon, for god's sake." He scooted to the open door and dangled his legs over the side, like a kid sitting on a too-tall chair. The ground was fifty feet down, but because everything was overgrown, I could hardly see the grass below. If either of us fell, we would disappear into the leaves as if we were diving through the surface of a pond.

"You gonna melt in the rain?" Lee crumpled over. *"I'm melting, melting. . . ."* He whined like the green-skinned Wicked Witch.

"No, but I'm usually inside at night."

"Well, that's your first mistake right there." Lee unwrapped the sandwich and inspected it. "What kind of jelly is this?"

"Strawberry jam."

He sneered. "You couldn't use grape like a normal human being?"

"I *made* this jam. Well, Emma and I made it. She had a Brownie project."

Lee's eyes lit up. "Ooh! Did you bring brownies?"

"No," I said with a smile.

He shook his head as he licked some of the jam that squished through the slices of whole-grain bread. "Not bad for an amateur." He swallowed the whole thing in about four bites. "Got any water?"

I rummaged around in my backpack. "Somewhere . . ."

"Never mind." Leaning his head out the door of the fort, he stuck out his tongue to catch rain in his mouth. He was nearly off the edge, holding on to nothing and in danger of sliding off and down. Way down.

I grabbed hold of his elbows and pulled him in. He toppled backward and collapsed onto my feet, his face grinning up at me, inches from mine. "What the hell, Middie?"

I let him drop him on the floor. "Acid rain," I teased.

"Ha! Good one!" he said, pointing a finger at me as he sat up again. "You're thinking of my health, and that's funny."

I had to duck a little as I investigated the tree fort, seeing as how it was originally built to accommodate young boys. It was pretty bare bones as far as "man caves" go. Shaky Wi-Fi signal. No electricity, of course. And that hole? Directly in the center of the fort. Each time I passed under it, I got a shower of water on my hair.

"Hey, what is that?" I heard Lee ask. When I glanced over at him, I saw him jut his chin in the direction of a child-size table, a relic from the boys' youth. "Underneath. There's a stack of something."

I lifted the small table up, uncovering a hidden pile of comic books. I picked up a handful of them and fanned them toward Lee. "Spider-Man. Superman. Richie Rich?"

Lee clapped his hands. "Yes! Bring 'em here!" He was next to the open door again but this time kept his feet inside. He saw me hesitate and then sighed. "There is *no* light over there. How can we read them?"

"We're reading them?"

"What else do you do in a tree fort? You eat sandwiches and read comics."

Lee took the stack from me as I sat down and then, with a wicked grin, held up a copy of *Playboy*. "I know what I'm reading tonight."

Oh yes, I blushed—fifty shades of red. "Lee!"

"It was between Superman and Spider-Man." He held up the other comic books to show me. "Boys will be boys. You want me to read you one of the fascinating and informative articles?"

"Uh, no. Just keep it to yourself." I quickly looked away.

"Have you never seen porn before?" He sounded incredulous.

"I have two sisters. When would I see *Playboy*?"

"Well, there's Nate."

"Nate did not look at porn."

Lee threw back his head and laughed so loud and long that I was afraid we'd be caught by the neighbor who owned this tree. "Oh yeah, right. Nate didn't look at porn." He paged through the magazine, his eyes lingering on every photograph. "Trust me, every guy looks at porn."

I refused to let him get to me, so I picked up a Superman comic and thumbed through it. I had to shift closer to Lee in order to share the beam of moonlight coming through the open door of the tree fort, but I avoided the magazine in his hands. "Nate didn't. And if he did, I don't need to know that."

"Aw, come on. Naked bodies are beautiful." I squirmed like a kid; I couldn't help it—and Lee reveled in my discomfort, ostentatiously flipping the pages of the glossy magazine and making little moaning sounds. "Oh yeah, that's nice," he said to the airbrushed models. "Very, *very* nice." He opened the centerfold and turned the magazine sideways. "Now, those can't be real, can they?" He leaned next to me and thrust the centerfold in my face. "What do you think? Real or fake?"

I shut my eyes. "Stop it!"

"What do you think, honestly? I want a woman's opinion."

I felt a smile on my lips. In spite of myself, Lee could make me laugh. "I have no opinion. I don't know."

"They're awfully . . . full?" he went on. "Kind of puffy, which makes them look really weird." He tsked. "I don't know. Why would a pretty girl do that? The bigger the better, I suppose some guys like that. Not me. I like the au naturel look. No enhancements needed. If they're flat, they're flat, you know?"

"Oh my god, Lee, stop talking about breasts!" My hand flew to my mouth, covering my giggles.

Lee feigned shock. "Breasts? How crass of you, Meredith. I'm talking about her lips. It looks like she's had collagen injections."

I tore the magazine from his hands and was about to fling it away when I stopped and looked at the model. She did have puffy lips, it was true, and they didn't look natural. "You're right," I conceded. "They do look enhanced."

Lee held up his hands. "See? That's all I was talking about." Then he narrowed his gaze. "Now what about her breasts—"

"Lee! Stop!" This time I did toss aside the magazine. It landed back underneath the tiny table.

"Shhh!" He placed a finger to his lips. "Do you want to get us kicked out?" He rolled back on his butt, doing awkward somersaults until he landed in a corner of the tree fort. Only two of the corners were dry. He sat in one and I took the other. The distance between us was about eight feet; if we each stretched our legs in front of us, our toes would touch. I pulled my knees up to my chest and listened to the rain falling lightly on the leaves. According to my phone, it was nearly midnight. I'd managed to sneak out the back staircase near my room just after my parents went to bed.

"First night in a tree fort?" Lee asked quietly. When I nodded yes, he glanced around him, up at the ceiling, at the walls and door. My eyes adjusted to the darkness and I could see a smile tease out dimples in his cheeks. I'd never noticed them before. "Not so bad, huh?"

"A little cold, but yeah, not bad." I hugged my legs tighter and rested my chin between my knees. I felt my eyes begin to close but each time I shivered, I woke up again. At least the rain had stopped.

"You tired?"

"Mm-hmm. Yeah."

"I'll read you a story."

I heard a rustle of paper and I started to protest. "No porn, please."

His laugh was light. "No porn." He cleared his throat and adopted a Serious Broadcaster's voice. "When last we saw Superman, he was being crushed by Lex Luthor in outer space." Then he became Lee again. "In this first panel, Superman's squished between two asteroids the size of houses and he's gritting his teeth like he's constipated."

"What . . . !"

His eyes, meeting mine, danced merrily. "I gotta say, whenever Superman's in trouble, he looks like he's shitting bricks."

"Oh my god, Lee," I said with a laugh. I felt my cheeks warm with a blush again, although thankfully not as much as with the *Playboy* magazine.

"I can stop if you want," he said.

"No, no. Don't stop," I said quickly. "It's fun. I like it." As Lee started to describe the comic panels again, I felt sleep descend like a blanket.

". . . and then *pow! Bam!* Superman's fist flies through the air, cracking the asteroid apart . . ."

I nestled my head against my knees and curled my hair over my neck.

"'Think you can destroy *me*, Superman? Ha!'" Lee's voice rose and fell, adding a cackle here for the villain and a basso profundo there for our hero. It was like listening to a radio play but one being performed just for me.

"I kind of like Lex Luthor," I heard him say at one point.

I answered him drowsily. "Hmm? He's the bad guy. You can't like him."

"Nah. He's just misunderstood."

I woke the next morning laying on my side with a hooded sweatshirt—Lee's, I realized—draped over me like a blanket. Sunlight warmed my cheeks through the hole in the tree fort's roof. In the corner opposite me, Lee was curled into a fetal position, wearing just a short-sleeved T-shirt with his jeans. He was using the stack of comic books as a pillow; his hands gripped the Superman he'd been reading aloud to me.

I had no idea when he'd given me his sweatshirt, but he must have been freezing all night. I stood and stretched, feeling every ache and cramp from sleeping overnight in a rotting tree house. In the sunlight, it looked like Tarzan's home in a jungle. The leaves and vines crawling up the fort were slick with rain from the night before and the place smelled like peanut butter.

I inched closer to Lee and saw three empty Saran wrappers and one half-eaten sandwich next to the comics. A ring of strawberry jam lined his lips and a speck of sleep drool dribbled from the corner of his mouth. I was about to wake him when I had a better idea. I found my cell phone and snapped a picture of him fast asleep.

I tapped the screen to send it to his cell along with the message, *thx 4 great nite.*

I was in chemistry a few days later when I got Lee's next text: *movies 2nite, sneak in back*

Unfortunately, I'd forgotten to put my phone on vibrate, so it beeped loudly.

"Whose phone was that?" the teacher roared, startling me. I quickly stuffed my phone back into my purse, but it was too late. His bald head swiveled from one side of the room to the other and he cast a sharp eye for the culprit. Class was held in the only lecture hall at the school, a room with a pitched floor so we had to look down at the white board and giant periodic table. Unlike conventional classrooms, we couldn't hide behind anyone in chemistry. Mr. Mitchell could see every single one of us.

And he saw me.

"I'm sorry, Mr. Mitchell," I started to say, but he cut me off.

"No need, Middie," he said, his voice softening when he realized it was my phone. "Please be aware of it for the future."

The class began to murmur and Mr. Mitchell rapped his knuckles on the podium for attention. "That was not license for all of you to start chitchatting! Especially after that last exam." He glared at everyone and went back to the board.

Behind me I heard whispers and then someone said, "Be nice. This must be really hard for her."

Another voice clucked. "She doesn't look that upset to me."

It hurt to hear that, even if one of the girls was defending me. I wanted to turn to them and say, *Do I have to be crying constantly in order to feel pain? Do you think it's easy to avoid every tiny thing that reminds me of Nate every moment?* But I didn't. I kept my head down and let my hair fall across my eyes, willing myself not to weep.

A few hours later I met Lee outside the movie theater, one of the newest buildings in town, with four screens and a very busy concession stand.

"Not the back door," he cautioned me, "the side one." When I found him in the parking lot near his Vespa, he clarified, "Everyone who wants to sneak into the movies goes through the emergency exit in the back." He led me toward a giant Dumpster, which was about fifteen feet from a nondescript black metal door with no handle on the exterior, so when it was shut, it blended in with the rest of the building.

Sure enough, as we watched for a few minutes, a couple of ten-year-old-boys tried to sneak in through the emergency exit of one of the theaters. Almost instantaneously, they were escorted out by one of the ushers in a maroon vest and matching pants.

"Don't worry," Lee said. "That won't be us."

"God, I hope not." The thought of being chased away like a stray dog sounded humiliating. "So what do we do? How do we get in?"

We walked over to the wall and Lee grinned maniacally as if I were about to join a secret club of mental patients. "Watch this door. The ushers take the trash out between movies. You have about thirty seconds from the time they walk out, go over to the Dumpster, and then turn around." He wobbled his hand in the air. "More or less."

I tried to stay calm on the outside while my heart was beating hard in my chest. I was a good girl. Good girls didn't sneak into the movies without paying. "Then what?"

His smile creased the corners of his eyes. "So serious, Meredith Daniels. I'll take you into battle with me any day."

"Just go on, before I lose my nerve."

"By the way, I appreciate that you wore all black. Just like a ninja."

I dropped my arms to my sides. "I didn't know!" Black cotton pants and a black tank just seemed easiest to put together. And yeah, maybe I was trying to think stealthy.

"Once we get in, follow me to the right." Lee gestured in the air, drawing an invisible map. "Stick close to the wall until we get through the employee entrance and into the lobby. Then we're golden. We're behind the ticket dude and we can go anywhere we want." He paused and chewed on his lip. "You sure you're ready for this?"

"I'm a ninja, remember?" I waved my hands in the air as if I were doing a martial arts move, karate chop.

"If you say *Hai-ya!* I'm leaving you right here, right now."

Next to us, the door clicked open and I heard Lee cheer quietly. "Sweet! Tiny girl, big bag. Let's go." He grabbed my hand and flattened himself against the wall. Our hips were side by side, our shoulders pressed together. My nose twitched as I smelled cigarette smoke in Lee's hair and on his clothes. *Liza smokes. They were probably together.*

The metal door swung open fully and the girl taking out the trash kicked a wooden wedge under it to prop it open. She was about five feet tall with spiky pink hair and lots of piercings. She struggled with the bag but eventually managed to fling it over her shoulder and half drag it to the Dumpster.

I watched her for a moment, mesmerized by the pretty cotton-candy color of her hair, until I heard Lee whisper urgently. "Meredith! Come on!" He was at the door ahead of me, waiting, his hand outstretched toward me. I felt like my feet were stuck in cement and I couldn't move them. The girl was at the trash bin, struggling to open the lid, and soon she would be finished and headed back to the building. I had to move now—or never.

I lunged myself at Lee just as the girl turned, seeing us both. Her eyes flew open and she planted her fists on her hips. "Hey! You can't do that!"

Part of me thought it was odd that a quirky, counterculture chick like this one would be yelling at us while another part thought, *Go! Now!* I ran into the back of Lee and he pulled me along the wall, inside the theater, through the employee entrance. We stumbled into the lobby, grinning in relief.

I glanced around us, half expecting a swarm of usher police to come after us, but no one did. Crowds stood in line for popcorn, but we were safely behind the counter. Before the pink-haired girl could find us, we hurried into the nearest theater. We slid into the first pair of empty seats we could find and tucked ourselves down. I couldn't tell what was playing but it was something action-y. Cars screeched and horns honked. An alien ship flew through the air firing lasers at the humans running for cover.

In the dark, Lee grinned and his white teeth lit up the

space between us. "Must be that Victorian drama everyone's been talking about," he whispered gleefully.

I felt giddy too. I'd done it. I'd sneaked into the movies. It made me insanely happy that Lee was happy. It probably shouldn't have, but it did.

"Give me your phone," he said quietly. "I wanna commemorate this."

I shook my head. "Nuh-uh. We just got here. I don't want to get kicked out."

He frowned. "Killjoy." Then he held his hand in front of us and leaned his head close to mine. "Click," he whispered, as if he were taking a real picture. "Gotcha."

CHAPTER *twelve*

"Oh my god, finally!" Haley exclaimed when I was at my locker, pulling out books for morning classes. She leaned into me. "Where have you *been*?"

I looked around me. "Um . . . school?"

"You have not. And I would know, because I have been here for the past week"—she pointed first at her chest and then at mine—"and you have not."

It hadn't been a week. It couldn't have been. Haley was being her melodramatic self. "You're crazy, Hale. Where else would I be?"

She hugged her book bag to her chest and leaned in closer. "At the movies. With Lee Ryan."

I felt a blush color my cheeks and I stuck my head into my locker to escape my friend's inquisitive gaze. "How did you hear that?"

"Short? Pink hair? That's my brother Cal's girlfriend."

"You know her?"

"She knows *you*. What were you thinking?" Haley asked. "Sneaking into a movie theater?" She shook her head. "That sounds like something *I* might try. But you?"

I pulled my head out of the locker and stared hard at Haley. She shrank back a bit. I so wanted to say, *Why not me?* Instead I closed my locker, trying very hard not to slam it shut. "Pretty hot today, huh?" I said. "Just like summer again. Indian summer."

Haley kept her lips pressed together. She was pissed, but she didn't want to be. I'd been keeping secrets from my best friend and she didn't like it. Neither did I.

"Are you walking with me to homeroom?"

She nodded, slightly warily, and we walked down the hallway in silence. Outside homeroom, she stopped. "But what about Lee?"

At the mention of his name, images flooded my brain: the waterfall hike, the tree house sleepover . . . more secrets I'd been keeping from her.

I shrugged. "He was Nate's friend."

"And . . . ?"

"He was there too." I couldn't look at her. I couldn't. I knew the question in her eyes would make me uncomfortable. She wouldn't be able to help herself: she would *have* to ask me. That was what a best friend *did*. I walked into the classroom and took a seat at the back. Another student stopped Haley at the door, asking a question about field hockey practice, and I took that time to slip away.

Our homeroom teacher, Ms. Delaney, pushed through everyone at the door with a hurried *Excuse me* and, as the first bell rang, she tapped her hand lazily on the sign at the front of the room: a black-and-white drawing of an old-fashioned flip phone with a red circle and slash. I reached into my purse and found mine to shut it off.

There was a message from Lee: *day off, wanna come?*

I glanced up at the clock, at the sweeping red hand counting down the minute until the second bell rang, when everyone needed to be in their seats, ready to shout, *Present!* I felt my hands shake as I held the phone, staring at the text.

Respond or ignore?

Across the room Haley laughed at her field hockey friend's joke; behind me, other students finished their last text messages before shutting their phones off. The homeroom teacher was powering down her Kindle. The clock's red second hand reached nine, ten . . .

Dry, crackling heat radiated through the uncovered windows and from body to body. It was suddenly summer again, for a day or two at least.

My fingers tapped a quick reply: *yes*

Almost instantly, he wrote back: *outside now*

I hesitated only a fraction of a second and then rose from my chair just as the last bell echoed in the hallway. "Ms. Delaney, I need to leave—"

"Middie, what are you—" She started to talk over me.

"—now because I'm not feeling very well—"

"—doing out of your seat—"

"—my mother is coming to get me—"

"—when you know we're starting—" She stopped. Gray eyes blinked a few times behind rectangular lenses. "Oh. Yes, of course. By all means, take all the time you need."

I gathered my books and my purse and scurried out of the classroom, deftly avoiding Haley's laser-like gaze. I made a mental note to shut my phone off. I knew I would be on the receiving end of some questioning texts.

Lee was waiting for me in the pickup circle at the front of the school and I had a fleeting memory of him whisking me away on that first day when we heard about Nate's death. Was it so very long ago?

I hopped on the back of the Vespa and grabbed hold of the chrome trim without a word. The air was as dry as dust; it crackled with a last-ditch attempt at summer, a promise of cornstalks and pumpkins and hot cocoa with marshmallows in the not-too-distant future. Those days were just over the horizon, but not now, not today.

I vaguely recognized the long driveway Lee turned into; it was a place I knew after dark, but it looked different in daylight. Dayton Feed, where we'd had our senior year kickoff party six weeks ago. Ahead was the giant barn, its sides weathered and graying, bushes dried and growing over its signage.

Lee whizzed past the barn and headed farther toward the back of the farm. A fence ahead wore a rusted metal sign that said No Trespassing. *Naturally,* I thought with a smile. Where else would Lee go but a place that was off-limits?

We parked the Vespa and hopped the fence easily. Through brush and branches and trees, we emerged in front of a swimming hole I'd never seen before. Water from a bubbling creek gently flowed between two rocky banks, cooling the air and the grassy shore. The pool was not as deep as the one under the waterfall had been, but it was wider and more placid.

I drank it all in: the solitude, the moist air, the breeze on my skin. It was beautiful.

Lee peeled off his sneakers and socks and tossed them on a tree branch. "You wanna go in?"

"I didn't bring a suit."

"Neither did I." He grabbed the bottom of his T-shirt and pulled it over his head as if I weren't even there. His chest was scrawny compared to Nate's and his shoulders rounded rather than squared. He caught me looking and grinned. "Yeah, I'm a hunk, huh?" He shrugged, feigning nonchalance. "Whatever. Someday my soft, skinny body will be in fashion and everyone will want to look like me."

So. Skinny-dipping.

Could I?

I stared down at my outfit: I'd chosen a long-sleeved navy blue T-shirt and dark blue jeans at the start of the day, not knowing how warm it would get. I could feel the heavy cotton clinging to my back with sweat; my underarms were damp and sticky. I was dying for a dip in the creek.

I heard Lee unbuckle his belt, and I quickly shut my eyes. But he'd decided to adopt a bit of modesty and duck behind a bush to finish undressing.

I started with my shoes, heeling them off one by one and then unrolling my socks. *Pants or shirt?* I wondered. Which should I take off first?

Take off? a wise little voice in my head yelped. Why on earth was I taking anything off in front of a stranger?

But he wasn't a stranger. He was a friend now. And he was nearly undressed himself. I pulled off my shirt, slipped out of my jeans, and stopped. Keep on the bra and panties? Jeans over wet underwear sounded like a bad combination, so I whipped it all off just as Lee came out from behind the bush.

I jumped in, wading until the water was as high as my waist, and then I ducked down, letting it cover me up to my neck. Freezing at first, it didn't take long for my body to adjust to the temperature. I dipped my head back to wet my ponytail and felt the heat rise off me like steam from hot pavement.

A moment later, Lee walked out from behind the bushes

and I started to turn my head, but then I noticed—

"You're wearing underwear!" I said, pointing an arm toward his green plaid boxer shorts.

His eyes widened in delighted shock. "And you're . . . *not?*" He rubbed his hands together like a villain in a cartoon. "This is so much more than I expected!"

"No! No, no, no. This isn't fair!" I cried.

"Meredith Daniels, why the hell did you take off all your clothes?"

"Because I thought . . . I . . . thought . . . you were going to?"

Lee walked toward me, one eyebrow raised suavely. "I think you were projecting," he said. "You *want* to see me naked."

I felt my cheeks burn. "Oh dear lord, no," I told him. "That is the furthest thing from my mind."

Is it? the little voice asked me.

Shut up, little voice.

Lee turned and walked out of the creek and back to the bushes.

"Wait! Where are you going?" As I watched, Lee's boxers flew over the top of the bush. "Oh my god. . . ." I dropped fully under the water then, knowing what was coming next. How long could I hold my breath? Twenty seconds? Thirty? A minute?

I heard a gentle splash and felt the water ripple around me. Slowly, I lifted my head out of the creek, one eye squeezed shut as if glimpsing him naked with only one eye would somehow be less shocking than with both.

Lee had waded in to his waist . . .

Well, nearly to his waist.

My blush spread down my neck and chest and I thanked god I was mostly underwater. I had no idea how much of my body was flushed with embarrassment.

Lee swam around me. "Ever been here before?"

I shook my head as he did a silly dog paddle. "Nope."

"Ever skinny-dipped before?"

"Would you stop saying naked words?" I asked. I wrapped my arms around myself, careful not to make even a moment's contact with Lee.

"So that's a no."

"Right. No."

His circle became smaller and smaller; he was about three feet away from me and getting closer. It was as if he were daring me to move away from him. Or to not move away . . .

I did a kind of breaststroke till my knees were able to touch the bottom. Then I crawled, making sure that all vital parts were still submerged, toward the far rocky bank. The water was shallower there, and I could comfortably sit on the sandy bottom.

Lee took it in stride and began to swim more in earnest. Every so often his naked butt would break the surface of the water, giving me a glimpse of shockingly bright white skin.

"Hey, Meredith!" he called between breaths. "Wanna see me do the backstroke?"

I held my hand over my eyes, not trusting myself to simply close them. "No!"

"You sure? I'm really good at—"

"No, no, no, no!"

He paddled over to me and rested on his knees. His chest was above the water, slick and wet but drying quickly under the sun. "I can't believe you took your clothes off in front of me," he said with a sly sideways glance. "Usually it takes a lot of sweet-talking to get a girl to do that."

He wanted to see me blush. I wouldn't oblige. "First of all, I didn't take them off in front of you—"

"You think those tree branches were an impenetrable shield?" he asked.

"And second of all, I thought *you* were taking *your* clothes off, and I didn't want you to be the only freak in the pond."

"Aw, that's so sweet of you. You didn't want me to be naked all alone."

"For the love of— Stop saying 'naked.'"

On the other side of the swimming hole, my phone rang, trilling the first few notes of Haley's disco ringtone.

"I'll get it for you." He began to rise, but I quickly grabbed his shoulder and pushed him back into the water.

"No!"

"Okay, get it yourself."

"She can go to voice mail."

Lee shaded his eyes and stared out over the creek as if he could see my phone from here. "You can't stay in here forever."

"I know."

"You'll wrinkle up," he said with a cluck of his tongue. "Like your mama."

I splashed some water at him. "What?"

"*What* what? Did you not hear me? I said—"

"I know what you said, and it was kind of mean."

"Geez," he drawled. "I was only joking." He splashed water back at me and it went right up my nose.

I coughed it out and shouted, "Screw you, Ryan!" as I shoveled handfuls of creek water at him.

He shoveled it back. "Screw *you*, Daniels!"

Back and forth it went, some childish taunts were thrown, and maybe there was a brief glimpse of some skin or body part I might not have wished to flash, but it wasn't as if Lee could cover anything up either.

"Screw it all!" Lee yelled. "And screw Nate Bingham!" His shout echoed against the rocky banks of the swimming hole.

I stopped, my hands cupped to throw water. I was only partially submerged, head and shoulders above the surface, so I sank down onto my knees again to hide. "Lee . . ."

"Screw . . ." Lee slammed his hands hard against the surface, aiming a tidal wave of water away from me and back toward the shore. "Nate . . ." He turned to face the rocks and I heard a hitch in his voice.

"It was a stupid place for him to go. Goddamn it." He slapped at the water. "A stupid thing for him to do." And again. "I told him that. Like, who fucking cares about kids in goddamn Honduras, you know? Who cares?" Lee held his arms up to the sky as if posing his question to the universe.

I felt a chill run up my spine and I remained as motionless as I could. "Nate cared—"

Lee whipped around and aimed a finger at me. "No, he did not. He did not care." His eyes were rimmed with red; water ran down his cheeks like fat tears. "He cared about going to college and to medical school—"

"And this was supposed to help him do that!"

"No!" Lee shook his head from side to side. "He could have stayed here and done a ton of other shit that would have been just as helpful. He didn't have to leave. Fuck him. Fuck. Him." He sank down into the water and let it cover his head. A few bubbles rose to the surface and then stopped.

I waited. If I could hold my breath for a minute, how long could he? The air was still and quiet; nothing disturbed the solitude of the creek. I began to panic at the thought that Lee could drown—could he? Could he drown himself by sheer willpower? We were miles away from help. Not a soul knew we were here.

A second minute passed and nearly a third and still, Lee remained below the surface.

That was it. I lunged for him, dragging him up out of the water and pushing him toward the shore. Leaning over him,

I pressed my hand against his bare chest, ready to start CPR if necessary.

His eyes fluttered open and he coughed a few times, spitting water up and over his chin. He pushed back against the shore and sat up, coughing.

I paddled back and away from him. "We're even now. You saved my ass—"

"And you saved my flabby white one."

He was trying to get out of this with a joke, but I wouldn't let him. "What was that? What the hell did you think you were doing?"

He shrugged, silent.

"And that bullshit about Nate. Why would you say that?"

Lee tried to swim away from me, but I grabbed his arm and forced him to look at me. "Why are you so angry?"

"Middie, you're the girlfriend."

"So? What does that mean?"

He sighed and squirmed. "You've got a million people worrying about you, caring about you. Who am I? Huh? I'm no one."

"You were his friend."

"His *best* friend. My heart got broken just like yours. And there is not a single person who gives a shit." He wiped a hand across his eyes as if he were erasing the emotions I could see in them so clearly.

Lee had never shown me this side of himself before. I wanted to reach out to him—to let him know that *I* cared.

We were side by side under the water, so very, very close to each other.

But Lee couldn't let the conversation remain serious. "So, hey, thanks for taking off all your clothes with me. This was awesome. Very therapeutic."

"Glad I could help."

"You want to do this again, you just . . ." He mimed dialing a phone and mouthed, *Call me.*

"Uh-huh."

I followed him to the other side, hunched over to cover myself. I had to figure out how I was going to get out, get dry, and get dressed without him seeing me. When Lee got to the water's edge, he ran to the bushes where his clothes were hanging and ducked out of sight.

"Close your eyes!" I called to Lee. "I'm coming out."

"Please. You don't have anything I haven't seen before."

"Maybe I do."

"What is it? A third nipple? An extra toe?" His head popped up again. "Now, *that* I would have to see."

"Stop. Go back and close your eyes. Now," I growled. I waited until he was completely hidden by the bushes and then I dashed to the edge of the shore, grabbed my clothes, and stumbled to the widest tree I could find. I was dripping wet and reluctant to put on my dry clothes, but I didn't have much of a choice. Finally, I finished dressing and emerged from behind the trees to find Lee staring balefully at the creek. I felt like I was interrupting something.

"You ready to go?" I asked as I gathered my purse and took a quick look at my messages. *Ten* texts from Haley, two voice mails.

Lee nodded and we headed back to the Vespa through the woods. "Thanks for coming to the creek."

"So you always wanted to skinny-dip with Nate?" I teased him.

Lee looked surprised. "I always wanted to come to this swimming hole," he said. "*You* were the one who turned it into a strip joint."

I laughed as we stepped into the brutal heat from the cool of the woods. "You want a photo to commemorate this?" I asked when we got to his scooter.

He grinned. "Yeah, okay. But get my good side this time." He leaned in close to me as I held the phone in front of us. I felt his warm cheek against my cool one. The smell of the freshwater creek clung to his face and arms. "Naked cheese!"

I burst into laughter, my eyes squeezing shut as the camera clicked. *Oh yeah, that's gonna be one great photo.*

CHAPTER thirteen

Haley and I navigated a crowded cafeteria a couple of days later as a team of school council members were decorating the room for Halloween. Black and orange streamers fell in crisscrossing swaths while paper skeletons danced on the walls.

"So you were deep into studying—is that what you're telling me?" Haley asked as we both dodged glittery black cats made of crepe paper.

"Chemistry," I said, nearly blushing at the memory of Lee naked in the creek. "So many pop quizzes, you know?"

"Uh-huh."

"I just needed some more time with the books, so I shut

my phone off," I went on. "Didn't even see your message till last night."

Haley slid into an empty chair at our table. I hated lying to my best friend, but I knew it would just make her mad to know the truth. *Studying* was a better alternative to *skinny-dipping with Lee*.

"Messa*ges*," she said, emphasizing the last syllable. "Yeah, okay. As long as you're all right." She held my gaze for a long moment, scrutinizing me even as she unpacked her lunch. "You look . . . I don't know . . . refreshed?"

I nodded and quickly glanced into my own bagged lunch before she could read anything on my face. "Oh yeah. Got some extra sleep."

Haley smiled. "Good. Sleep is good."

"Hey! Did you see the decorations?" Katrina asked as she sat opposite us at the table. Debra took a seat seconds later.

"I think the giant jack-o'-lantern is new this year," Haley said as she bobbed her head toward the caf entrance, where a couple of girls were maneuvering a big soft-sided pumpkin. "Cute."

"Halloween is my very favorite holiday," Katrina said, although this was not news to us at all.

"Because we celebrate things that are orange? Like your hair?" Debra teased.

"Ha, ha. I've been working on the haunted house." Katrina immediately got down to business, pulling a small notebook out of her purse and opening it to a page filled with blue pen scribbles. She pushed aside her salad to make room for her notes.

Every year she, Debra, and Haley volunteered to work at a haunted house that raised money for local charities. They dressed up as witches and vampires to scare kids and their parents, who paid a few bucks to walk through an old house decorated like something from *The Addams Family*.

"I don't want to be a witch this year," Haley said. "I'd rather be a zombie."

Katrina consulted her notebook. "Okay, I think we can do that."

"Oh, me too!" Debra said.

"You can't both be zombies."

"Why not?"

"Because I need some witches too. Every haunted house *has* to have a witch."

Listening to them gently bicker about costumes and makeup reminded me that this year I wouldn't be celebrating Halloween like I normally did: with Nate, handing out candy at his parents' house. Maybe this was the year to try something new.

"Hey, I'll be a witch," I heard myself say. The girls turned to me.

"You will?" Katrina asked. When I nodded, she picked up her pen and began jotting notes. "Awesome!"

I felt Haley's inquisitive eyes on me. "Really? You never do the haunted house."

"This year is different, you know? I want to try something new."

A grin spread across Haley's face. She looked as if I'd told her she'd won the lottery. "You are going to have so much fun. I promise!"

"Oh yeah! We have the best time," Debra said. "We scare all the kids—"

"And their parents too!" Katrina added. "Remember that guy last year? Totally flipped out when Haley jumped out of the closet. I thought he was having a heart attack."

For the rest of the lunch period, we talked about costumes and hairstyles, how to apply wounds, whether to buy or rent a cape, and so on. Debra and Haley were going to be zombies, shambling the grounds in tattered clothes and mud-streaked shoes, while I would take Haley's place as the witch in the closet, jumping out at unsuspecting guests.

The more Katrina told me about my assignment, the more I began to sweat the details. Was this really my thing? Could I pull it off? Or would I embarrass myself and my friends? Just as I opened my mouth, ready to take it back, to tell them I'd changed my mind, Katrina said, "Our last haunted house together!"

And Haley added, "Our last Halloween together!"

I glanced around the table at the three of them, my best girlfriends. Of course I could do this. The bell rang, but we were still engrossed in the haunted house.

Haley turned to me as we walked out. "I'll show you how to lunge. You might want to start doing some squats to prepare yourself."

"Yeah, it's a long night," Debra said.

"But so worth it," Katrina said with a grin. "This will be awesome!"

"Whoo-hoo!" Haley said and then she looked at me and lifted my hand to high-five hers. "That's right. Whoo-hoo!"

Putting together a witch's costume was a lot harder than I'd imagined, but fortunately Emma could earn a badge for helping me sew, although I probably spent more time teaching her *how* to sew than she actually sewed. She also had lots of ideas for how I should scream and say *Boo!*

"You can practice on me," she offered.

"Don't you want to be surprised at the haunted house?"

She shook her head. "No. I don't like surprises like that." She wagged her finger at me. "And don't be too scary."

I swallowed my laugh and made a solemn promise. "Not too scary. Got it."

By the time Halloween rolled around, I thought I was pretty well prepared. I had a crazy black wig with streaks of white in it, a pointed hat that came down past my ears, and a heavy velvet cape I'd borrowed from Katrina. A black dress from Debra over high-heeled boots finished the outfit, but the look wasn't complete until I'd hollowed out my cheeks with green-tinted makeup and added gray lips.

Lee texted me just as I was touching up a fake mole on my chin: *trick r treat?*

I quickly texted him back with a photo of the mole.

His response: *needs more hair*

Laughing, I wrote him: *ewww*

Gotta see this. Where?

I sent him the address, adding: *u can bring liza*

Maybe

Maybe he'd come? Or maybe he'd bring Liza? Before I had a chance to text him back, my phone exploded with a flurry of calls from the girls. Katrina was on her way, picking each of us up so we could arrive together at the haunted house and "bond" on the ride over. More likely, as Debra put it, she just didn't want any of us to be late.

Debra's zombie makeup was fantastic, as was Haley's. They'd followed an online tutorial for just the right amount of undead and they'd shredded some old jeans and flannel shirts, which they wore over torn T-shirts. Both of them looked liked they'd died during the Nirvana grunge era. Katrina was a vampire, and she'd sprayed and teased her hair until it was an airy red nest.

To put us in the mood, Haley led us all in singing "This Is Halloween," which was the only Halloween-themed song we knew besides "Thriller." By the time we arrived, we were shouting "Halloween! Halloween! Halloween!" at the top of our lungs and sweating off our carefully applied makeup.

"Oh my god, there's already a line!" Debra said as

Katrina pulled up. True enough, a long line of kids and their parents snaked from the front entrance down the sidewalk. "There must be fifty people here and it's not even dark yet."

I started to get nervous, seeing all those kids. Would I be scary enough? Too scary? I felt Haley by my side, felt her squeeze my arm. "I'm so glad you came," she whispered. "This will be a blast."

An image popped into my mind of the little kids coming to Nate's house on Halloween night. While his parents went out with his brother and sisters, we stayed home to hand out candy and make out on the couch.

I felt a little wistful seeing these kids in their costumes. This would be a different experience, for sure, but I was ready for it. I wanted it. I squeezed her back. "Me too!"

The wind gusted, sending dry leaves skittering across our path—nature's own special effect. As we got closer to the house, we could hear man-made creaks and groans; wisps of dry ice gave the path a creepy vibe and made the air feel crisp.

Inside, strands of fake spiderwebs hung from the rafters and fake black spiders ate fake black flies. The hallway was pitch-dark in places, lit only by electric candles in pumpkins. Haley giggled beside me, and her nervous laughter was contagious.

"This is amazing!" she whispered loudly. "Do you love it?"

"I love it!"

"Hi!" Katrina's face appeared between our shoulders and we screamed and then collapsed into fits of giggles again. "You guys go back there." She pointed to the other end of the hallway where there was a door underneath the stairs. "When you hear people coming, jump out and scream!"

Haley grabbed my hand and we ran down to the staircase, throwing ourselves through the small doorway. There was barely enough room for both of us to be there, let alone one with a tall, pointed hat.

We huddled inside like we were playing hide-and-seek. Haley kept peeking out the door. "What are you going to say?" she asked me.

"I think I'll just scream. What about you?"

"Braiiiiins!" She half closed her eyes and reached an arm through the door. We heard a small boy yelp. Haley's eyes widened and she snatched her hand back. "Sorry!"

"Oh my god! You scarred him for life!"

"He shouldn't be there, then!"

We fell over onto each other, laughing like kids.

"Shhh! Here comes another." Haley shoved me toward the door. "Go, your turn!"

"Me? Why me? I thought we were doing this together!"

"Go, go!"

I took a breath and lunged out the door, screaming and raising my arms over my head. Two boys about Emma's age yelled and fell backward. I quickly retreated and Haley closed the door.

"You did it!"

"I did it! Oh my god!"

"Did it feel good?"

"It felt awesome!"

Haley laughed. "Sometimes it's fun to just scream."

I remembered Lee screaming at the pond last week. Fun, cathartic, whatever you wanted to call it, it felt good to let loose.

Haley squealed and hugged me. "I'm so glad you came out with us tonight."

"Yeah?"

"Yeah. We like hanging out with you."

I felt my mouth open. "You do?" It was hard to take her seriously with her pale zombie makeup and fake open neck wounds, but I knew what she meant.

"Well, don't get a big head about it," she teased me with a sly smile.

"That's not my head, that's my hat!" I said, and we both started laughing again.

Haley whispered-sang, "I am the one hiding under your stairs . . ."

"Fingers like snakes and spiders in my hair . . ."

"This is Halloween, this is Halloween . . ." Our voices grew louder, filling the small closet. "Halloween, Halloween!"

Haley flung open the door and we threw ourselves out into the hallway with our arms over our heads, falling on top of a small group of kids and parents, who ran away laughing and screaming.

All except one: Lee. He stood in the middle of the hallway, his mouth agape and his eyes crinkling with amusement. His gaze traveled from my hat to my boots and then took in Haley beside me. We stood facing each other for a long moment; screams and shouts echoed in the old house and feet stomped on creaky floorboards.

I looked at Lee, raised my fingers like claws, and said, "Boo!"

Taking my cue, Haley's arms shot out in front of her and she reached for Lee's head. "Braiiiiins!"

His face split into a grin and he roared with laughter. "Not much of a meal," he said. "More like a snack."

Haley didn't break character, groaning and swaying, limp fingers swiping the air around Lee. "Unhhhhhhh . . ."

"Nice hat," he said, bobbing his chin at me. "You should wear one more often."

But like Haley, I tried to stay in character, remaining as witchlike as I could. "I'll get you, my pretty!"

"That mole . . ." Lee pointed to a spot on his chin. "Yeah, right there. Get that looked at, huh?"

I tried not to smile, but it was hard not to when Lee was doing his best to make me laugh. Fortunately another group was coming down the hallway, so I pushed him away with both hands. "And your little dog too!"

He glanced back at me, grinning again, and I was glad the hideous green makeup covered my blush. I let Haley pull me back into the closet to reset for the next group, but my thoughts lingered on Lee. I was irrationally happy to have made him laugh.

I readied myself to lunge, elbows tensed like springs, when another thought popped into my head: I didn't see Liza.

"Boo!"

CHAPTER *fourteen*

When my sister Allison was thirteen, she had a brief infatuation with boho-chic: gypsy blouses and long floral skirts, scuffed cowboy boots over leggings, huge sunglasses and layers of hair. But her interest waned when her friends teased her about looking like a homeless Mary-Kate Olsen. Soon all of her embroidered blouses and handkerchief skirts were relegated to the back of her closet.

I was reminded of this phase of my sister's life when I was searching for an outfit the week after Halloween. It had been fun dressing up, stepping out of my fashion comfort zone, and frankly, nothing inspired me in my half of the closet. My usual jeans-shirt-sneakers attire, although comfortable and reliable, felt dull. Each time my hands reached for a top, my brain rejected it: *boring, predictable, safe*.

My eyes were drawn to Allison's cream-colored top with three-quarter sleeves that flared just below the elbows. The heart-shaped neckline was embroidered in peach and jade green, and it plunged much deeper than my usual T-shirts did. I twirled in front of the vanity mirror, admiring how the loose sleeves fluttered in the breeze. The embroidered edging drew the eye in and down while the neckline hinted at cleavage that, well, wasn't there.

I like this. I liked the way the crinkly cotton felt on my shoulders, how the bottom hem fell just at my hips. I reached farther into the closet and found a skirt with layers of filmy crepe and chiffon. Was it too pretty for me? Too ornate? I rolled the waistband over twice to make the skirt a little shorter. It paired perfectly with the blouse. I added short leather boots and stepped back in front of the mirror.

Still good, but there was one thing out of place. I reached back and pulled the elastic out of my hair, letting it fall over my shoulders and down my back. It had been so long since I'd worn it down, without even a barrette to hold any of it away from my face. But a severe ponytail was not what this outfit called for.

With a new-to-me outfit and the loan of my mother's car, the day ahead held such promise—until I hit school. Moments after the second bell rang, one of the secretaries from the principal's office interrupted the roll call, handing

Ms. Delaney a green piece of paper. Green meant it was official, something that needed attention right away. Ms. Delaney read the note and then her eyes glanced up, finding me. She crooked her finger and I rose automatically.

Under her breath, she said, "Mr. Z needs to see you in his office now." She showed me the paper. *ASAP* was written in black ink. "Take this in case anyone stops you for being out of class."

I took the paper uncertainly. I'd never been called to admin for anything in my entire life.

Mr. Z welcomed me warmly, his tone a major contrast to the official order in my hand. "Come in, Middie. I'm glad you could make it," he called.

There was a choice?

The last time I'd been in his office had been the day we all heard about Nate. My gaze found the couch I'd sat on then, the corner of the desk I'd wept over. I felt a shudder roll through my spine—*Why am I here? Did something else happen?*

"Please sit down, Middie. I just want to take a few minutes to catch up."

I lowered myself into the only empty chair in the office and perched on its edge.

Mr. Z clasped his hands together on top of a pile of papers and books on his desk and his chin grazed the tops of his fingers. "Has everything been . . . okay? Have things been . . . getting better?" His eyebrows lifted hopefully.

"What do you mean?"

"Well, Middie, you haven't been in class regularly."

He sounded just like Haley. "Sure I have."

"Actually, you haven't. And it seems you haven't turned in some assignments as well."

That can't be. I was going to classes, doing my homework. Wasn't I? I tried to think back to the last time I was in front of my computer. A day? Two?

"Your SAT prep coach said you've missed some afterschool sessions too," he went on. "And your college applications? Are they getting done?"

Getting done. As if little writing gnomes were sneaking in at night to take care of everything for me. I frowned, irritated by the question.

No, not the question, I realized, but the way it was being asked. "Mr. Z, can I go back to class now?" I rose from the chair. I was done.

"In a minute, Middie, in a minute."

I sighed very loudly, but he paid no mind.

"You didn't attend the grief counseling sessions we offered after Nate's death, did you?" he asked.

I shook my head no.

He chose his words carefully. "Are you receiving counseling . . . elsewhere?"

"No," I replied in a flat voice. "I'm not."

"I see . . . Do you not believe it could be . . . of benefit to you?" He pushed his glasses up higher on his nose, magnifying his eyes and lashes and a few old-person skin tags.

"I don't think I need it."

"That's exactly when it's most helpful."

I edged away from the desk. I was not interested in seeing a counselor, in being "therapized," in hearing someone say all the stupid trite things that people in mourning were told. The things people said to me every day.

How I needed time to heal. How I needed to accept the death of my loved one and learn how to go on living. How, in time—

"Everything will be fine," Mr. Z said in a tone he probably thought was soothing. "You just need some time. . . ."

Whatever he said after that was drowned out by the pulse pounding at my temples. I was tired of being placated by my family and teachers. I was tired of hearing them speaking in saccharine tones.

"Everything will *not* be fine!" I said more loudly than I'd intended. "Nate is dead and nothing is going to bring him back."

"Middie—"

"Mr. Z, you just don't understand. No one does. I . . . I . . ." My stomach felt queasy and my head spun. I didn't want to be here, having this conversation. I rushed out of his office, out of the high school, and headed straight for my mother's car in the parking lot. Hot tears stung my eyes, and it was hard to see as I drove. I wiped my sister's pretty blouse across my eyes, smearing mascara all over the fluttery sleeves.

I found Lee at his house, at the garage in back, head buried in the engine of the Mustang. *Nate's Mustang.* I thought about composing myself before I caught his attention but changed my mind. He'd seen me—all of me, warts and all; raccoon eyes were barely a blip on the radar. "Hey."

He glanced up from under the hood and his eyes narrowed. "You're crying?"

"Yeah."

"All right."

I liked that he left it at that. He didn't pry. Didn't try to soothe me.

He gestured to the toolbox sitting on the concrete step next to the door where I was standing. "Grab me a crescent wrench, would you?"

I stared down into the toolbox, at the collection of metal and rubber and had no idea what I was looking for, but at least I had a task. I hitched up my skirt and bent down. "What's a crescent wrench?"

"It looks kind of like . . . Pac-Man on a stick."

I tried to picture the little yellow moon-shaped character that scarfed up all the dots while evading multicolored ghosties. I searched the toolbox for anything resembling Pac-Man.

"Ms. Pac-Man was better." Lee's voice echoed under the hood. "She had a bow in her hair."

"Got it!" The wrench was round on the outside, flat inside the "mouth." I handed it to Lee, who used it on . . . the carburetor? The radiator? I knew nothing about cars.

He wiped his fingers on the front of a T-shirt that was streaked with oil and grease and hung loosely outside his pants, emphasizing his lean frame. *I know what he looks like under that shirt,* I thought. I felt my face flush immediately and I looked away, staring instead at the cluttered walls behind me. The work space was disorganized and dirty, a far cry from all of Nate's meticulously kept boxes at his home; he'd obviously not had much of an influence on his best friend.

A calendar from 1987 hung beside a rack of rusty gardening tools, which reminded me, guiltily, that I hadn't been to Roseburg Farms in a while. The brightest spot among all the dusty knickknacks and baby food jars filled with nuts and bolts was a sheet of lined notebook paper with a simple outline drawing of a horse in midcanter, back hooves flying, tail and mane up, tacked to the wall with a strip of clear tape.

"Hey, can you get me that Red Bull?" Lee asked me.

Four slim red, silver, and blue cans sat on a wooden stool as if they were on an altar. I picked one up—empty, as were the second and third. The fourth was half-filled. I handed it to Lee and he tossed it back in one long swallow.

"You drank *all* of those?" I asked incredulously. "It's not even ten."

He thumped his chest with a fist and let out a burp. "That's late."

"How early were you up?"

He lazily leaned his butt on the Mustang's chrome

bumper. "'Up' implies . . ." He belched again. "That there was a down. And there was no down." He aimed a pointed gaze at the cans. "Those tinny skinny friends of mine made sure there was no down."

My eyes searched his face. "You've been awake all night?" He had the beginnings of bags under his eyes and his cheekbones looked sharper and more pronounced than usual—but there was an odd twitch in the corners of his eyes and a jerky quality to his gestures that made him look like a living scarecrow.

He tossed the empty can overhand like a basketball, and it landed in a wire wastebasket with an aluminum *plink*. "I want to finish this. You gonna help me or not?"

"Help?" I hesitated. "I don't know—"

"That *is* why you came here, right? To help me with the car?" He leaned closer, bathing me in thick caffeinated breath and holding my gaze so long as if to dare me to contradict him.

I couldn't find any words. I wasn't sure why I'd come over, why I'd left school, why I'd suddenly needed the space and time to breathe . . . and why I'd known I'd find that here with Lee. "The car, yeah."

"Then get over here and help me with this alternator belt," he said.

"The what?"

"There's a long belt, called a serpentine, and it fits around here." He thrust a hand deep into the back of the engine.

"And here. And here. It connects everything. Water pump, air pump, power steering, and the alternator, of course."

"Of course."

"Didn't used to be this way," he said, his voice picking up speed as he explained everything to me. "This car used to have five belts, each one handling a separate thing. But that was a pain in the ass and those belts were hard to replace, so Nate and I upgraded it to a single belt." Lee held up a forefinger. "You look nice, by the way."

Startled, I glanced down at my boots. "I do?"

"Yeah, the dress and the hair . . ." He waved a grease-stained hand at my outfit.

"It's a skirt and top, not a dress."

"Whatever. It's nice, that's all."

"Well, thank y—"

"Bring me the manual, huh? It's in the glove compartment."

As I slid into the passenger seat, I flipped down the visor and checked my reflection in the small rectangular mirror. I wet my finger and wiped off the raccoon eyes, noticing, *huh*, my hair did look nice for a change. I turned the visor back up quickly and caught Lee staring at me in the crack of space between the hood and windshield. When our eyes met, he stood abruptly and went back to work. "The manual, Meredith. Come on."

I felt a smile tickle my lips.

We worked for the rest of the day, breaking only for a fast

sandwich and soda. I managed to keep the grease and grime from Allison's clothes, but regular soap and water would not wash off the oily residue on my hands. They needed to be scrubbed.

Finally, at around five in the afternoon, Lee pronounced the work done. We'd not only replaced the alternator belt, but we'd also flushed the coolant lines and radiator and retrofitted the air filters. "If it doesn't work now, well . . . ."

"It never will?"

Lee scoffed at me. "You're such a pessimist! If it doesn't work now, I'll have to try something else." He walked over to the passenger-side door and held it open for me. "Go on, get in."

"We're going for a ride now?" I felt oddly nervous. I so badly wanted the car to work. For Lee . . . for Nate . . .

"In," he repeated. And I obliged.

I heard the garage door rise with a clatter and as I waited for Lee to return, my gaze again fell on the drawing of the horse on the wall. It was so simply rendered, just a bold black outline of a horse, yet it felt vivid and alive. As soon as Lee got into the car, I pointed to it. "What is that?"

"That's a horse."

"Well, duh. You like horses, I take it."

"Yeah." He held up the key chain with the Ford logo on one side and the Mustang logo on the other. "Nate and me . . . We were gonna get tattoos." He said this in an almost whisper, as if speaking it aloud would make it untrue.

"Seriously?" Nate had *never* said anything to me about wanting a tattoo. Then again, he'd never said anything about this car either.

Lee pulled up the sleeve of his left arm and rubbed his right hand against the bare skin. "Right here."

"Tattoos?" I still couldn't wrap my mind around that. I felt laughter bubble up in me. "Nate?" I shook my head. "No way. Just . . . no."

Lee was insistent. "You didn't know him like I did. He *wanted* ink."

I lifted one eyebrow. "Ink?"

"Yes, Miss Meredith Daniels. That is what it's called. Getting inked."

I crossed my arms over my chest. "Well, I in no way believe that Nate wanted to get *inked*. You? Sure, but him?"

A bemused look crossed Lee's face. "Me, but not Nate? Why?"

"It's permanent, Lee. A tattoo is forever."

"Not always, but okay. So what?"

"So what if you change your mind?"

Lee drummed his fingers against his chin in thought. "So . . . ?"

"So? So!" I let my hands drop into my lap as dramatically as I could.

Lee turned to face me, closing the distance between us to just a foot or so. "Who cares if you change your mind? The way I see it, say yes now and deal with the shit later."

He grinned as he shoved the key into the ignition and then stopped. He took my hand and held it over the key. Our fingers trembled with excitement. "Ready? One, two—"

"Three!" I said. We both held our breath as the key clicked past start, paused, and then the engine roared to life! The smile on Lee's face was as bright as I'd ever seen it. It lit up the dark circles under his eyes and erased the shadows on his cheeks and jaw. He nodded, a goofy grin on his face like a little kid's. "It works!"

"Whoo-hoo!" I shouted. I clapped my hands. Silly, but I couldn't help it! The day's work paid off—the Mustang was running.

Suddenly I felt Lee's arms around me, hugging me close. The scent of grease and dried sweat and Red Bull clung to him, clung to me, as the skin on our necks met and our cheeks touched. I felt his palm against my back. My own hands had wandered to the back of his neck and were clasped there, holding him.

I froze in place, not wanting to move, not trusting myself to stay still. *This is not a hug,* I told myself, *not a real hug.* This was a friendly, congratulatory embrace.

It was Lee who cut it short, who pulled back and gripped the steering wheel with both hands. He said nothing, but I saw his lips twitch, as they had before. He glanced at me briefly. "Ready?"

I nodded, willing my heartbeat to slow, forcing my brain to focus. It was sleep deprivation and Red Bull, I told myself.

Oh, wait, that's him, not me. What's my excuse?

Lee shifted the car into reverse and eased it out of the garage. The thrill of the Mustang actually moving quickly overshadowed any weirdness. This was all about the car and nothing more.

We were halfway down the long driveway, headed toward the main road, when Lee stopped the car and let it idle in neutral. He got out, walked over to the passenger side, and opened my door. "Move over, you're driving," he said. He tried to smoosh me over with both hands.

"What? I can't!" It was a stick shift, and I had only driven an automatic. I'd never learned a manual transmission.

"You and your four-letter words," he said. "'Won't.' 'Can't.' Go on. Or I'll sit on top of you."

I crawled behind the wheel and stared down at the floor, a stranger in a very strange land. Brake, accelerator . . . and clutch? What on earth was I supposed to do with that? I turned to Lee helplessly. "I . . . I . . ."

"Just try," he said. "What's the worst that could happen?"

"I drive the car into a tree and we die."

He threw back his head, laughing. "Oh my god, no. You'll only stall."

"Oh." I cocked my head to one side. "You're sure?"

He wobbled a hand in the air. "Fifty percent. We'll know for sure in a minute."

I stared at the gearshift. I didn't even know where to begin.

"The clutch," Lee said helpfully. "Put your foot down on that—no, your left foot."

"My left . . . ? But I do everything with my right."

"The clutch is with your left. Your right foot is on the brake. So do that. Like, now." He was so patient, so encouraging. Maybe I could do this.

Left on clutch, right on brake. "Okay." I was holding on to the steering wheel for dear life. I was pretty sure my knees were locked too.

"Now put your right hand on the gearshift. You're gonna slide it into first gear. Then while you let your foot up off the clutch, take your right foot off the brake and put it on the gas."

"Wait, wait, wait! That's too many things!" My hands felt clammy and wet on the wheel and my feet were jammed so hard against the pedals that I thought I'd actually put them through the floorboard.

"You can do this," Lee said calmly. "You're smart—"

"Not like this."

"—and I'm right here."

I felt my heart thumping in my chest. *Oh god, oh god, oh god . . .* I took a breath and did what Lee said: clutch, shift, gas . . . the car lurched forward and died. I yelped. "Oh no! I broke it!"

Lee chuckled. "Like I said, you only stalled. Try it again. Come on, you can do it."

Fine, all right. I braced myself for a second go at it.

Clutch, shift, gas. Stall.

And again. Clutch, shift, gas. Stall.

"Damn it!" I shouted at the windshield. "Why isn't this working?"

Lee tried not to laugh, but I could see the merry twinkling in his eyes.

"You can just stop that right now," I told him.

"I will. It's just . . ."

"What?"

"It's funny to see you get upset."

"Funny?" I felt myself start to fume. "You like watching me fail?"

"It's a *car*," he drawled. "Who *cares*?"

"Yes, but . . ." *But I want to be good at it.* I crossed my arms and leaned back in the driver's seat, pouting. "Forget it. You drive."

Lee's eyes widened. "That's it? Damn, you give up easily."

"I told you—"

"Yeah, you told me." He shook his head. "Try it again. Just once more. For me?" He batted his lashes coquettishly.

"Ugh, fine. Once more." I started the car. Clutch. Shift. Gas.

And stall with the force of a hundred ponies.

"Damn it!" I screamed. "I am never doing this again. Ever!"

Lee said nothing but got out and walked around the back of the car. I scooted across the seat, settling into the warmth he left behind. *Let him drive this thing,* I thought. After all, it was his now.

I heard the trunk open and Lee returned to the front seat with a small cooler. He opened the lid and pulled out a beer. "Do you always carry a cooler of alcohol in your trunk?"

Lee uncapped the bottle with an opener on his key chain and handed it to me. "Normally I drive a Vespa, so no, I don't. But I had a feeling I'd get this thing rolling and I knew I'd want to celebrate."

"With me?"

"Actually," he said with a snort, "I didn't plan on sharing." He pulled out another beer and aimed the neck at me. "So you better not drink all of them."

I held the bottle up to the waning sunlight. "You know, I drink maybe once a year, if that."

"Bullshit. I saw you at that party. You had a beer in your hand."

"I didn't drink it, Sherlock."

He sighed. "Great. These are good beers and I just wasted one on you. At least take a sip and toast the car, huh? Can you do that?" He tapped the neck of his beer to mine. "To our awesome mechanical skills."

I raised the bottle to my lips, bracing myself for a bitter brew. But it wasn't the usual flat, watery stuff from a party keg. It was nutty-flavored and a little sweet and the bubbles tickled the roof of my mouth and tongue.

I took three more swallows before I paused for a breath,

holding the chilled bottle against my chest. "Um, that's pretty good."

"Yeah, this is my mom's favorite too. When she's around."

Mom. Lee never spoke about her.

"Oh?" I said as neutrally as possible.

He tipped his head back and drank half the bottle in one long gulp. "I'll bet you never had a mom who was single *and* married, huh?"

"I, um . . . No. My mom is just married. You know, to my dad." I sipped some more of my beer, hoping I could encourage him to keep talking. If he wanted to.

"You see, Sherry Ryan is married to my dad, and Sherry Livingston is not married to my dad. They look like the same woman, but only from the outside." Lee finished the rest of his beer and slowly peeled the label off the bottle. "When my dad's in town, I get to see Sherry Ryan, and when he's not, Sherry Livingston sneaks in."

"Do you mean—"

"She fucks around when he's away. Yeah." He took another swallow. The bluntness of his words took my breath away. Luckily, Lee didn't mind the silence.

"Fortunately for Sherry Livingston, my dad would rather not be here anyway, so she pretty much gets the run of the house."

His laugh was short, more like a gruff exhale. I didn't know what to say, so I kept quiet and motionless. A moment later he reached into the cooler for a second beer and a frown creased his face. "You need another."

"Oh no, I'm good. See?" I sloshed the beer in my bottle from side to side to prove it wasn't empty, but when I looked, only a couple of swallows remained. "How did that happen?"

"I told you. My mom knows her beer. Drink up." He placed a finger at the bottom of my bottle and tilted the mouth of it toward me.

I swallowed, thinking, thinking. "What about your father?" I asked when I'd finished. "Doesn't he care that your mom is sleeping around?"

"Who said my mom is sleeping around?" Lee snapped. "Did I say that? No. I said *Sherry Livingston* is sleeping around. That's not my mom." He gulped down some more beer and finished with an *ahh*.

"Okay." Lee was so very close to revealing more of himself, but he'd stopped just short of too much.

I reached into the cooler and took out another beer. Lee silently handed me the opener, and I uncapped the bottle like a pro. I held it up to him, and he allowed a hint of a smile as he clinked ceremoniously. We sipped at the same time. I tried to match him, swallow for swallow, but had to stop before I choked—I was still a lightweight when it came to alcohol.

"We need to name her," Lee said, patting the seat. "What do ya think?"

"Name . . . the car?" My head was beginning to swim. All this beer on a nearly empty stomach was not smart, but I wanted to be in the moment. I wanted to be spontaneous and fun.

"Yeah, what should her name be?" Lee ran a hand lovingly along the steering wheel and gearbox.

"Christine?" I blurted out and then started laughing like a fiend.

Lee's mouth opened in shock. "Meredith, do you think our car is evil?"

Our car?

"Maybe. She didn't let me drive her, so . . ."

His laughter filled the car. "You're blaming your crappy driving skills on Christine?"

"So we've named her, then?"

"Well . . . Christine wasn't a Mustang, you know."

"If Stephen King were younger when he wrote the book, maybe it would have been."

Lee looked amazed. "You are so wise, Meredith Daniels."

My head lolled on my neck as I turned to him. The second beer was definitely taking effect. "I like that you call me by my whole name," I said.

"You do?" He stared, examining me. "Why?"

"Because . . . it's my name." I laughed. I wrinkled my nose. "I don't like Middie. Or *Yoko*." I tried to hold his gaze, but my eyes were having trouble focusing. "It makes me feel bad when you say that." I leaned my head against the cushioned rest and kicked off my boots before pulling my knees up and placing my feet on the dash. "You think Christine minds?"

"Nah. Christine's cool."

I drank some more of the beer, taking tiny little sips instead of big gulps. I knew I was getting drunk, could feel my head getting lighter, could hear my voice slur, but I didn't want to stop. I didn't want to plan what was going to happen. I didn't want to worry about the future.

Say yes now and deal with shit later.

"Am I being spontaneous and fun?"

"A little bit."

I slapped a weak hand at his chest. "Just a little? I'm drinking beer in an evil car. What more can I do?"

"You could . . . get a tattoo."

"Oh, no way! No, no, no." I shook my head from side to side and stamped my bare feet on the glove compartment in front of me. "Think of something else."

"Hmmm . . . nope, there is nothing else."

"Well, I am not getting *inked*," I declared. My voice was loud, even to my ears. I was definitely buzzed, if not actually drunk. I needed to breathe some fresh air, but the window was closed. "Can you roll down the window?"

"It's not electric," Lee said.

"Oh." I stared at the old-fashioned handle, unable to think straight, willing it to move on its own.

"Here, I got it," Lee said, reaching across me to roll it

down. As he leaned over me, I felt an overwhelming urge to sniff at him, to inhale him, to suck up his scent, his hair, his skin—to exist in the moment, this moment.

But a small part of me worried that I wouldn't stop there, and that would be wrong—for me, for Lee, for Liza.

For Nate.

I pressed my palms against the seat and gripped the leather tightly, holding my breath, holding every nerve still until I felt a rush of fresh air against my face and Lee returned to his own side.

I rested my chin against the open window like a dog. The breeze lifted my hair away from my face, and I closed my eyes to it. "I guess I can't be spontaneous," I said. "I'm not what you want me to be."

I heard Lee's voice behind me. It sounded so very far away. "I don't want you to be anything. I just want you to be whoever you are, Meredith."

I smiled. "Your girlfriend is very lucky," I said. "Do you love her?"

"I do love her."

"Is she okay with you hanging out with me?"

Lee laughed softly. "She's cool with it."

"I like her. She's nice. But she shouldn't smoke." I clucked my tongue, or at least I thought I did. It stuck there for a moment, as if all my saliva had dried up. I reached for the beer and took another sip to unstick my tongue.

"She's funny too. And smart. And beautiful."

"Yeah?" Another swallow of beer and I felt my body slide down in the seat. "I wish I could be like her."

"I wish you could too," he said. "She's the only one who cares about me."

I felt my heart lurch. I opened my eyes and swiveled my head toward him. The car spun woozily and my stomach skittered. "That's not true. I care."

He looked at me but said nothing.

"I care," I said again, trying to sit up. "I'm your friend."

"I heard you the first time."

"So . . ."

"So because you say you care, I should . . . what? Say that I care too?"

"Um . . . don't you?" I guess I'd assumed he *did* care about me, about my opinion, about my feelings. He'd done everything I'd expect from someone who did.

But maybe, maybe I was wrong.

The effort of trying to hold a conversation, to keep myself upright, was suddenly too much, and I sank down, my head slamming against the metal prongs holding the cushioned headrest. "Oww . . . ," I moaned. That was gonna hurt in the morning.

My eyelashes felt like they weighed a hundred pounds each; they pulled my lids down like shades. . . .

Shades, memories, images of the past. . . .

I felt Lee's hand on my cheek, felt his warm palm hold my chin. "I'm sorry about all of this. I just keep thinking you're going to change your mind. Stop talking to me. Then it will all be the way it was before."

"Shhh. . . ."

I curled tighter into myself. *I'm not changing my mind. I know what* forever *means.*

CHAPTER *fifteen*

This is what a hangover is.

Although I'd never had one before in my life, I knew instantly that the churning nausea and insane pressure on my head and chest were classic symptoms of someone who had had one too many. It felt like an elephant was crushing my rib cage, *after* he had stomped all over my face.

As I started to move around a little, desperate for water, even the smallest tic threatened to trigger a tsunami of queasiness. I panicked when I couldn't move my legs, until I realized they were simply tangled up in my nightgown.

Nightgown? What the hell? I hadn't worn a nightgown since I'd started high school, when Haley declared at a slumber party that my pretty Lanz cotton gowns were old-fashioned and completely lame. This one was all white, thin seersucker with an embroidered bodice and a light pink satin ribbon threaded through the eyelets along the borders of the shoulder straps.

But why was I wearing it? I couldn't imagine having had the brain function to seek out this nightgown rather than pulling on sweatpants and a T-shirt—or simply collapsing into bed without getting changed at all.

Across the room I saw my purse and the clothes I'd been wearing. How had I gotten home? Had I driven here? Against my nauseous stomach's better judgment, I ran to the window and looked down at the driveway. *Oh, thank god!* My mother's car was still in one piece.

I stared at it for a full minute or more, but my brain was an absolute blank. As I pulled out some clothes for school, I mentally walked through the previous day: homeroom, Mr. Z, Lee, beer . . .

"Oh my god! What the . . .?" I glanced down at my bare upper arm and saw the black outline of a horse on it.

A tattoo? About four inches wide and two high, it looked exactly like the drawing hanging in Lee's garage. I rubbed a finger across it but it, like the rest of my body, was sore to the touch, bloated and puffy.

Lee! How could he bring me to a tattoo parlor when I was drunk? I threw on jeans and a T-shirt and tore out of my bedroom, stopping in the bathroom long enough to toss back some aspirin for my pounding headache.

In the kitchen, I steeled myself to face the music with my parents, but the place was empty. A note in my mom's handwriting sat next to her car keys on the counter:

M, didn't want to wake you. You needed the rest. Take car to school when you're up.

Oh yeah, no. I was *not* going to school. I grabbed the keys and hurried to the car. I drove first to Lee's house. The Mustang was there, but the Vespa was gone, so I sped off to Lookingglass. With every mile, my anger grew exponentially. I practiced everything I wanted to say to him, shouting every profane word I could think of to the windshield. Passing cars must have thought I was an escaped lunatic.

How could he do this to me? How could I explain this to my friends and family? A tattoo, honestly? I pulled into the lot in front of the charter tour shack, kicking up gravel as if I were in an action movie. Hand on door, curses in mouth—I stopped short when I saw a "Back in 10" sign on the window. *Damn him!*

And, oh my god, my head. The aspirin was kind of working, but I needed more. Caffeine. Water. I needed coffee. I hurried to the convenience store across the street.

The bell on the door announcing my arrival sounded like cymbals crashing around my ears. I nearly cringed when Liza's cheerful voice called out, "Hi there!"

I tiptoed across the floor so my Nikes wouldn't squeak on the freshly cleaned linoleum. "Hi . . . ," I said softly.

"Could I have a very large coffee?"

Liza's wide blue eyes took me in from head to toe; the look on her face said she knew I was having a bad morning. She brought a finger to her lips, shushing herself, and set about very quietly making me some coffee.

I leaned against the counter, cradling my head in my hands. Liza was dressed in mostly purple again; she was a girl with a favorite color, that was for sure. Her hair was held back from her pink-cheeked face with a purple polka-dotted headband, showing off dangly plastic earrings with white dots on a purple background.

As I watched her hips sashay from side to side while she poured my coffee, I felt an irrational twinge of jealousy shoot through me. *Lee loves her? What does he see in her?* Sure she was attractive and she had a pleasant smile and a cheery outlook on life. But she smoked, which was gross, and she liked *purple*, for god's sake.

I shook my head. Whatever. I didn't care. I couldn't care. Lee was a jerk. If anything, I should be warning *her* about him. My hand went absentmindedly to the tattoo. I carefully peeled my sleeve up to peek at it, and as I did so, I heard a sharp gasp.

Liza's face drained of color. She slid my coffee across the counter in silence, her eyes flicking from my arm to the cash register very quickly. "One forty-five," she said loudly.

I fished two bucks out of my wallet and handed them to her.

"Cream and sugar are over there." She jutted her chin past me and dropped my change on the counter with a clatter. I scooped it up and put it in the tip jar, hoping Karma would let my generosity make up for my harsh thoughts of her.

I dumped some sugar and milk into the coffee until it was the color of sand and cool enough to drink.

"You, uh, you just get that tattoo?" Liza asked in a shaky voice.

I nodded and took a big hot gulp, scalding the roof of my mouth.

"Oh." Her eyes blinked a few times as if she were trying to focus. "So, both of you, huh?" Not so much a question as a statement of defeat. She meant Lee. We'd apparently *both* gotten tattoos last night. Brilliant.

"Is that why you're here?" she asked. Her head snapped up and her gaze narrowed at a figure crossing the street outside the shop window. Lee was loping awkwardly across the street, leading with his knees and head, body following.

Finally. I started for the door and then turned back. "It's not what you think."

A glimmer of hope lit up her face. "Really?"

"We're just friends."

"Oh." She rolled her eyes. "I get that too. 'Just friends, Liza. Can't be more than that.'" She lowered her voice, mimicking Lee. "God, I hate that about him. He's so . . . closed off, you know?"

"Wait . . . you're not his girlfriend?"

Liza shook her head and her dangly polka dots shook too. "Liza and Lee sounds good, though, doesn't it? Lee and Liza, Liza and Lee." She shrugged and looked down at her feet, as if she'd revealed too much. "Maybe someday. Who knows."

I was out the door at the tail end of her words. He'd tattooed my arm without my consent. Why should it surprise me he'd lied about Liza being his girlfriend? I charged after him, my anger refueled by fresh coffee and a sugar rush.

I slammed my palm against the door and called out his name. He came around the back behind the counter with a bewildered look on his face. "No school today?"

"How could you do this to me?" I said. My anger set every nerve on edge, making me feel raw and exposed. I thrust my arm at him and pulled up my sleeve, as if to show him the evidence of my pain.

He started to reply but smiled instead, which infuriated me more!

"Lee! I'm serious. I trusted you!"

He held my gaze for a long moment and then unleashed on me. "You came over to *my* house, *uninvited*, drank all my beer, and now you're pissed at me? I had to drive you home, sneak you inside without your parents waking up, and then *walk* all the way home at two in the morning."

I was incredulous. "That is nothing compared to a tattoo!"

"*You* were the one who wanted it. You said you wanted what Nate wanted."

"Bullshit! I would never have said that." But even as I spoke the words, a sliver of doubt crept into my mind. *Did I say that?*

Lee said nothing but grabbed my arm with a soft grunt, pulling me through the back door and into the small court-yard behind the shack. I dug my heels in like a stubborn dog, but he urged me forward step by step.

"Let go of me!" I shouted, trying to wrench my arm free, but he held fast. Across the street, I caught a hint of move-ment in the window of the convenience store and knew Liza was watching.

Still holding me in place, Lee reached for a hose that was coiled on the ground and squeezed the nozzle, send-ing a spray of water into the air. Then in one swift move, he tucked me behind him, pulled up first my sleeve and then his own, to show a matching horse on his left biceps. With the two tattoos side by side, he aimed the hose against our skin. The cold water was a shock to my system, waking me up more fully than any amount of coffee could.

"What the hell are you doing?" I screamed. "Leave me alone!" I squirmed and twisted but it was no use. A very long ten seconds later, Lee shut off the hose and released me. I stood there, my arm dripping wet, one shoe soaked through to my sock. My shirt and jeans wet on one side. "Why did you do that?"

He took a step closer and, cupping one palm under my elbow, slowly and gently rubbed the tattoo on my arm. I watched as the ink disappeared. First the tail, then the hooves, and so on, until there was nothing left but a faint outline of the horse's head. He placed my hand on his "tattoo" and I did the same, rubbing some of the ink off with my fingertips. "It's a Sharpie," he said. "It's not forever."

"Oh." I felt like a total idiot.

"You might want to take a shower before you accuse me of something."

"I . . . I thought . . ."

"How could you think that?" Lee asked in a quiet voice. "I would never do that to you."

I looked up from Lee's arm, from Lee's hand on mine, to search his face for any signs of guile or teasing. But there was nothing there. I heard an echo of his voice in my head.

I had a crush on her for years.

She's the only one who cares about me.

My girl is clever and funny and beautiful.

And Liza's voice mocking him:

Just friends. Can't be more than that.

"It wasn't Liza you were talking about," I said. "So who were you . . ."

I felt the space between us close, felt a wall of heat build as Lee pulled me into him.

He dropped his chin to his chest, folding me into his arms, and his face lowered to mine. My lips melted into his, and we kissed, first gently and then with more force, more insistence. My arms were at his back, my hips pressing into him as he wrapped himself around me, nearly swallowing me with his body.

I felt the warmth of his mouth, the electricity of our tongues. My eyes fluttered open and I glanced over his shoulder, my vision catching Liza at the window. I should have cared, but I didn't. I didn't want to care about anything but this kiss, this embrace, this connection. I never wanted it to end.

He pulled back slightly, and his breath came in short gasps. I could feel his heart beating through his T-shirt, doubling mine.

"What . . . ," I started to say, but he shook his head and kissed me again.

I let my mind become a blank, let all the cares and worries slip from my consciousness, let my hands find what they wanted to find, touch what they wanted to touch.

Lee's palm was at my neck. I collapsed under him and we tumbled as one against the side of the shack. I felt the back of my shirt become damp from the wet shingles as Lee pressed himself to me. His mouth left my lips to nuzzle my ear and neck and shoulder, and his hands wandered from the sides of my waist toward my hips and—

Enough, I thought. That was far enough.

But it wasn't. I needed more.

I took Lee's hand and entwined my fingers in his,

gripping my palm to his tightly as if we were fighting each other, our hands and arms at war. He took both of my hands and held them above my shoulders, pinning me to the side of the shack.

He paused, brushing his lips against my cheek. I opened my eyes and made him look at me.

"Kiss me again," I said.

His smile was sly, teasing. "No."

"Yes. Kiss me again." I gripped his hands harder, curling his arms around my back, waiting for him to give in.

"No," he said. "*You* kiss *me*."

I grinned and whirled him around so I had him pinned to the side of the shack. I tilted my chin up and leaned into him, crushing my mouth to his. I didn't—wouldn't—let him go.

But I didn't think he minded much.

Finally, the urgency left us, like a water faucet, once gushing, slowly trickling to a stop. My heartbeat slowed, energy spent. I took a deep breath but was reluctant to sever the connection between us. I rested my head against Lee's chest and felt his breath rise and fall under my cheek.

"Meredith—"

"No. Please. No." I was afraid to look at him, afraid to see in his face what this was, what it meant to him. It wasn't the same for him as it was for me—it couldn't be.

"But—"

"I have to go."

He pushed me away from him, holding me at arm's

length. "Now? Seriously?"

I eased myself out of his embrace, carefully peeling his hands away from my waist. "I . . . I can't do this. Whatever this is."

"This. You mean 'us'?"

I winced. *Us.* Was there an *us*? Could there be? When Nate . . .

Nate is gone, a voice inside me said.

No. This wasn't okay. Not yet.

I backed away, my gaze on my feet. "I'll . . ."

"Call me when you've joined the circus?" Lee cut me off with just a hint of sarcasm in his voice.

"Still working on that magic act," I muttered. I hurried off, head down.

As I left, I heard Lee say, "You sure know how to disappear."

In the shade box I gave Nate was a small slip of paper, a receipt for a locker at an ice rink. It was a Winter Olympics year, and everyone at our junior high school was into snow and ice sports. Until that day, Nate and I had been friends only. He was a year ahead of me, already a freshman at the high school. When it was time to go home, it didn't take me long to unlace my skates and slide my feet into my Nikes, but for some reason, Nate was a slowpoke. I remembered how he took his time, first with each sock, then with each shoe. At last, he stood and put on his jacket and gloves, slapped a baseball cap on his head—and then leaned down and planted a kiss right on my lips. I was so surprised that I didn't even close my eyes.

His lips, so new to mine, were soft and gentle, and his hands were on my elbows, holding me down as if I might float away. Although it could not have lasted more than a second or two, that kiss—my first kiss—was seared into my memory.

Until now. Until Lee. Was I ready to replace that memory? I didn't ever want to forget Nate, but I was afraid I couldn't ever forget Lee.

CHAPTER *sixteen*

The day of my campus tour sneaked up on me. Although I tried to get out of it, my mother insisted. "Go to Portland. Have fun with Allison. And when you come back, I bet you'll jump right back into everything with gusto!"

Somehow, she assumed (as everyone did) I'd be back to normal eventually.

I had the feeling that "normal" meant something entirely different now.

Allison was meeting me at Lewis & Clark to walk the tour with me and ask questions I might not think of. Frankly, the only thing I was thinking of was Lee. I couldn't get him out of my mind.

My mom was right, though she didn't know why. I needed distance. It was too easy to run to Lee whenever I was feeling down. And now, after what had happened between us . . . I needed space more than ever.

I'd been to Lewis & Clark once before with Nate, but as I drove through the gates and winding roads, it looked more foreign to me than I'd expected. I hardly recognized anything at all.

Through the entire tour, I felt like I was in a daze. The buildings were charming, the landscape pretty, and the students seemed perfectly smart and nice. And yet . . .

It didn't feel right.

It might have been right for Nate, or for Nate and me, but not for me.

Not for me alone.

After the tour, Allison and I found a tiny coffee shop with a sidewalk sign declaring "Love You a Latte!" I let her order for me while I nabbed a table by the window that faced out on the parking lot. I glanced around me, at the tables crowded with students. The air was electric. There was the buzz of caffeine and sugar, combined with demands for quiet hissed by the few students who were actually studying.

I waited until my sister was fully absorbed in ordering coffee before I took out my phone. I'd been patient during the tour, listening to our guide, but now I had to know: Did Lee try to contact me? I held my breath as I turned on my phone, tapping my toes on the tile floor while it tried to find a signal. Ten seconds passed, twenty, a minute, but even as the bars inched upward, not one message loaded. Not a single new voice mail or text. I scrolled through old ones just to be sure, but there was nothing.

My heart sank and I slumped against the chair.

How could he not have called me? The way we left each other . . . didn't he care?

If he were Nate, he would have called.

But if he were Nate, I wouldn't have . . .

I blushed, remembering our kiss. Remembering *my* kiss. I'd never been so aggressive with Nate, so *insistent*.

Allison interrupted my thoughts as she slid a giant paper cup of coffee across the table at me and tossed some sugar packets after it. "Cute baristas here," she said with a grin. "They give you free shots of espresso when you give them your phone number."

"You didn't."

She took the plastic lid off her cup and blew across the creamy surface of her coffee, cooling it down. "I gave him *a* number. Just not mine." After a few sips, she sat back in her chair and said, "Ahh. That's better. Now you can talk to me."

"Who said I have anything to talk about?"

"Please. Mom told me everything."

Everything? I stared into my coffee, wishing I could dive right down to the bottom and submerge myself with the melting sugar. "Then you don't need me to tell you."

"Skipping school, not handing in assignments—that's not like you, Mid."

I glanced up sharply. "They *told* me I didn't have to go," I said, my voice rising. "They *told* me to take it easy and not stress."

My sister wore a sliver of a smile, as if she understood exactly what I was saying. "Yeah, but they didn't expect *you* to take them up on it, at least not for very long. They expected *you* to go right back to normal."

"Is that what this is all about?" I waved my hands around the coffee shop, taking in the campus, the students. "Making me normal again?"

"Sure." Allison laughed. "A road trip to Portland is just the ticket." Her smile ebbed. "Maybe it wouldn't be such a bad thing to come here. Nate picked it for a reason. *You* picked it for a reason—"

"I picked it *because of* Nate."

"So? That doesn't mean it's not a good choice for *you*."

My sister didn't usually consider my feelings. "When did you get all nice and philosophical?"

"I have no idea. Maybe it was that women's studies class I took last year."

"What if I don't want to go to college at all?"

"Like, take a gap year? Yeah, you could do that."

"No, I mean, not go at all. Or maybe go. But later. I don't know. Do I have to know?"

"Um, you have to go to college." She sipped her coffee and checked out a couple of guys who'd just walked in. Her eyes followed them to the counter.

"Not everyone does."

"Don't be an idiot. Mom and Dad will kill you if you don't go somewhere."

We both heard my phone buzz, a signal that a text was coming in. *Lee?*

My sister grabbed it and gasped. "Uh-oh."

I snatched it out of her hands and tapped the screen. But it wasn't Lee. It was . . .

"Wesley? Who's Wesley?" I opened the text and found a message that was clearly *not* meant for me. *Hey expresso grl!*

"'Expresso'?" I said with a laugh. "Is this"—I glanced up at the counter, where a boy who was clearly too young for Allison lifted two fingers at us—"that guy?" When my sister nodded, I roared. "'Expresso'! With an *x*. Oh my god. He *makes* them, for god's sake. Ali, you gave him *my* number? How could you?"

Allison whipped the phone away and her fingers flew over the screen. "I don't know. It was the first one that came to mind."

I shook my head. "You better get rid of him. I do *not* need some coffee clown who can't spell sending me texts."

"Yeah, yeah," she said, waving me away. She tapped Send and then sat back in the booth. "So, you getting into my old boho clothes?"

"How did you know I was wearing them?"

"Emma texted me."

"She doesn't even have a phone!"

"They're not exactly *you*, but . . ." Allison's fingers absently tapped the screen of my phone and she turned it sideways, an expression of surprise on her face. She paged the screen with her finger—again, and again, and . . .

Oh, shit. My selfies with Lee.

I lunged over the table. "Ali, hey, give it here," I said, but she held it out of my grasp, twisting away from me. She kept her eyes on the phone the entire time.

"Thanks for last night . . . Middie, what the . . ." She paged through a couple of more pictures and then glanced up at me. "What. The. Fuck. What is this?"

She held the phone with her fingertips like it was made of plutonium.

"I can explain, Ali. Lee—"

"Lee Ryan," she said with a nod. "That's who this is."

"I can explain."

"You said that already."

"He's not a bad guy," I said, trying not to sound incredibly defensive. "He's just"—I remembered what Lee said about Lex Luthor—"misunderstood."

Allison folded her arms. "So the lazy-awkward-stoner thing is *not* true?"

"He's actually got a job, and . . . and he doesn't smoke

pot," I said. Sure, there was the "awkward" part, but . . . "He's really helped me."

"Yeah, I can see that." Allison gazed at me disdainfully, looking down her nose. It reminded me of when we were kids and I wasn't doing what she wanted.

I wanted to laugh. Lee would have laughed, but I gathered joking would not be well tolerated.

"Nate *just* died," my sister said with intentional cruelty. "Do you know what this looks like?"

I thought of telling her how he'd comforted me without coddling me, encouraged me without patronizing me. But the photos told a different story. An incomplete one.

I turned my face from hers. No matter how much I explained myself, how many times I defended my actions, I would just look more guilty.

It would look, even more, like I was betraying Nate.

"It's not like that," I told her simply. "It isn't."

"It's called a 'rebound.' Whatever you think it is, that's all it is. For both of you. It's not real." My sister rose from the table and slurped down the rest of her coffee. "I gotta hit the road." She leaned down and gave me a hug before she left, calling over her shoulder as if it was an afterthought, "Drive carefully, okay?"

I gazed down at the screen on my phone. Still no word from Lee.

She's right, I thought. *Allison is right.*

I was a terrible person. I had betrayed Nate.

Over something that was really nothing at all. There couldn't be an "us." There could be no "Lee and me." I had to let it go—let *him* go—and get back to school and my friends and my real life.

CHAPTER *seventeen*

Chemistry exams, AP English papers, calculus pop quizzes, and loads and loads of SAT practice tests. Three weeks were easily filled with schoolwork and hanging out with Haley and my friends.

I did everything everyone asked and more. I cheered on Haley at her field hockey games and spent my afternoons at the farm. When Emma's Brownie troop needed a chaperone for a field trip to the science museum, I volunteered. And at Thanksgiving, I cleaned the kitchen. I wasn't exactly the best cook, but scrubbing pots and pans I could handle.

I took the SAT for real and bombed. But that wasn't much of a surprise. Everyone said the first time was the worst and that I just needed to study more. I promised my parents—and myself—that I would take it again and do better.

By the end of November, normal had returned to my life even if my life hadn't exactly returned to normal.

I forgot about Lee. I stopped checking my phone for text messages, stopped waking at three in the morning expecting a call, stopped thinking about the last time I saw him. His hands on my waist, his breath on my neck . . . So maybe I hadn't entirely forgotten, but I was trying.

On the Sunday after Thanksgiving, day broke quietly, with everyone sleeping in and only an occasional car on the road. I started with a light jog and every muscle in my body creaked. I hadn't gone for a run in weeks.

The wind whipped my ponytail across my face and I felt a few droplets of rain on my cheeks. Dark clouds swirled above me, volatile and threatening, but I kept running. I remembered the night in the tree house and heard Lee's voice, asking me if I would melt in the rain.

No. Not me. Meredith Daniels does not melt.

Very quickly, other voices jumped into my head: my mother, my friends, my sister and teachers . . .

What do you want, Middie?

What are you doing for the rest of your life, Middie?

When are you going to go back to normal, Middie?

Normal.

Meaning, back to the person I was.

But why did they want me to be that person? That person was who she was mostly because of Nate Bingham. *He* was the one who planned everything. *He* was the one who had life all figured out. Without him . . . who was I?

No. I could never go back to the person I was.

Because there was no Nate anymore. And that person didn't exist without him.

I rounded a corner and headed toward a familiar fork in the road. If only decisions in life were as easy as that: seeing a fork and choosing one side or the other. Nate's death was a decision that was made for me—but that didn't mean that I had to allow everyone else to make my decisions for me too.

If I didn't know what I wanted yet, that was okay. What lesson was I supposed to learn from all of this if it wasn't to *live* rather than *plan*?

Say yes now and deal with the shit later.

I jogged in place in front of Lee's house while I texted: *u up? I'm here*

No response. Well, what did I expect? He hadn't heard from me in almost a month.

Rain began to fall more steadily now. I texted again and waited some more, but after ten minutes, it looked like he wasn't coming down.

I wandered over to the garage to take a last peek at the Mustang. The side door was unlocked, so I tiptoed inside. The car was pristine and beautiful. The chrome, the clean lines, the restored leather—it was old yet timeless, a true classic. We'd fixed this car, and that fixed me.

I felt like Lee had let me in on a secret, one that only Nate knew: Lee was a great friend. I finally saw in him what Nate had, what he had appreciated in Lee while he was alive.

"Planning on stealing it?" I heard behind me.

Lee stood at the top step near the door, his body in silhouette, rain falling softly behind him.

"It'd be kind of hard, since she still won't let me drive her," I joked.

With his face in shadow, I had no idea if he was smiling or scowling. "You never called," he said. "You . . . disappeared."

I wanted to make a joke. *I'm a magician, remember?*

"I'm here now."

"Yeah, you are."

We took a few tentative steps toward each other. My mind and pulse raced: Was this the right thing?

I didn't know. And I didn't care. This was my choice *right now*.

I quickened my last few paces, grabbed his shoulders, and kissed him. My head swam and my heart fluttered in my chest as he responded, kissing me back with all the intensity I had hoped for.

That you came here for, I admitted to myself.

"Are you real?" I said quietly. "Allison said this wasn't real."

He answered with his lips. Our bodies pressed together, melting, folding, winding around each other—our voices hushed. I felt his breath in my ear, heard my name whispered, my real name, not that stupid, stupid nickname, and all the tension in my body eased away.

Lee had no expectations *of* me, no plans *for* me. He understood and accepted me. No one else did.

One of us opened the car door and one of us pulled the other in and it didn't matter which because we both felt the same way. We both wanted the same thing. We kissed—by turns passionately and sweetly and urgently—and laughed, at ourselves and the rain. I tasted minty toothpaste on his tongue and smiled to myself, imagining him brushing his teeth in those minutes before he came down to meet me. It was the thought of him nervously wondering if this might happen that made it easy to stop caring where he ended and I began.

At long last, our mouths parted and we rested, still wrapped together, arms and legs entwined. Lee cracked open one of the fogged-up windows, and a cool breeze blew through the car and across our skin, slick with sweat. With a shiver, I curled closer to him and rested my head on his bare chest. I could feel his heart beating beneath his ribs, gradually slowing to its normal pace. I reached up and traced my finger along his jaw to his lips and he kissed the tip of it, then goofily tried to bite it. I snatched it back with a laugh and planted a fat kiss on his lips instead.

"I'm running away to join the circus," I said. "Wanna come?"

He grinned slyly and dropped a rain of kisses on my neck and shoulder. "I thought you'd never ask."

I heard my phone ring with a text message and I thought about silencing it, but then, nearly simultaneously, Lee's did too. We searched the floor for our clothes, giggling like little kids as we rummaged through the clumsy pile of shirts and pants until we finally located our phones.

I saw the expression on Lee's face before I'd had a chance to read my message. His mouth dropped open and his eyes blinked rapidly. "Lee? Is something . . ."

And then I looked at my message. From Nate's mother:

Nate is coming home with me.

"Oh my god," I whispered.

Lee and I exchanged a glance. *Is this a joke?* We stared at our phones. It was a truly evil one, if so. But it had been sent from Mrs. Bingham's phone.

Could it be? Could Nate really be alive?

In the aftermath of the massacre in that tiny Honduran village, bodies had been burned beyond recognition. The rebels held the village for over a week, refusing to allow authorities in to identify the bodies and giving reporters limited access to the area. Everyone had assumed Nate was among the dead.

Everyone except his mother. She'd never given up hope—unlike us. She'd stayed in Honduras long past the point of rationality.

For a very long moment, we were motionless in the

garage. The only sound was the rain on the roof, the drip and drizzle on the window glass. And our breath, a soft sigh.

We dressed in silence, each absorbed by our own thoughts, and slipped out of the car, one at a time. When Lee closed the door, it was as if he was shutting away what had just happened between us, closing it up as if it were a thing we could tuck away.

Our eyes met and then suddenly, Lee grinned. "He's alive." He swept me up in his arms, a gigantic bear hug of an embrace, and a far cry from the passion we'd shared.

He spun me around the garage, whooping with happiness and relief and gratitude. "That dude is one tough motherfucker."

I gasped and giggled. Nate was not just tough; he was a miracle. "Do you think it's real?"

"Why wouldn't it be? If anyone could make it out there in the jungle, it's my man."

My phone buzzed again: Haley. And again: my mother. And again: Allison.

And again, and again, and again. My inbox was crowded with the happy news. When I got to twenty-five messages, I finally let myself believe it could be true.

"He's alive, he's alive, he's alive!" I sang as I grabbed Lee's hands and we twirled around the Mustang. Our Mustang. Nate's Mustang.

"Jungle warrior!" Lee threw his head back and laughed. "Oh man, I can't wait to see that dude."

Bzz . . . bzz . . . bzz . . . More texts, more names, more relief. "Hang on. I gotta send some notes back." I looked at Lee. "You?"

He shook his head. "Nah. Just the one."

"Oh. Yeah. Well, that's the important one, anyway." I stepped closer to the door to read the messages in the rainy daylight. Behind me, Lee was at the wooden bench, holding fast to his phone, gripping it tightly as if the message might slip away.

In the middle of texting, my phone rang with a call. "Hey, Mom . . . Yeah, yeah! I got it too. . . ." My mother shrieked on the other end of the phone; her voice bubbled over with excitement. "I know! I can't believe it! Is it on the news? . . . Oh, I, uh, I went for a run." I glanced over my shoulder at Lee. He had something else in his hand now—a paper. The horse he'd drawn. Our tattoo. Nate's tattoo.

"Our house? Now? Yeah, yeah, I'll be there as soon as I can." I laughed. "Rain? Who cares? I'm on my way!"

I said good-bye and pocketed my phone. "Nate's dad is at my house." Lee had his back to me, staring at the drawing. I paused at the door and glanced back. "I gotta go. Hey?"

He walked slowly toward me and I waited until he stood by my side, staring out the door at the rain. I felt his hand take mine, felt his fingers lightly twine around my palm, his nails graze the soft pads of my thumb and forefinger. His touch relaxed me, soothed me, as small and delicate as the gesture was.

My arm started to reach around his waist, but a phone call interrupted me. I glanced at the number and tapped the screen to answer. "Hey, Dad, yeah, I'm on my way." I tilted my chin toward the sky; the clouds were shifting quickly and a single patch of blue was directly overhead. I mouthed to Lee, *Gotta go,* and then I took the call on the road, beginning my jog. By the time I turned back to look at Lee, he had disappeared.

And now for my next trick, I thought. *I will make Nate reappear.*

Emma saw me first as I jogged up the driveway. She ran down to greet me and leaped into my arms. "Middie! Nate's coming home!"

"I know!" I hugged her tight and carried her inside.

"My wish came true!"

"Really? Is that what you wished for?"

She cocked her head to one side. "I wished it had never happened. So, kind of."

I dropped her to the floor in the kitchen and we ran into the living room where my parents and Nate's dad were joyously celebrating—and texting and phoning and emailing.

"Caroline called about half an hour ago," my mother told me as she poured coffee into mugs. "She told Tom that Global Outreach had finally gotten news of Nate. He'd fled the attack and run off with a couple of others into the jungle. At some point he contracted dengue fever, so he's still very weak and hasn't been able to give them the whole story. But he's alive. He's in a hospital, and he's safe." Her breath caught and she grabbed my hands for support. I knew she was feeling the same relief Nate's mom must be feeling now too. I helped her bring coffee to Dad and Mr. Bingham.

Nate's dad embraced me and took the tale from my mom. "We won't know the extent of his injuries until Caroline gets a chance to see him and talk to him. But he's *alive*, and that's all that matters."

"How long?" my dad asked.

"Five days? A week? The Honduran government would like him to help them identify some of the attackers, if he can."

Emma elbowed me aside on the couch, placing herself between me and Mom. "Will he still be a doctor when he comes home?" she asked Mr. Bingham.

"Oh yes, I'm sure he will be."

A frown creased Emma's forehead. "But it's so dangerous. He could get killed again."

"Again" shook me, but Mr. Bingham ignored it. "The doctor part isn't dangerous, Emma. It's where he was."

"Ohhh . . ." She nodded as understanding dawned. "Then make sure he doesn't go anywhere. He should stay here with us forever."

"Here? In Roseburg?" I asked.

"Yeah. And never go anywhere else." Then she tugged on my sleeve; her gaze at me was stern. "And you too. Don't go anywhere."

I put my arm around her shoulders and hugged her to me. "Okay. We'll all stay here all the time."

Emma thought for a moment and then raised one finger. "Except for Girl Scout camp. I have to go to that."

Even as I laughed, emotions crowded my head and my mind buzzed with anticipation. Nate was alive! He would be home in a week, maybe less.

Not much later, we said good-bye to Nate's dad, who was eager to get home and make arrangements for his trip. He would meet his wife in Honduras and together they'd bring Nate back. "Caroline was right," I heard him tell my parents as they walked him to his car. "I should hate myself for giving up so easily, but I'm just so grateful he's alive."

My gut clenched at those words. I had done the same thing. But it didn't matter now; that was our past, and Nate's return was our future.

Outside, it had stopped raining, and I breathed in the fresh air, rich with the fragrance of late autumn. I studied the scenery with Nate's eyes. What would he see when he returned? The summer was officially gone; winter was on the horizon. At Roseburg Farms, it would be time for winter vegetables, for turnips and spinach and radishes. At school, we were starting basketball season, Nate's favorite sport.

I felt my phone vibrate in my pocket. A text from Allison: *yay!*

I grinned, texting her back. *Soooo happy!!*

It's over, right?

What did she mean?

Lee? Is that what she meant? I felt my pulse quicken and part of me wanted to respond childishly. *I know what I'm doing!* But maybe that's not what she meant. Maybe "over" meant Nate's ordeal in Central America. Whichever it was, I typed: *It's all good.*

I was Nate's girlfriend. I was happy he was home. Lee was Nate's best friend. He was happy too.

My cheeks burned as I thought of the car, of us. It *was* over. It had to be.

Right?

CHAPTER *eighteen*

At school, the entire student body was uplifted by the stunning news. Any lingering solemnity about Nate's death—his disappearance, we were all calling it now—was gone, replaced by relief and excitement that he was returning as a hero.

During lunch, Haley and I sat with Katrina and Debra, discussing winter formal, a dance scheduled for late January that everyone began planning before Christmas.

Katrina waved a plastic fork around the cafeteria, pointing out possible candidates for dates. "What about Dave's friend, the one who just transferred here?"

"Isn't he a sophomore?" Debra asked.

"But he was on the football team."

"JV." Debra rolled her eyes. "Please."

"JV is better than no V." Katrina smirked and the girls roared with laughter.

I loved hearing my friends laugh.

"What about you, Hale?" Katrina was asking. "Thoughts?"

My best friend shrugged. "Maybe Rick, I don't know."

"What happened to Senior Year Boyfriend?" I asked her.

"Oh yeah, well, who says there can't be boyfriends, plural?"

Katrina lifted her fist, wrapped around a plastic fork, and bumped Haley's. "Amen to that."

My gaze was drawn to the next table over, where a group of guys sat, the kind who looked like they'd be more comfortable reenacting *Game of Thrones* with papier-mâché swords than attending a dance with girls.

". . . and Nate will go, right, Mid?" Haley asked me.

"What's that?" I tore my attention away from the boys.

"You and Nate? You're bringing him, right?"

"Um, I guess so," I answered slowly. "We'll have to see how he feels when he gets back."

My friends nodded wisely and sympathetically. "Of course, you have to give him time to heal," Debra said. "But obviously you can't go with anyone else."

The lunch bell buzzed and the girls quickly finished their salads and sodas. Over at the next table, one of the gamers slid his iPad into his backpack and stood up. "The guy's nineteen, survives a massacre, lives by his wits in the jungle and returns? *That* is an amazing story. Book, movie, maybe a TV series."

"HBO?"

"Netflix."

Nate, I thought. They were talking about Nate. I picked up my tray and followed my friends out the door. *He's coming home. He's really coming home.*

I had my head buried in my SAT study guide as I waited outside the school for my mother to pick me up. A familiar voice called to me.

"Yo, what's up?"

Lee dropped the kickstand on his Vespa in front of me as naturally as could be. "Oh, hey," I managed to stammer. I stood but kept my books clutched to my chest, keeping distance between us.

Lee slid off the Vespa and leaned in a little too close; I could smell the residue of his shaving cream on his skin and the laundry soap in his T-shirt. I had a sudden urge to shoot my hand out and press it to the back of his neck, to pull him close to me and feel his lips on mine. I quickly stepped back.

"What are you doing here?"

"You're a friend. We're friends, right?" He cocked an eye at me.

I nodded. I couldn't speak. We were friends. We could

only be friends. Even after what had happened in the car, that was all we could be.

"So, I saw you sitting there and decided to say hello."

I glanced around, checking for bystanders in a way I hoped wasn't obvious. "Hi."

"I was thinking maybe a trip to the pond."

The pond. My face flushed, thinking about skinny-dipping with Lee. "Oh, um . . ."

"Friends, right?" he asked, his gaze boring into me.

"Yes," I said quickly. "But . . ."

"But?"

"It's cold," I said lamely.

"Not *that* cold."

I glanced back at the school, as if it could call me back inside or tell me not to go—but no one came rushing out to stop me. While Lee started up the Vespa, I texted my mom: *getting ride from haley's mom.*

I straddled the scooter behind Lee and wrapped my arms around his chest. He leaned back into me and I breathed in his scent. He no longer smelled of cigarettes; there was no trace of Liza, no "girlfriend."

No one but us.

In minutes we were at Dayton Feed, eagerly trekking into the woods toward the pond. With every step, I felt giddy, remembering the last time we were here. But as soon as we were out of the sun, the temperature dropped fifteen degrees, and the closer we got to the water, the colder it became. The back of my neck tickled as the wind tossed my hair.

Wrong, the little voice said. *This is wrong.*

This wasn't about swimming. This was a choice—a test. One answer meant one thing; the other meant something completely different.

I didn't want to go in. Not if it was going to change everything.

But if Lee was waiting for my answer, you'd never know it. He seemed completely carefree. Like he was just game for a dip.

He heeled off his sneakers at the water's edge and waved me over. "Come on! How bad could it be?"

I unlaced my Nikes and peeled off my socks but hesitated when I was down to my bare feet. Had it been this cold last time we were here? The isolation of the pond from the rest of the farm had been a blessing in the heat of late summer, but now, six weeks later, it was more of a curse.

Lee rolled up his jeans to the knees and began to wade in, and I shivered in anticipation. "Holy shit! It's freezing!" he howled.

He reached a hand for me and pulled me into the pond. I shrieked as the water hit my ankles and splashed at my calves. A shudder ran up my spine and neck, shocking me as if it were an electrical field I'd stepped into. I dropped Lee's hand and dashed back to shore, shaking my head. "Sorry, sorry, no."

Lee stared forlornly over his shoulder at me.

If only we had left our memories intact, tucked away as safely in our minds as the ones in Nate's boxes.

It had changed. The weather. The pond. Us.

It had to. For the past three months, we had lived in a bubble of our own making, comforting each other, knowing what the other needed, providing what no one else could.

But Nate would be home soon and things couldn't be the same anymore.

"We should never have tried to come here again," I told him.

"Don't worry about it," he muttered, stuffing his feet back into his shoes. "We're leaving."

After the pond, Lee and I limited our communication to text messages—all about Nate.

Did you hear from his parents? he would ask me.

Did you walk Rocky? I would ask him.

When do you think . . .

What about . . .

Should we . . .

It was . . . businesslike. Polite. I felt like we were figuring out who we were to each other, who we would be to each other, but texting was cold and impersonal and every typed message pushed us further apart. Every time I saw his name on my phone, my heart beat faster, but inevitably the message was benign. And mostly began with the word "Nate."

Stop thinking about him, I told myself. *Stop thinking about it. . . .*

But I couldn't.

I had to clear the air. I had to before Nate returned, and maybe it was selfish, but I had to see him again. One morning, I jogged over to his house before school, knowing he wouldn't have left for work yet.

"I want to drive Christine," I told him when he stared at me quizzically.

"I don't know about—"

"Just once. For Nate."

He rubbed the back of his head with his palm as he thought. A cowlick stuck up at the crown and my hand began to reach toward him as if I could press it down into place, to touch him once more, but I stopped myself. I felt my face flush and I turned from him so he couldn't see.

"Okay but not for long." Lee backed the car out of the garage and then slid over to let me take his seat.

I tried to remember what he'd told me last time, about how to shift smoothly, how to use the clutch with my left foot instead of my right.

He sat on the far side of the bench seat, his back to the window, staring at me.

"Okay, if you do that, I'm gonna stall," I said. "I know it."

"What am I doing?"

I blushed, glared down at the speedometer. "Staring. You're—"

"You won't stall. Just do what I told you." He chewed a finger, the only thing that indicated he was as nervous as I was. I sat there with the engine running in neutral, the windshield fogging up, my hands gripping the wheel so tightly I thought my fingers would break.

"Meredith . . ."

I heard him call my name, but I couldn't answer. *What am I doing here? What am I doing?* I wondered. My eyes filled with tears and my throat felt like it was closing up. I could barely breathe.

"Meredith?"

I felt Lee slide over. He wiped a fallen tear from my cheek and held his palm under my chin, gently pulling me to him, pressing his lips to mine. I tasted salt on his lips and sugary, milky coffee on his tongue. I crawled on top of his lap. Kissed him back and let him cover my face and neck with a flurry of kisses. The windows fogged all around us, creating a steamy cocoon.

The space between us heated, the air was thick and warm and alive. I felt Lee's hands under my shirt, his palm on my belly. "This," I gasped. "This is—"

He took a breath and eased me back behind the wheel. "I'm gonna take you home now," he said. He slid the button on the air vent open and almost instantly, the windows began to clear.

"What? Now?" I yelped. But I knew it had to be now. We had to stop before this went further than it should. That we had taken it to this place was my fault. I'd known at the pond that our relationship, whatever it was, couldn't go on. But I had to test it. I had to see how I felt. How Lee felt.

The answer was . . . upsetting.

I shook my head. "I'll run home," I told him as I opened the driver's-side door. A rush of cool air against my face was a dose of reality. I took off down the driveway, headed home. I wanted to turn back, to glance over my shoulder to see if Lee was watching, but I didn't dare. If he was, I might be tempted to run back, and if he wasn't, my heart might break a little.

Dinner with the family came and went. Emma talked nonstop about Girl Scouts. Dad was on a kale kick. Mom wanted to know if I'd wear one of Allison's dresses for winter formal. I attacked my homework and near midnight, crawled under the covers, and shut off the light.

Not long after I closed my eyes, I heard my phone buzz with a text.

It was from Lee: *miss u.*

I sat up in bed and pulled my knees to my chest under the sheet, my hands clinging to my nightgown. My emotions were a roller coaster: What did he want from me? Part of me was angry that he could make me feel this way, while another part wanted more. More passion, more life, more Lee.

A flash of light caught my eye as I stared at the phone. Not lightning or moonlight, and certainly not a street lamp. It was coming from our neighbor's tree. The tree fort. Lee.

I tapped the screen for his number and while I waited for the crappy Wi-Fi to connect, I hesitated. What would I say?

I miss you.

I want you.

I lo—

He answered, his voice husky and low.

"Read to me?" I said.

I heard him clear his throat. "When last we saw our intrepid photographer, Peter Parker," he enunciated like a broadcaster, "he was chasing down a criminal mastermind with his camera." The rustle of a page, of the wind blowing through the holes in the fort. "Here we see Peter in his regular clothes," Lee said in his normal voice. "And, man, what a dork! Like that Mary Jane would ever pick him over Spider-Man. I mean, come on. . . ."

As he went on through the story, my eyes began to close. I settled my head on the pillow, imagining my head against his chest and my knees curled over his lap.

In the morning, I awoke with my phone buzzing in my hand. I grinned. It had to be Lee.

"Hey, you!" I said with a smile in my voice.

"Middie? Hi! It's me!"

Oh my god. It was Nate. My heart nearly leaped out of my chest. "Nate! Oh my . . . oh my . . ." I felt like I was hyperventilating. "Where are you? What—?"

"I'm on my way home." The line was clear, unlike the last time we'd spoken when he was in Honduras, but he still sounded faraway. "Tomorrow, I think." He began coughing into the phone, an awful sound, as if his lungs were filled with fluid.

Nate's mom came on the line. "Hi, sweetie, Nate just wanted to touch base with you, but he's really got to rest. We're in San Diego now, should be back tomorrow. Love to your family, okay?"

The call ended and I stared at the phone in my hand. It was real. He was real.

CHAPTER *nineteen*

It didn't take long for the whole town to find out when Nate's plane was arriving. Word quickly spread and by mid-afternoon, the Binghams' house was filled with friends and relatives eager to welcome him. At one point, each room on the first floor was packed to capacity and I could barely turn around.

"Middie!" I heard Haley shout my name from the front hallway. She squeezed through the crowd, hands reaching toward me. I grabbed her fingers and pulled, wrenching her free from the group as if I were snatching her from the grip of quicksand.

"This is insane," Haley said as she stood in a circle and

turned around, admiring the WELCOME HOME, NATE sign my sister and I had put up. We'd also taken all the flowers and plants people had sent Nate and arranged them in the windows so the sun shone on them as if they were an indoor garden. I thought we'd done a pretty good job.

I felt a crush of people behind and around me as more guests entered the Bingham home, jostling us against each other. Haley giggled when her chin bumped into my shoulder. "This is fun. Kind of like a mosh pit without the sweat."

She was right. The house buzzed with energy: Scotty and the twins were back from their grandparents' house, shouting and running through the house with their friends, while my own parents were enjoying playing hosts in a really nice kitchen.

Suddenly there was a sharp yelp and the front door flew open. "He's here!" someone shouted. The crowd surged around us and I lost Haley in an avalanche of guests.

My heart started to race as the seconds and minutes ticked past. There were so many people blocking my view that I couldn't see a thing! And rising on my toes like Haley did wasn't enough for me. Just as I heard a commotion on the outside landing—

"Nate! You're here!"

"Oh my god, Nate!"

"Nate! Dude! Awesome!"

I felt a hand grasp mine and tug me back a step.

"What the—?" My head whipped around and I came

face-to-face with Lee. He gripped my fingers tightly even as he glanced over my head at the door. "What are you doing here?" But in asking that, I heard the jealousy in my voice. Nate was Lee's best friend; why wouldn't he be here?

"I came to check on Rocky, make sure he got fed." His gaze was not on me as he spoke but on the door.

"Oh. Well, I think so."

Lee pressed his hand against my back; I felt the air sizzle between us and I wanted to lean into him, but I didn't dare give in to the temptation. Nate's parents were wheeling Nate in, and the guests parted to make way for them. I caught a glimpse first of the wheelchair and then Nate's feet in his sneakers. My gaze traveled up to his legs and waist and his hands resting on the chair's arms. He looked like he was swimming in his jeans and T-shirt—so thin and frail—and then I saw his face and gasped. He was gaunt, nearly skeletal after weeks in the jungle and sick with fever; his hair had been cut very short very recently, so it stuck up awkwardly over his ears. His eyes were sunken, hollowed out like the eyes of a jack-o'-lantern. He appeared overwhelmed by everyone in the house, although he managed a weak smile.

And then he saw me and his haunted eyes lit up. My name was on his lips and he reached for me. I let go of Lee's hand and rushed forward, throwing my arms around Nate's shoulders, careful not to break him. I heard scattered applause and a couple of wolf whistles when we kissed. Even Nate's lips were fragile: thinner than ever, cracked and dry.

"I can't believe you're here," I whispered to him. "You're alive. You're really alive." I buried my head—carefully—in his neck and breathed him in. He smelled like Nate, like he always did. Same deodorant and shaving cream and shampoo. A flood of memories came back to me with his scent, and it was as if he'd never left.

"Middie, god, I missed you." His voice, although low, was strong and clear. His bony fingers wrapped around my wrists and his eyes found mine.

"Me too," I said, quickly averting my gaze. I *did* miss him, but I felt awful saying it. Allison was right: I was a terrible person. But I would make up for it.

"Sorry to break up the lovefest," Mr. Bingham said with a grin. "Let's get Nate over to the couch so he can sit there instead of on this metal contraption."

"Oh! Sorry!" I stepped back to allow Nate's dad to wheel him into the living room and I fully expected to find Lee not far behind me, but when I turned to look, he was gone. I didn't have time to wonder where he went because Mr. Bingham needed help with Nate. I jumped in to assist and earned a grateful nod. It was the least I could do.

Once Nate was on the couch, no fewer than five people offered to fetch a drink, a pillow, a plate of food, and to each, Nate smiled and said thank you. He patted the spot beside him on the couch and I sat, feeling like the queen next to her triumphant but world-weary king. I held one of his hands with both of mine. It felt so natural to have him next to me, shoulder to shoulder, his hip pressed to mine.

Could this be a dream? I wondered. Could it be true he was home? I gently squeezed his fingers and he squeezed back, catching my eye with a subtle grin.

"Nate," one of Nate's old basketball friends called to him. "You gonna tell us how you kicked ass down there, or are we gonna have to wait till they make a movie about it?"

Everyone laughed, including Nate, but I could tell they were anxiously awaiting Nate's tale. And so was I! The more we knew about how he survived, the more real it would become to have him home.

But Nate's mother intervened. "Nate can't talk for very long. He tires quickly, so not too many questions, okay?"

The crowd grumbled good-naturedly, but they accepted Mrs. Bingham's word as law. They would take whatever crumbs they could get.

Nate sipped water from a glass someone handed him and then cleared his throat before he began. "I thought I was dead," he said. "The fire, the guns . . . But the worst part was the screaming. Children were crying for their parents; moms and dads were shouting their kids' names. It was . . . it was awful." Nate paused as if he were hearing those voices again.

The room fell silent until Nate went on. "They thought I was dead too. But I'd only broken my leg when a wall collapsed on it." He hesitated again, and we could see on his face that he was reliving the scene. I wished I could stop him, tell him to forget all those terrible things, since he was home now and safe, but I too was desperate to know what had happened. "I managed to grab my backpack and escape when they'd left my hut. Two men were with me for about a half mile, but, um, they didn't make it." He bowed his head.

"Where did you go?" Nate's cousin Brad asked. He was perched on the couch arm on the other side of Nate, hanging on every word. "How far did you run?"

Nate looked down at his lap. "I think . . . I think the final figure was twenty-five miles? Something like that. It was pretty far," he said with a laugh. "My leg was killing me!" He tapped his left thigh with his palm. "This is the one. Broke my femur."

"Ouch!" one of his friends said. "Your femur? That's a total bitch, man."

"Brutal," Nate agreed. "I could have bled out if my femoral artery had ruptured."

"Doctor Nate, heal thyself!" someone shouted and there were scattered laughs.

"Yeah, well, not yet," he said ruefully. "They say I might have a limp for the rest of my life." He turned to me with a smile, an optimistic grin that said nothing was going to get him down. "I don't believe it. I think I'll be back to my morning runs with Middie in no time." He leaned over and kissed my cheek and the group in the living room sighed, "Aww!"

No sooner had Nate begun his tale than he started to fade from the effort of speaking. Mrs. Bingham swooped in like a mama bird and began to shoo everyone into the kitchen or outdoors. She opened her son's hand and dropped in a half dozen pills: narcotics for pain, antibiotics for the virus. He swallowed them with his water and settled down into the couch.

Many of the guests started to leave, recognizing Nate's need to rest. I wondered if I should go too, but Nate held fast to my arm.

"I'm not going anywhere," I said, nestling my head against his shoulder.

"Neither am I," he said. "Ever again."

"Emma will be happy to hear that. She told me she wished this had never happened and now that you're back, that means her wish came true."

"That's cute," Nate replied. "I guess."

"I think she wants to marry you," I teased him.

Nate cocked an eyebrow. "Is she a Girl Scout now?"

"Not yet."

"Tell her she has to wait until she's a Girl Scout and then I'll marry her." He began to giggle over this and I realized the painkillers had kicked in fast. His eyes began to close and his chin bobbed. His laughter was infectious. Pretty soon we were both in stitches for absolutely no reason, but it felt good to laugh, to feel normal with Nate.

"Hey, man, where ya been?" we heard. Lee stood in

front of us, hands in the pockets of his jeans.

"Dude!" Nate said. "What's up, dude?" He sounded buzzed-on-the-way-to-drunk and his eyes blinked slowly. He reached up with both hands for Lee, tried to pull him down into an embrace, but the grab was clumsy and Lee ended up stumbling forward and landing on me with his head practically in my lap. I felt myself blush and hoped Nate didn't notice. Lee's gaze avoided mine as he muttered an apology and stood up.

"Oh, sorry, man, you okay?" Nate slurred, his eyes closing.

Lee nodded. "Yeah, I'm good. What about you?"

I watched this exchange like a fly on the wall of a boys' secret clubhouse. They goofed on each other, joking about Nate's lame leg and bad haircut. "What'd they use, a scythe? You look like shit."

Nate's smile was lopsided and silly and he took the teasing in stride. "You wish you had a Honduran barber, dude. I think I'm *only* gonna get my hair cut by a Honduran barber. Forever and ever." And he laughed soundlessly, which made Lee and I exchange a glance before we too burst into laughter.

Finally, Nate began to doze off and his shoulders slumped forward. I felt his hand go slack in mine and knew that he was asleep.

Lee stared at Nate for a long time and then the smile slipped off his face. "See ya," he said, pivoting on his heel toward the door. I watched him go, feeling an ache in the pit of my stomach.

"Middie?" Nate mumbled. His eyes fluttered open and closed a few times.

"Hmmm? Right here, Nate."

There was a long pause. "Middie, I love you."

I pressed my lips to Nate's forehead. "I love you too."

Later, as I tried to sleep, images of Nate in his wheelchair fought with pictures of Lee for space in my mind, and one thought kept pulsing through, over and over: *He's home. He's really home.*

With Nate's return, my life swung into gear and I was suddenly swamped—but in a good way, since it gave me time to help Nate and kept my mind off Lee.

Three of my afternoons each week were spent taking Nate to his physical therapy. The other two I spent at SAT prep classes; the retest was coming up fast and I was nowhere near ready for it—again. Nate offered to barter study aid for driving and I gladly accepted.

Seeing Nate in the wheelchair was the hardest part for me. He'd lost twenty pounds when he was in the jungle, practically all of it muscle. I knew he was still Nate on the inside, but on the outside, he was a different person. A different boyfriend. He would tease me about my vocabulary and then, a minute later, grip my arm with both hands as he tried to stand up.

I felt helpless with him. I hadn't ever known Nate as anything other than a strong, confident guy. He'd had it all: good looks and athletic skill, brains and humble charm. He would probably always be optimistic—that was in his nature—but now there was an edge of fear. And it was that fear that made me worry for his health, both mentally and physically. More than once, he tried to embrace me but I kept my distance, not wanting to injure him. A soft peck on the lips here, a gentle hug there . . . Eventually we would be back to normal, I told myself. Eventually we would be the old Nate and Middie.

When it was time for Nate's exercises, I was allowed in the PT room to cheer him on. After a week of observing, his therapist let me guide him as he walked the parallel bars and lifted weights. It was a challenge for Nate at first, because his muscles had lost so much tone, but we kept at it.

"That's it, Nate! One more set!" I would call to him as he worked his quads, lifting the padded weights with his ankles. "Eight, nine, ten, done."

When he rested, it was my turn to work out. "Okay, complete this sentence."

I perched on an exercise ball with a pen and paper. "Go."

Nate read sample questions from a tablet. "There is no doubt that Larry is a genuine *blank*. He excels at telling stories that fascinate his listeners." He pointed at me. "Is Larry a braggart, dilettante, pilferer, prevaricator, or raconteur?"

"Hmm . . . who's Larry? Friend of yours from the basketball team?"

Nate grinned. "When did we get so funny?"

"Me? Funny?"

"Quit stalling and answer the question." He picked up a free weight and did a few biceps curls.

"All right, Larry is . . . a prevaricator?"

"Buzzzzz! Wrong! He's a raconteur. A prevaricator is a liar."

"A liar tells stories."

Nate counted out a half dozen more reps before responding. "Yeah, I guess, but it's the wrong answer."

I tossed my pen and paper to the floor and helped Nate move to another piece of equipment. "This is why I will fail the SAT. Again."

"You won't fail." His glance at me was stern. "I'm going to help you."

That was the old Nate, the can-do Nate, the Nate who was determined to continue on his path—on our path. I couldn't deny him that. He'd suffered through so much. I swallowed my doubt and nodded. "Right. I won't fail."

Nate was the very definition of "indomitable spirit." While he could suddenly become exhausted, which was the residual effect of the dengue fever he'd contracted, he was always upbeat and self-assured. He did every set of reps without complaint. He took his meds and his naps in equal measure. And he responded to a ton of emails and phone calls from people who wanted to wish him well. He'd even gotten an email from a professor at Lewis & Clark inviting him to speak to a group of students in their off-campus study program.

When it became too much, he would sink back on one of the weight benches and close his eyes. "Middie, tell me something. Anything."

That was when I'd bring out my phone and read to him the text messages I'd tried to send. "This one is just *x*s and *o*s. You know, tic-tac-toe."

He laughed. "You are very silly, Middie."

"Too silly?"

"Just silly enough."

But I was careful to self-edit. When Nate shared pictures of Honduran landscapes, I showed him Emma in her uniform or my selfies with Haley on our first day of school. My photos of waterfalls and ponds and tree forts didn't exist, just as his photos of the village children and GO doctors who died didn't either. We both had secrets to keep.

Watching him work as hard as he did, dedicated and focused and determined as he was, I couldn't *not* work hard myself. When I wasn't with Nate, I threw myself into my classes, studying every night. But one thing continued to elude me: my college application to Lewis & Clark. Nate was so certain we would go together, but I . . . wasn't. Not anymore.

After three weeks of rehab, Nate had put on ten pounds

of muscle and was no longer as gaunt and weak as he'd been when he first came home. He could walk on his own, using a cane when he was tired, but he still had a limp. The therapist told Nate he was going to cut him back to just two appointments per week and let Nate do some work on his own at home.

"Nate, this is awesome!" I told him on the drive home. "No more daily PT."

Nate was not happy at all. "This is bullshit," he said and was silent for the rest of the ride. At his house, he refused my help, slamming the car door and starting up the path to his house by himself.

I offered to make him a snack, but he snapped at me. "I don't need your pity." He threw the cane down on the floor and limped to the kitchen where he opened the fridge door and leaned against it, his breathing heavy.

"Why are you so angry?" I couldn't ever remember seeing Nate upset like this. He was always so mild-tempered that any outburst felt like a total eruption.

He answered without looking at me, his eyes scanning the shelves of the refrigerator. "You heard what the therapist said."

Had I missed something? "He's cutting back. That's good, isn't it?"

"No, it's not. And it's not 'awesome' either," he said, sarcastically. "It means he's done whatever he can do and that's it. Twice a week is not gonna help me get any better."

Bewildered, I simply stood there and let my arms hang. "Two days a week is—"

"Three days less than it needs to be." He slammed the door shut, but it closed with a soft *whoosh*. "How can I get back to the way I was if I'm not doing therapy every single damn day? I don't want to stop until I'm better."

"You are!" I thrust a hand at him. "You're walking!"

"It's not the same! I'm not the same!" He turned and stared at me, and while his cheeks had filled in somewhat from getting his fill of his mom's good cooking, his eyes were still troubled, still fearful, still at odds with the old Nate. "What do you care? You gave up on me too."

Stunned, I couldn't speak. *What did that mean?*

"The only time you've touched me since I came back was when my dad wheeled me into the house that very first day," he said, his voice growing quiet and hoarse. "You haven't hugged me or kissed me. *Really* kissed me." He glanced over his shoulder, out the window. The sun was setting in the backyard and the air was growing cold, but the twins and Scotty were happily playing on the swing set with Mrs. Bingham.

I didn't know what to say. This was a new side, a vulnerable side, to Nate that I hadn't ever seen. "I . . . I didn't want to hurt you," I said.

He turned to me. "I'm not gonna break."

"I know," I said, feeling suddenly and intensely shy. I leaned against the center island, aware of the distance between Nate and me. The few feet from one end of the kitchen to the other felt like the miles between Central America and Roseburg.

The fear I'd heard in his voice I saw now in the lines on his face. As much as we wanted to believe nothing had changed, some things had. It was Nate's limp on the outside, and his heartache on the inside.

I'd thought helping Nate with his PT, supporting him and encouraging him, was enough to take care of him. But he could have gotten all that from his friends and relatives; that wasn't the kind of care he needed from *me*.

I crossed the kitchen in short strides and wrapped my arms around Nate's waist from behind. We stood there for a moment like that; I felt the roughness of his bony spine under my cheek, the outline of his ribs under my hands. Finally, he turned to face me and he took my head in his hands, tilting my chin up before he pressed his mouth to mine.

I closed my eyes and felt summer return. With every kiss, another day was erased. With every touch, another painful memory was taken away. His hands brushed my hair from my neck and slid down my back and his hips met mine.

Nate, my Nate . . . He'd been the love of my life for five years, my friend for ten. I knew him better than anyone, maybe better than I knew myself.

"I want things to be the way they were," he said quietly.

I nodded. "I do too. Just exactly the way they were."

Relief flooded Nate's face. *Just like old times,* I read in his eyes.

I wondered what he could read in mine. I did want things back the way they were—if only I could erase the memories of what had come between.

CHAPTER twenty

It was remarkably easy to fall back into the rhythm Nate and I had before he left. Within a month, my daily routine returned to its old pattern of school-Nate-study-sleep and repeat. There was no room for anything, or anyone, else.

Nate too wanted everything back in order, and he resumed his volunteer work at the farm as quickly as he could. His fan club was thrilled to have him back. They nearly mowed him down when we drove up one Friday afternoon. In no time at all, they were exchanging advice about the best canes and how to get out of bed without falling.

I tried to join in, but Nate sternly aimed a finger at my backpack. "Aren't the SATs calling you?"

While he let the other volunteers regale him with sto-ries about squash that looked like the heads of presidents, I studied. From time to time, Nate would glance over at me and smile, never once betraying a desire to flee. There was none of the vulnerability I'd seen at his house the other day. It startled me how different he was from Lee, who covered up his insecurities with goofy non sequiturs and awkward jokes. Where Nate went with the flow of conversation, Lee flailed in its waters.

On the way home, Nate quizzed me on vocabulary words.

"Anachronistic."

"Um . . . out-of-date?"

"Correct. Sagacity."

I tried to pare down the word to its root. Was "saga" the base word? "Long?"

"No."

"Boring?"

"No, it's—"

"Wait! I got it. Big?"

"Middie, you won't get it," he said with a sigh.

"What . . . Why not? Don't you think I'm smart enough?"

Nate was quick to shake his head. "All I meant was you were on the wrong track. You were thinking 'saga.'"

I glanced sharply at him. "How did you know that?"

He laughed. "How long have I known you? I could see it in your face."

"You saw 'saga' in my face?" I couldn't help but smile.

"What did it look like?"

Nate scrunched up his nose and narrowed his eyebrows. "I did *not* look like that."

"Nah, I'm joking." He took my right hand from the wheel and held it in his, caressing my palm and fingers. "I just know you so well. I know what you're thinking." He kissed my hand as if he were my prince. "I thought about you all the time when I was lost." His voice softened. "Every night when I was in the jungle, I imagined you here. I imagined us here. Together. Running. Talking. And *other* things," he added, which made me blush.

"Yeah?"

"Yeah."

Ahead was a stop sign, and I suddenly realized where I was. If I turned left, I would head toward Lee's house. To the right, Nate's. I'd been here before, this fork in the road. And I'd made a different choice. I put my turn signal on and drove to Nate's.

"You're having dinner with us tomorrow, aren't you? Like we always do?" he asked as I pulled the car up the driveway. Each year, Nate's family celebrated Christmas Eve out at a restaurant and then went home to get the house ready for Santa to visit. For the past five years, I had been included. "We're trying a new Italian restaurant."

"Sounds delicious." Of course I had to go. It was tradition.

As I backed out the driveway and into the street, I saw a flash of blue in my rearview mirror and glanced up. A scooter—Lee's Vespa. My heart began to thump in my chest. I wanted to wait to see where he was going— would he pass me, follow me, ignore me? But another car swerved around him and the driver started to lay on his horn, urging me on.

I hadn't seen him since the party at Nate's house. No texts, naturally, no calls, no invitations to do something crazy . . . It was as if our relationship—whatever it was—had never existed for him. I slowed my car down and pulled over to the shoulder, waiting for the impatient driver behind me to pass, and then I glanced in my side mirror.

Lee was gone. Had he turned up Nate's driveway? He and Nate *were* friends, after all.

And what are we? What could Lee and I possibly be to each other now that Nate was back? We'd never figured that out.

That night I fell asleep with my books surrounding me and my laptop on, only to awaken at three in the morning in a sweaty panic. I was going to fail: school, the SAT, and Nate. I was going to disappoint everyone in my life.

I dug my phone out of my purse to read a message I desperately needed.

breathe

Christmas Eve dinner was at a small Italian restaurant in town. Nate's family was dressed up in their best clothes; even Scotty wore a jacket and tie. But all the fancy attire in the world couldn't hide the holiday energy the kids brought with them. The only thing that kept them seated was the promise that Santa would only visit if they were good.

After we were seated, the waiter and house manager appeared at our table, beaming with delight. Both men were in their forties, mustachioed brothers with immaculately white shirts and sharply pressed black pants.

"We saw your name on the reservation list." The manager thrust his hand at Nate. "You're Nate Bingham, aren't you?" Nate barely had a chance to nod before the man's face split into a grin. "Son, you're a hero." His brother, standing at his elbow, bobbed his head in agreement.

Nate demurred, even as his parents patted his shoulder and whispered encouraging words. "But I didn't do anything. A hero saves people."

"You saved *yourself*," the manager said. "Your dinner is on me tonight."

"On *us*," his brother added.

"I insist—"

"*We* insist."

"Thank you so much," Nate's mother said. "That is very kind of you."

A moment later, the brothers brought sodas and a bottle of wine to our table. "On the house."

Nate's dad was gracious. "You are very generous, thank you."

"Wow, free stuff!" Scotty said as he claimed a soda for

himself. Mrs. Bingham split a can of soda for the twins, pouring a small amount for each of them, while Mr. Bingham poured wine into the rest of the glasses.

"None for me," I told him. "I'm driving."

"You can have some of my soda," Scotty said. "It was free."

I laughed and thanked him for the Coke. "You being nice for Santa?"

Scotty narrowed his eyes at me. "Middie, there's no such thing as—"

"Scotty! Hey, why don't you tell me what you want to eat?" Mr. Bingham said quickly before he could spill the beans.

The whole family was in high spirits: Nate's parents were thrilled he was home for Christmas. They couldn't take their eyes off him, couldn't take their hands off him. Mrs. Bingham was constantly touching Nate's cheek and forehead, checking for fever. Mr. Bingham sneaked sideways glances at him, as if worried he would suddenly disappear again. And through the entire meal, I felt Nate's hand on my hand, fingers reaching for mine, for extra assurance that he was here.

Around nine, Nate's parents packed the kids up and hustled them back to the house to get ready for Santa's visit. I held up my glass of soda to remind them I would be fine to drive Nate home as soon as we were finished with dessert.

"Take your time," Mr. Bingham said. "We've got to make cookies for Santa."

Just after they'd left, the restaurant manager brought an elderly couple to our table, introducing them as regulars who'd heard about Nate and wanted to tell him how proud they were of him. Nate thanked them both, as graciously as his parents had, holding his tongue until they'd left. "I didn't defend our country," he said to me when they were out of earshot. His words were slurred; I didn't realize how much wine he'd had to drink. "I didn't even save a kitten from a burning building." His eyes held mine. "I just got lucky. I managed to play dead, and then I escaped when no one was looking."

"It wasn't just luck—"

"It was! Those guys may have killed a lot of people, but they weren't the sharpest tools in the shed, you know. They were dumb. I took advantage of it and I ran away." He blinked back tears. "I didn't save anyone. They were all dead. I didn't do anything."

"You *couldn't* do anything," I said to him. "It wasn't that you chose not to."

"I know, but . . ."

"But what?" I reached across the table and took his hand in mine. "Nate, you were lucky to have survived at all. And you can talk about your experience and maybe that will help even more people. Maybe you could write a book."

He squeezed my hand. A tear fell from his eye and he wiped it away with a linen napkin that had a stain of red sauce, like the kiss of a ruby lipstick. "I don't want to go anywhere," he said urgently, holding fast to my fingers.

"You mean, like college? Or med school?"

"I mean, I don't want to do any more Global Outreach work. I want to stay here with you and I want things to be the way they were before." He sounded a bit like Emma with her wishes. "We still have our plans, right?" he asked. He leaned over the table and grabbed my hands. "You and me? College and med school and marriage and family?"

I snorted a laugh. "Med school for *you*, not me."

But he was serious. "We've talked about this our whole lives. Our future is with each other."

"Of course it is," I heard myself say automatically. "Absolutely, one hundred percent."

He kissed my hands and I felt another tear fall from his cheek and onto my fingers. He was so positive about us. Even after all that had happened to him, he still wanted to be with me.

On the ride home, Nate rolled the window down, cool air on his face, holding my hand the entire time. When we got to his house, we stayed in the car for a bit longer, our arms wrapped around each other, whispering and giggling until the windows fogged up. Nate drew a lazy finger in the steam on the windshield. *NM4eva*.

He lowered his head to my lap and stared up at me. "You're my rock, Middie. You were the one thing I could anchor myself to when I was delirious in the jungle."

"Really?" I felt my heart beat faster. While he'd been

dreaming of me, I'd abandoned him. I felt ashamed of myself. I wished I could take it all back, undo it all, just as Emma wanted. Make it all go back the way it was.

Nate pulled me to him, pressing his hand at the back of my neck and kissing me deeply, passionately.

Lee.

My eyes flew open and I pulled back from Nate. *Whoa, what the hell was that?*

Nate, upside down, looked quizzical. "Middie? You okay?"

"Um, yeah, yeah. . . ." I closed my eyes and sent the image of Lee—his scent, his voice, his taste—away from me and concentrated on Nate. I let him kiss me again, his tongue lightly tickling mine, his lips lingering on my neck and earlobe, my cheeks and chin.

Lee, I thought again, and this time I did sit back and take stock. What on earth was happening?

Nate sat up but kept his arms on either side of me. "Bad pasta?"

"Uh, yeah, maybe." I didn't feel sick to my stomach, but there was definitely something wrong with me. I should not be thinking about Lee.

Nate held the back of his hand to my forehead. "You feel a little warm. Maybe you should go home and get some sleep."

I nodded. "Okay." When he started to get out, I did too, but he stopped me.

"I'm a big boy. I can walk in by myself."

"You sure?"

"I'm sure." He came over to my side of the car and bent down to kiss me through the window. Just a quick peck on the lips. "Merry Christmas. I hope Santa brings Emma everything she wants."

I waited until he'd slowly made his way inside the house and turned out the front light on the landing. Then I backed my mom's car out of the driveway and headed home. I left the windows rolled down and stuck my head out like a dog with its ears flapping in the breeze.

Lee was creeping back into my thoughts, into my world, and I had to make it stop. Nate loved me, and I wanted to love him back. I couldn't keep planning our future together if my present was all fucked up.

Just before bed, I pulled out my phone and found Lee's last text to me. I took a deep breath and clicked Reply.

It's meredith. merry xmas

I paused. I wanted to send him a text that he couldn't help but reply to. If he did, then I would know . . . something. If he didn't . . . I would know that too.

joining the circus, wanna come?

Text in haste, repent in leisure? I clicked Send and quickly shoved the phone back into my purse, then finished undressing for bed. Five minutes later, there was no reply from Lee.

Twenty minutes, nothing.

An hour, still nothing.

When I awoke in the morning, the only thing I saw on my phone was the tiny word Delivered. He'd gotten it.

And I'd gotten my answer.

CHAPTER twenty-one

When I didn't hear back from Lee, I was actually relieved. Lee's presence in my life was unstable, an unknown—who needed that? With Nate, I knew exactly where we were headed and what I was supposed to do. And if I didn't, there were plenty of people to remind me.

We were two days away from New Year's Eve, on holiday break, when Haley brought up party plans while we were at the Matchbox, a coffee shop not far from the high school.

"There are at least three that I know of," she told Katrina, Debra, and me over hot chocolate and handmade marshmallows. It was our annual tradition to meet at the intimate café to exchange Christmas gifts but really we simply liked hanging out in a place that wasn't a cafeteria crowded with a million other students. The coffee shop, especially in winter, was a quiet oasis with a background music of espresso being ground and milk being frothed. Today, we watched wet snow fall lightly outside the plate glass window, the fat flakes melting as soon as they hit the sidewalk.

"One is superdressy," Haley said. "One is my parents'." She rolled her eyes. "And one is—"

"Mine!" Katrina said, grinning and holding her hand up.

"Not completely yours," Haley said. "It's your sister's place, isn't it?"

Katrina nodded. "Yeah, but she and her husband are totally cool. They said we can drink if we don't go anywhere."

"Ooh, champagne?" Haley asked.

"Only if you bring it," Katrina said with a laugh.

Debra tapped her spoon on the table absently. "Who's going to be there? Like, guys our age or their age?"

"Does it matter?"

"Well, yeah. I don't want to get a new outfit if it's just going to be guys we know."

"There'll probably be more college guys than regular guys," Katrina said, looking up at the ceiling of the café as if she were mentally calculating the ages of the party guests.

"And how many of us? Like, what's the ratio?"

Katrina lifted one curious eyebrow. "Are you about to use *math* for a party?"

Debra looked down at her hands and arms in astonishment. "Why, yes, I think I am," she said, and we all laughed.

Haley glanced over at me. "What about you, Mid? You gonna come out with us this year?"

"Well—"

"Last New Year's Eve party of high school," she teased.

"Oh my god, you have to! We'll have so much fun!" Debra said, adding, "You can wear my dress again, like you did at Halloween."

I laughed. "That was a costume."

"You can make it into a sexy dress," Katrina said. "Just don't wear the green makeup again."

"You can wear whatever you want," Haley said. "And so can Nate."

Nate. I tried to imagine him at a big New Year's Eve party. I shook my head. "It's too soon, I think. He just got back and he gets tired pretty fast."

"Oh, right, yeah," Debra said quickly. "You should do what he wants. He's the one who's been away."

Been away. "I think we'll probably just hang at his house like we usually do."

Katrina leaned into my shoulder. "And watch the *ball* drop?" she snickered.

"Yeah, actually, we will."

"Ugh, boring."

"But romantic," Haley said. "It's sweet. Just the two of you."

"Not *just* the two of us. His parents will be there."

"Well, if you change your mind, there are three parties to choose from." Haley stopped and shook her head. "Hmm, just two. I'm not going to wear a superfancy dress like it's the formal or something."

"And *I'm* not going to your parents' party," Debra said.

"Then it's *my* party!" Katrina beamed with delight. "Party! Party! Party!"

The girls cheered, filling the small café with laughter, and I couldn't help but join in. *Party, party, party,* I thought. It did sound like fun. I wondered if I could convince Nate to go.

"Aw, Mid, I'm sorry," Nate said when I arrived at his house on New Year's Eve. "I really don't think I want to go to a party. Can't it just be you and me tonight?"

Even though I knew that would be his response, I'd dressed up a little nicer than usual, just in case, wearing a lacy long skirt over black boots and a V-neck white-and-black embroidered top. Yeah, I was a little disappointed. Not that I *didn't* want it to be just the two of us, but with his parents and Scotty and the twins around, it was mostly *not* the two of us.

Still, I bobbed my head with a smile. "Sure, of course."

"They'll go to bed early," he said with a sly grin. He pulled me down to him on the sofa.

"Were you reading my mind?" I blushed as he took me in his arms.

Nate brushed his lips against my cheek. His gaze held mine forcefully, as if to prove to me his inner strength was greater than his physical limitations.

"I want it back," he said. "I want all of it back just the way it was." He looked at me expectantly, and I whispered, "So do I."

He bent toward me, placing a kiss firmly on my lips, his hands on my back and his fingers in my hair. Just as things began to heat up, we heard voices in the kitchen.

"Can I stay up till midnight?" Scotty asked.

"If he gets to, we get to too!" one of the twins said indignantly.

"No one is staying up till midnight," Mr. Bingham replied.

"Why not? Nate and Middie are."

Mrs. Bingham's voice rose above the others. "When you're twelve you can stay up until twelve."

"What can we do if we're not twelve?" Scotty wanted to know.

"Make popcorn."

I whispered to Nate, "I'm so glad we're older than twelve."

Then one of the girls said, "Can we watch TV with Nate and Middie?"

Nate looked at me. "Are we watching TV?"

"Ask first," Mr. Bingham said.

"Nate!" the twins shouted. "Can we come in and watch TV with you?"

Nate and I exchanged a glance and a shrug. "You mind?"

I shook my head. "Of course not."

As the twins bounded in, I rearranged myself on the couch, detangling my skirt from Nate's legs. *All dressed up and no place to go,* I thought.

Or was I? This *was* my place.

For the next three hours, we played Monopoly with the girls and video games on Scotty's Xbox. We ate popcorn and chocolate kisses and watched the ball drop in Times Square at nine West Coast time, which was the best compromise Nate's parents could come up with for the kids. After celebrating with sparkling apple cider and playing another round of Monopoly, Scotty and the girls managed to eke out an extra couple of hours before they were sent off to bed. Mr. and Mrs. Bingham finally left us alone just before twelve.

We were both beat. Nate's grin was tired as he sprawled back on the couch. "This being-normal thing is exhausting. I hope it gets better."

I leaned my head on his shoulder. "Every day will get better until *you're* better."

"You think so?"

"I know so." I turned to look at him. He had a smudge of chocolate on his chin from one of the candies. I wiped it off with my thumb and licked it. Suddenly, Nate dove toward me, his lips on my mouth, his tongue darting out to taste the chocolate on my lips. His hands were on my waist and he was pulling me onto his lap, folding himself over me on the couch. I stretched my legs along the length of the sofa and felt Nate do the same, aligning his hips and his legs to mine. I heard his voice whisper my name, a sweet, melancholy sigh, just before he kissed a gentle trail down my neck. *Not so tired after all,* I thought, smiling to myself.

I let my hands follow a path along his shoulder and back, down the side of his waist and slope of his hip. We were getting back to the way things were before—finally. And even though Nate's body felt different beside mine, it was him. I felt myself sigh in return. *"Nate . . ."*

I wanted Nate's kisses to make me forget everything else, to let me sink into him and never return, which was almost close to happening when the doorbell rang. Nate looked at me. "It's almost midnight. Who's coming here on New Year's Eve?"

"No idea."

The door opened. "Yo, Happy New Year."

I shot up to a sitting position, but Nate merely grinned. "Lee, dude, come in."

Lee? I felt myself stiffen as I glanced at Nate. "Were you expecting him?"

He shrugged. "You never know with Lee."

Part of me wanted to stand when he walked in—a hug? A half kiss? What did friends like us do? My mind raced, trying to recall how we were with each other before Nate left. We barely knew who the other was—would we be like that again? Should we?

Lee solved that conundrum by remaining at the edge of the rug, hands stuffed in the pockets of his ripped jeans. Despite the cold weather, he wore only a Windbreaker over a T-shirt and his ink-covered sneakers.

"Hey, Lee," I said with a smile. "Happy New Year." Nate tucked his fingers around mine, and I felt his solidarity with me. We were a couple. Lee was a third wheel. If anything I should feel sorry for him. "You want some sparkling cider?"

Lee's hazel eyes barely registered my presence before alighting upon Nate. "Dude, you're not at a party."

Nate leaned forward on the couch and slung an arm around my shoulder. "Neither are you."

Lee opened his jacket and showed us a bottle of beer tucked inside. I recognized the brand and felt my cheeks warm as I remembered drinking it with him. "I take the party with me wherever I go."

"Classy," I said, but again, Lee ignored me.

He opened the other side of his jacket. Another beer. "Got one with your name on it. Come on, let's go."

"We're kind of hanging out," I told him. "Alone."

"I'll get him back by midnight, Yoko. Don't you fret."

"It's almost midnight now." I heard my voice harden.

"Well, sure, if you're celebrating in this time zone."

I turned to look at Nate, but he was watching Lee. "What do you have in mind?"

Lee's eyes twinkled. "Maybe a drive?"

Nate clapped his hands once. "Yes!" He stood uncertainly but refused my help.

"Are you going? Really?"

"Just for a few minutes," he said, pecking me on the cheek. He started to leave the room. "I gotta get a sweater. Entertain Lee while I'm gone."

My face flushed beet red and I glanced down at my feet. "You sure? I can go—"

He put his hands on my arms. "You don't have to do everything for me. I'll be down in two seconds." He left the room and I expected . . .

What, Middie? What could possibly happen?

I hadn't seen Lee in person since Nate's party, and I wasn't sure what to expect, but it wasn't this. He wasn't talking to me, wasn't looking at me, wasn't even acknowledging my existence.

Jerk, I thought. Well, if he wanted cool, then I would give him cool.

"How's work?" I asked. "Business good?" *That was nice,* I thought. A very nice, casual thing to say.

I heard a crinkle of a chocolate kiss being unwrapped. *Rude jerk. Whatever.*

"Guess not too many people want to go hiking now, huh?"

He drowned out the second half of my sentence with more wrapper noise.

So irritating. I turned to him, mouth open, about to call him out on his rudeness—and met his gaze. Suddenly my nerves were like live wires. I could feel every word in my mouth as if it were in a foreign language, as if I'd never spoken it before.

The room felt supercharged, the air electrified. And yet, the only word I could use to describe Lee's mood was "bored." He chewed the chocolate candy as if he were eating cardboard. There was absolutely nothing in his face that showed he was engaged, interested, or even present.

I cast a glance down my body—was I the only one feeling this? Was Lee completely immune to the energy between us? He couldn't be.

But his eyes were so vacant, so absent. His gaze flicked over me briefly before he rolled up the tin foil and hooked it above my head and into an empty cup on the coffee table.

"Two points!" Nate called from the staircase. Lee and I turned.

"Shoulda gone pro," Lee said with a lopsided grin.

"Shoulda played JV," Nate replied.

"Eh, high school ball is overrated."

Nate opened the door and a blast of cold air swept through the foyer. He stared down the driveway and a grin spread across his face. "Is that it?"

The Mustang.

"It is," Lee told Nate proudly. He slapped Nate on the back, boxing me out. "I told you it'd be done in no time."

"Holy shit, it looks awesome!"

"Well, come on, let's drive."

I grabbed my jacket and started to follow them out the

door, my hand firmly in Nate's, when Lee stopped us. "Uh-uh, just us, Yoko."

"But . . . we're friends, aren't we? All three of us?" I asked. I could feel my heart thumping behind my ribs as I waited for an answer. *Friends, we're friends.*

"Yeah, of course we're friends," Nate replied matter-of-factly.

We both looked at Lee, who reluctantly shrugged his shoulders. "Friends, sure. Peachy keen, happy friend time. Whatever, dude, can we go?"

"So then . . . ?" I glanced at Nate, who looked torn. He also looked pretty excited to drive the car.

"It probably won't be that much fun," Nate said. "I mean, for *you*, since you can't drive stick."

"I can dr—" I stopped and looked straight at Lee. His gaze betrayed nothing. In that moment, I felt like I could have dropped the entire bomb on Nate—about Lee, about me, about us—and Lee could not have cared less. I was nothing to him now.

"What's that?" Nate wanted to know.

"Um, never mind." I shook my head and smiled with my lips pressed together.

Nate must have sensed my disappointment. "Maybe I should stay."

"No, go," I said, waving him away. "Have fun in the . . . What did you say it was?"

"Mustang. 1966," he said, his excitement bubbling over.

Gone was his exhaustion from a night with the family and in its place was a boyish glee at hopping in a sports car and driving fast. "Wait till you see it in daylight, Mid. Oh man, it's sweet."

"Sure," I said, trying to keep my tone light. "Another time."

Nate high-fived Lee and got an easy grin in return. "Dude, let's go."

"I'll be back for our kiss at midnight," Nate called to me as Lee urged him down the steps.

I heard them whooping as they raced off to the Mustang.

I closed the door and leaned back against it with all of my weight. An image of Lee and Nate in the newly restored car popped into my head and refused to leave. I kept thinking about Lee calling me "Yoko." *I* was the third wheel, not Lee.

CHAPTER twenty-two

With my head buried in my books for the first week of the new year, I hardly saw Nate at all. But one morning he surprised me with a phone call at five fifteen, our usual time for an early run. "Meet me downstairs in ten minutes," he told me. "Dress for rain."

I did, tiptoeing out the front door to see Nate slowly jogging up the driveway. I ran down to meet him, nearly crushing him with a hug. "You're running!"

"Well, not *running*, but kind of jogging and walking and stopping a lot," he said, a bit out of breath, his face flushed with the thrill of his success. "I have to be careful I don't step on a rock or in a pothole, but so far, so good."

"This is amazing!" I stared down at Nate's legs. "I knew you could do it."

"With *your* help," he said and kissed me on the lips as if this were any normal run instead of a monumental achievement. "Come on, let's go."

A light morning mist blew against my cheeks as we set out down the road at a comfortable pace. It wasn't fast enough to build up a sweat, but it was exciting to see Nate's progress just the same. He was cautious in his steps but not fearful, and every hundred yards or so, he would slow to a walk, swinging his upper body while he gave himself some time to breathe. I jogged in place next to him to stay warm.

We were quiet as we ran so Nate could conserve his energy. At this early hour, the sun was just peeking over the horizon, made gray by the thin layer of clouds, which would likely burn off by the time I had to go to school. Off in the distance I heard a few trucks, a horn honking, a plane, but on this back road we were surrounded by soaring pines stretching into the sky.

Not far from Nate's house, we slowed to a crawl and finally a stop. Nate paused, leaning both hands on his knees.

"You okay?" I asked, touching the back of his neck, which was slick with sweat and rain.

He nodded, sucking in air, and then exhaled. "I'm good. Although this would be a lot easier with a car." He added, "Like a cool Mustang."

"Oh, right, cool." I wondered how much I was supposed to

know about the car other than what I'd seen on New Year's Eve.

"That's ours, you know," he said proudly. "Lee and I fixed it up together."

Lee and I fixed it up together. I tried to keep my voice neutral. "You never mentioned it before."

"It was supposed to be a surprise," he said. "I'll show you how to drive it sometime. It's a manual transmission."

"Sure." I glanced down at my shoes and then back up at Nate. "You ready to go?"

The mist was gone, but there was still moisture in the air. My jacket and sweatpants clung to my legs and back and my ponytail kept sticking to my cheeks when the wind blew it against my face. I had a headband wrapped around my ears to keep them warm but wished I had added a scarf.

Nate stretched the backs of his calves and hamstrings and started to jog again. "Now that I'm back, you can concentrate on school again." He glanced sideways at me as we took off. "You are still applying to Lewis & Clark, right?"

"Well, yeah, of course I am," I said a little irritably. "Why would you say that?"

"Just checking."

For another quarter mile, we jogged silently, but the noises of the morning were stealing into our quiet bubble. Birds, dogs, people—their sounds dotted the landscape like drips of paint on a canvas.

"Middie . . ."

I stopped and turned to discover Nate was trailing behind

me by about a dozen paces. Somehow I'd run past him without realizing it. I jogged back a few steps to meet him.

"You can do this," he said. "We can do it together—you and me. If we stay on our path, the one we've wanted for years, we'll be fine."

"But what if I—" *Don't know what I want?*

Nate took my arm and pulled me close to him. His breath was on my neck as he held me by the waist. "Since our first date, I've loved you."

I didn't want to let him down—how could I do that to him? I felt a sudden rush of warmth as he embraced me, his lips on mine. I knew him so well I could close my eyes and see every detail on his face, like the single freckle over his left eye and the tiny crinkle at his temple when he was lost in thought.

"I was terrified I was lost forever, that I'd never find my way back, but I kept picturing you and that would calm me down." His voice dropped to a whisper. "Your face, your hands, your body . . ." He ran his hands along the sides of my waist and hips. "And I could see the future, our future. I knew that if I could just get back here, my life would have meaning."

My life would have meaning. Even at his worst moments, Nate was thinking of others, of a greater purpose.

My hands began to tremble and my eyes filled with tears. "I love you too." I leaned my head against his chest and listened to the steady pounding of his heart. We stood like that, swaying slightly from side to side, intimate yet comfortable, as we always had been with each other. Finally, Nate broke the silence.

"Tell you what . . . you write your college essay today—"

I groaned aloud, shaking my head. "Noooo . . ."

"—and I'll write my speech and then we'll go to the movies," Nate said. "My treat."

I cocked an eye, regarding him at arm's length. "Yeah?"

"Yeah."

"Popcorn?"

"With extra butter."

"And M&M's?"

"Hmmm . . ." He pretended he was thinking about it. "Maybe."

I tilted my chin haughtily. "It's yes—or no deal."

He laughed. "Okay then, it's yes. M&M's."

I kissed him with a loud smack on the lips. "Deal."

"Good." He gently turned me around, facing me back the way we came. "Go. Study. Finish your application."

I saluted him with two fingers. "Aye, aye, Captain." I ran off toward home just as the sun began to burn off the low-lying fog. It was the start to a beautiful day.

Tell us about an experience that defines you.

I knew in my heart that Nate's death in Honduras had been a defining moment for me, but now that he was back, did it still have the same impact?

I'd felt lost when he left, adrift when I thought he'd died. Every plan I'd had evaporated like morning mist at sunrise. I couldn't eat or drink, let alone think straight. It should have been no surprise I'd fallen into Lee's arms when it looked like I'd had no other choice.

No other choice, Middie? That's a bit harsh.

I stared at the application on my computer. No college wanted to read about my love life. No admissions rep was going to appreciate an essay on why I believed it was okay to kiss another guy.

What was that SAT word—"extrapolate"? I had to extrapolate the meaning from this experience. I had to find the purpose of it and apply it to my life, my circumstances.

There had been a brief moment when I'd seen an alternate future for myself, one that wasn't full of meaning someone else had applied to it. I'd been searching beyond my friends and family, beyond Haley and Emma and Allison, beyond Nate's volunteer work and his morning runs, beyond Nate . . . and I'd liked it. It was scary and unknown and nothing I'd done before.

And it had included Lee.

When life hands you lemons, make lemonade.

Good god, that was flippant.

The world I'd known collapsed one day in September.

Oh no, the admissions department would definitely misunderstand that.

I scrolled up and down the application, lazily spun my

finger on the mouse pad, but I still couldn't get my mind around the essay question.

Maybe I had nothing to say.

If I was worried Nate would ask me about my essay, I shouldn't have been: he was preoccupied with the speech he was writing for the study-abroad group. When he came to pick me up for the movies in his old truck, he was in mid-sentence as I opened the passenger-side door.

"Does it make sense to start with how I got involved in Global Outreach?" he asked me when I slid across the seat to kiss him hello.

"Um, yeah, I guess. Why not?"

He started the truck down the driveway, a thoughtful expression on his face. "It's not boring?" The truck rumbled over the gravelly end of the driveway, where it met the street. Nate paused and looked both ways before pulling out.

"I hate to say it, but I really think they want to hear the horrible stuff."

Nate's fingers gripped the steering wheel tighter and his gaze hardened. "I know. I'm just . . . not ready to talk about those things."

"Not even with me?"

He sighed. "I'm sorry, Middie. I don't want to burden you."

"It's not a burden," I said quickly. "I want to listen to you."

But he merely shook his head. I tried not to show my frustration, but I felt like he was shutting me out. If we were each other's closest friend, why wouldn't he want to tell me everything?

When we got to the theater, Nate parked in the back, near the Dumpster where Lee and I had sneaked in. I felt an odd sense of melancholy; it had been thrilling getting away with something.

The side door to the theater opened and a flash of pink caught my eye. The tiny girl with the big mouth was carrying out two bags of trash. Could we sneak in? I wondered suddenly. I tugged on Nate's arm and whispered, "Come on!"

Nate stumbled forward as I dragged him. "Huh?"

"We're going to sneak in," I said quietly, pointing to the open door. The girl was steps from the trash container; if we didn't move *now*, she would turn around and see us.

"Sneak? But why?" Nate wanted to know. "I already got tickets online."

I pulled him along, but his bad leg tripped on the pavement and he had to stop and shake it out. I glanced over my shoulder—ten more seconds and that pink-haired girl would finish and we'd be sunk. "Nate, come on," I said urgently. "It'll be fun."

"But the tickets," he said. Confusion creased his forehead. "I don't understand."

I heard the *whump* of the Dumpster top closing and saw pink out of the corner of my eye. She was done. It was too late. As she walked past us, the girl aimed a sour look at me, an unspoken *I'm watching you* in her eyes.

Nate looked at me. "You want to go in? Like normal people?" I let him lead me toward the front of the theater. "Lee was always trying to get me to sneak in with him. That guy was just asking to get caught."

I felt my cheeks grow warm. "That's probably what would have happened."

We queued up at a ticket kiosk and Nate held me from behind while we waited. "What are you wearing?" he asked, peering over my shoulder. I'd put together another of Allison's boho outfits, a flowing layered skirt and a long-sleeved top that tied at the wrists and cinched under the bodice.

"You like?" I twirled the skirt for him, expecting him to grin, but he was impassive.

"Not what I expected, but you always look pretty," he added, planting a kiss on the side of my cheek.

I stared down at the blouse and skirt and wondered if I'd made a mistake. Maybe Allison had given this up for a reason.

Once we were past the ticket taker, Nate handed me a stub. "I'll get in line for popcorn. You get in line for seats."

"You sure?"

"This is my treat, remember?" Then he pulled his phone out and handed it to me. "Here, you can play Fruit Ninja on my cell while you wait."

I took the phone and ticket and looked around for our theater. Fruit Ninja wasn't exactly my favorite game, but it was okay to pass the time. I swiped my finger across a few pineapples and coconuts, smashing them open with a *whoosh*, but just as quickly, I nailed some bombs and the game was over. I sighed and tapped the screen.

Nate's contacts were right on top. His mother, his father, me . . . and Lee.

Almost instantly, my face flushed and my palms started to sweat. I felt naked, transparent, as if anyone looking at me could see my pulse pounding. Could Nate?

I glanced down at the other end of the lobby and saw him chatting with some guys from high school. He would probably be there for a while longer.

Call him.

Could I?

Call him.

Lee was my friend. We were all friends, weren't we? That was what we'd agreed on New Year's Eve. Lee and Nate and I. Friends could call friends.

I slipped out of line and took a few steps away from the crowd as I pressed the CALL symbol on Lee's number. My fingers trembled and I shifted the phone from one hand to the other. There was a *whoosh*ing sound in my ear as if a sudden wind had blown through the theater. I could feel my heart thump three times for every ring.

"Yo, dude, where are you?"

My throat went dry; I opened my mouth but couldn't speak.

"Nate?" Lee's voice sounded anxious, bordering on panic. "You need help?"

"It's . . . It's me, it's Meredith." My voice cracked on my own name.

"Meredith?"

"Yeah, hi."

"Where's Nate? Is he all right?"

"Oh yeah, yeah, he's fine." My finger twisted a lock of my hair around and around. "He's in line getting popcorn."

There was a long pause. "You're at the movies?"

"Um, yeah."

"And you called me?"

"Well, yeah," I said with a short laugh. "You'll think this is really funny—"

"Meredith."

"When we got here, that pink-haired girl was taking out the trash—"

"Meredith."

"And she left the door open, right?" I started to talk faster, drowning him out. "So I told Nate we had to sneak in, you know, like you and I did that time and we were there, like right at the door, but then Nate stopped, you know, and the girl turned and came back and she looked right at me, like she totally knew what we were planning, so, of course, we couldn't do it." I stopped, having run out of story, run out of steam. My pulse pounded and I felt faint. Did the people around me know I was calling Lee? That my boyfriend was down the hall? That I was talking to a guy I'd slept with who was *not* my boyfriend?

"Meredith."

"No big deal, right? I was just calling you because it was funny." I twirled my finger in my hair and felt it pull against my scalp. "I thought you'd think it was funny."

"Meredith."

"What? What! You keep saying my name."

"Don't call me."

"Don't . . ."

"Don't call me."

"But—"

"And don't use Nate's phone. Jesus."

My mind spun. We were friends. He'd said we were friends, so it was okay that I called him. What was his problem? "It was funny," I said for the hundredth time. "The girl with the pink hair . . . looking at me . . ."

I heard Lee breathing on the other end of the phone.

"Lee, I—"

"Don't call me. Don't."

And then the call ended. I pulled the phone away from my ear and stared at the screen. It didn't say Call Failed or Call Lost.

Call Ended. Lee had hung up on me.

I had only meant to share a joke between friends. He was wrong. I pressed call again on Lee's number and waited. It went immediately to voice mail. "Yo, it's Lee. Leave a message."

Was that all I'd wanted from him? No. I wanted—no,

needed—I needed to talk to him. About us. About what had happened between us.

But we weren't friends. Lee and Nate were friends. Lee and I were not. I felt my cheeks grow hot and my eyes sting with tears. How stupid could I be? Calling Lee? And from Nate's phone? God, what an idiot! I stared at the phone in my hand as if I'd never seen a cell before.

Bodies swarmed around me, jostling me out of my reverie; the previous showing's audience emptied out of the theater, voices rising as they poured into the lobby. They laughed and cheered and whistled to each other. In groups and on dates, they checked their phones and took selfies in front of the movie posters.

At the other end of the theater, I saw Nate leave the concession stand, his arms filled with treats. I quickly erased the two calls from his phone's recent history and shoved it in my pocket.

I felt so alone. Shut out by Nate, shut off by Lee. What did I have? What did I want?

CHAPTER twenty-three

Our school's winter formal was more "semi" than "formal." Girls wore calf-length dresses, rather than floor-length, and boys wore jackets and ties, not tuxes. It was held in a decorated gym, not off-site, which made it similar to the homecoming dance, but we did traditionally have a buffet table and a live band. This year's formal had an '80s theme, but there was no way any of us were going to wear frosted hair or dresses with giant shoulder pads.

Haley's date was Brett Miller, a shy running back who had asked her out by text.

"Is that bad? That's not bad, is it?" Haley had called me one night the week before the dance. It was a welcome interruption from my studies.

"He seems like a nice guy. You like him?"

"I do. He's cute, and I like his blond crew cut and his freckles." Haley giggled over the phone. "And he says he likes to dance. And you know how I like to dance."

"Is he boyfriend material?"

I could sense her shrug. "Maybe. I don't know. Can we double with you and Nate?"

"Are you sure? It's your first date."

"I know! Maybe we should do a test run."

I laughed. "You'll be fine."

"You know what you're wearing?"

I stepped over to my closet and found the dress I'd worn last year, when Nate was a senior. It was a forest-green satin, just below the knee-length, with a scoop neck and cap sleeves. I'd paired it with green satin flats, although it had been raining that day so I'd ended up bringing the shoes with me in my purse and wearing boots in the car. Nate really liked the dress: simple and elegant. He probably wouldn't mind if I wore it again this year.

But *I* would.

". . . big fat curls with a curling iron," Haley was saying. "Corey Sanchez said she would loan me hers."

"I'm sure curls will look great on you."

"I hope so." Haley sounded worried, which was very unlike her. "I want to look good for my *date*," she said with a nervous giggle. "Ack! Date!"

"You'll be fine," I told her again. "We'll be there to help."

"I need you to be good role models!" she said.

"For Brett?"

"For me!"

By seven o'clock on Saturday night, the gymnasium had been transformed into a winter wonderland, complete with disco ball and dance floor, live band on a raised stage, and buffet table under one of the basketball hoops.

As soon as we arrived, Nate was swarmed by fans and friends, students and teachers, and even a few of the chaperones. Everyone wanted his attention. They all wanted to hear his story.

I found seats at a table not far from the dance floor and then took Haley with me to get food and drinks for all of us.

"Isn't this kind of cliché?" she asked me as we scooped pink punch from a bowl into paper cups. "The girls getting the guys food?"

"Nate's really tired, so I thought he should sit for a while."

"Ohh, you're being nice, not submissive. That's different."

I glanced down at the plate in my hands. I'd filled it with Nate's favorite foods: Doritos and cool ranch dip, BBQ spareribs, chicken nuggets and spicy mustard. That wasn't being cliché, was it? That was being nice.

I finished filling the plate and turned to look for Haley to walk back with me, but she was at the gym entrance with

Katrina and Debra. The three were comparing their dresses and shoes, taking photos and laughing. They spotted me and waved me over. I glanced at Nate, but he was deep in conversation with one of the chaperones. A few minutes with the girls wouldn't be a big deal.

"Middie, get in the middle!" Haley said.

"Hey, that rhymes!" Debra said with a slightly tipsy giggle. She leaned into Katrina and the two began laughing.

"Get in, get in!" Haley held up her phone and we all squeezed our faces together, getting as close as possible. "Say cheese!"

"Naked cheese!" I said, and immediately the girls roared with laughter. I clapped a hand over my mouth. That was Lee's, I remembered, from the skinny dip. I had no idea why it popped out, but—

"Feet selfie!" Debra said, and we all put our shoes next to each other so Haley could snap her phone over them.

"Lip selfie!" Katrina said, and we all mooshed our mouths side by side.

"Booty selfie!" Haley shouted. The four of us wiggled our butts next to one another and someone—not Haley—snapped a photo or ten.

By then, others had noticed us and had their phones out too, aimed at the four of us. Haley held her hand in front of her rear end. "Please, respect our butt privacy," she said and began laughing hysterically.

I held my hands in front of her butt too. "No more

pictures, please." And then we were all trying to cover each other up, arms and shoulders and backs and legs bumping into one another and we couldn't stop laughing. It was stupid silly, and maybe these pictures might end up on someone's Instagram, but who cared? It was senior year and this was winter formal, and we only got one chance at it, so why not make it fun?

I looked up and caught Nate's eye across the room. He was watching us intently, so I gave him a little wave and blew him a kiss, expecting he would at least grin back, but he frowned and went back to his conversation. I felt my enthusiasm flag a bit.

Well, okay, then.

". . . must have been a nightmare," the chaperone was saying to Nate when I got to the table with the plate of snacks. He had his foot on a chair and was leaning in toward Nate. "Damn, son, you were lucky the Devil had one eye closed."

"Yes, sir, it was pretty harrowing," Nate said. As usual, he appeared confident and comfortable in the presence of his fans, old and young.

"Maybe I should hang out with—" I started to say, but Nate pulled me down into a chair.

"Sit, Middie. I just want to be with you tonight."

Eventually the chaperones gave way to current basketball players, some of whom had played with Nate during his senior year. The conversation became a lot livelier and Nate loosened up.

"That play was *not* my idea," he told a former teammate. "Do you think I would ever send Jake up the center—you remember the size of that point guard! He was huge!"

The group laughed, but I was restless and bored. I searched the room for Haley and found her on the dance floor with Brett. Not far from her were Debra and Katrina, both of whom were dancing with guys I didn't know. The band was playing '80s covers, everything from Madonna and Michael Jackson to Culture Club and The Police.

The girls' skin glistened with sweat and their smiles lit up the small dance floor. I felt their energy and longed to join in. I turned to Nate, half rising from my chair. "Could you manage a dance?"

"Oh geez, I don't think so, Mid," he said to me. "Not my thing, you know that."

I did know that, but that was the past, the way it had always been. Couldn't we try something new, something a little more fun than sitting on the sidelines? "But you said you wanted to be with me tonight."

Nate's gaze flitted over my shoulder. "Maybe Lee will dance with you."

"Lee?" I whipped my head around to see Lee approaching the table. Alone. What was he doing here? Alumni didn't come to these dances, and Lee couldn't have been invited by a current student. Could he? I searched the room behind him but didn't see Liza anywhere either. I turned back to Nate. "I really don't think so."

"Lee? Hey, man, you want to dance with Middie?" Nate called to him.

I held my hand up, as if I could stop Lee in his tracks. I didn't even want to make eye contact. "I'm good. I can dance by myself."

He paused at the outer circle of the table. He was dressed completely inappropriately, as if he were headed for a concert instead of a formal: a powder-blue Captain America T-shirt under a slate-gray suit jacket, and, of course, jeans and his Converse low-tops.

He sipped from a paper cup that looked insanely small in his hand, as if he were suddenly a giant in the land of the little people. But it was only a Dixie cup, not a full-size one. He caught me looking at the cup. "They ran out of the regular ones," he explained. "And now I'm Gulliver in Lilliput."

I smiled. That was exactly what I was thinking. I was about to comment, but then I saw the blank look on his face and in his eyes, a vacant expressionless stare that told me he could not care one iota less than he did at that very moment. I felt my grin melt away.

We stood like that for another long minute, awkward and weird. He was swaying a bit, and I wasn't sure if he'd had a couple beers or if he wanted to dance.

I hadn't ever seen Lee dance. I had no idea if he could. Or would.

Haley and Brett came at us then, giddily hopping and goofing around. They both looked so ridiculous, but they were having such fun that I couldn't stop laughing. Beside me, Lee couldn't resist either; a sliver of a grin pierced his cold veneer. Haley and Brett grabbed us, pulling us out onto the dance floor with them, and then, miraculously, I was dancing with Lee.

Kind of. He didn't dance so much as step-touch, step-touch, and his arms sort of swung by his sides. We danced about three feet apart, our attention anywhere but on each other: Haley, Brett, the band, the disco ball, the crowd at the buffet.

My friends cheered and shouted for more just as the song ended.

"We've got a couple more songs coming up before we take a break," the lead singer of the band said into his mike. He looked a little like the '80s himself: spiky gelled hair, oversize shiny sports jacket with the sleeves pushed up to his elbows, skinny black pants and sneakers. "So why don't we slow it down a notch, okay, kids?"

Kids? Ugh. Even I groaned at that.

"One, two, three, four . . . ," he said, off mike, and the band began to play a soft ballad.

Just as Brett and Haley collapsed into each other's arms, I glanced at Lee, who met my gaze and then quickly looked away. My cue to leave. But the crowd wouldn't let me: suddenly there was a surge of slow-jamming couples on the dance floor, squeezing me in place. My back was up against Brett, and my front . . .

"Excuse me," Lee said. He was talking over my shoulder as he tried to maneuver around me, but it was nearly impossible. The couples were moving us closer and closer together, pressing us hip to hip, thigh to thigh. My face was inches from the lapel of his jacket, the slightly frayed edge brushing my nose and cheeks as I breathed. I could smell sweat mixed with deodorant, shaving cream with beer, and the sickly sweet scent of the pink punch on his lips.

I felt his hands on my elbows, guiding my arms around his waist, even as his gaze was far beyond me and the dance floor. I was stunned—after all he'd said on the phone? In the blink of an eye, our knees touched, our legs parted, our hips swayed. The heat between us was undeniable.

"I know this much is true . . ."

I glanced around at the couples on the floor: each of them was absorbed in the starry glow that surrounded them; they whispered and giggled, some wore goofy smiles, others were moon-faced and swoony. No one kissed—that was a no-no, along with grinding and twerking and any other vulgar displays—but I could feel the *wanting* to kiss and the *longing* to be kissed. It was like a virus being passed from couple to couple. I wondered if it would infect Lee and me.

"I know this much is true . . ."

My fingers interlaced at the small of his back, under his jacket. I could feel his heart thundering behind his rib cage and down his spine. My own pulse raced in rhythm with his, and I felt my skin tingle and tremble when he pressed his palms on my waist. From the neck down, we could not have been closer or more intimate, but . . .

"I know this much is . . ."

Suddenly he wrenched himself out of my arms and took off, his thin frame easily winding among the couples until he reached the edge of the dance floor.

Wait, Lee! I thought, but I couldn't call to him, couldn't shout his name.

So I ran.

I tried not to call attention to myself, tried not to make it appear as if I was running after him. I followed him past the buffet, through the gym entrance, and out the front door of the school.

As soon as we were out at the semicircle, I called his name. He stopped but didn't turn around. His arms hung by his sides and he looked off toward the parking lot. *Inches from a clean getaway,* his body language seemed to say.

I caught up to him but kept my distance. Fog swirled around the hem of my dress like wisps of smoke. "Lee, I—"

His cheeks were flush and his eyes red-rimmed. "Leave me alone, Meredith. Leave me. Alone."

"But we were just dancing—"

"Just stop, okay? Tell yourself whatever the fuck you want, but you were not *just* dancing with me." He snorted and shook his head. His hands twitched and trembled.

"Me? *You* were the one who—"

"Do you want me to tell Nate you cheated on him?" His

voice was cruel and his words clipped.

I felt my stomach drop to my feet. "I never cheated. We both thought he . . ."

"And after he came back, after we *knew* he was safe," Lee said, "what about then? What about your calls and texts *since then*?" He pulled his phone out and held it aloft.

"I didn't cheat," I said softly, casting my gaze away from the phone, away from the evidence. My eyes followed the trails of fog that spun around my legs and feet, tangling the lace edge of my skirt.

"You did and you still are," Lee replied.

"You're wrong. I love Nate."

Lee waved his hand back and forth between us. "Then what is this? Huh? What the fuck are you doing?"

"I . . ." I didn't know. I heard the words "I love Nate" and I knew they were true—

I know this much is . . .

—but I also knew how I felt when I was with Lee. And I knew he felt it too. I lifted my eyes from the ground and found his. For a split second, I saw fear and vulnerability behind his anger. "Lee—"

Just as quickly, he closed back up. "You're not supposed to be with me," he said coldly. "Don't you get it? The future is you and Nate. So just go ahead and get back to it. That's what you want, isn't it?"

I started toward him, my hand raised to his chest, but he hopped back and away as if I were on fire, spinning around and out of my reach. I felt like an idiot following him, but he was wrong in so many ways.

"Don't, Middie. Don't make me tell Nate." Lee shook his head, backing away from me and out of the circular driveway. "I can't hurt him like that. He's the best fucking friend I have in the world."

"It wasn't just me. It couldn't have been," I said quietly.

"I don't love you," he said. "I felt sorry for you. Nate is the one who loves you. Him. Not me. *Him*."

"Then what are you doing here, huh? Why did you come to a dance you weren't invited to? Do you normally crash high school parties?" I put my fists on my hips. "Oh yeah, that's right. You came to our senior party too. Guess you're just a loser with nothing better to do."

He turned without another word and walked toward his Vespa in the parking lot.

"Wait, Lee, I didn't mean that!" I watched, unwilling to believe he wouldn't have a change of heart, wouldn't at least glance back at me, but he didn't. The scooter disappeared, its taillights fading quickly in the foggy night.

I didn't know how long I stood there, long enough for the fog to re-form in Lee's spot, replacing him as if he'd never been there. I hugged my arms around my waist, suddenly feeling the cold, and turned back toward the school's entrance.

My breath hiccupped in my chest when I saw Nate standing at the top step, his weight leaning against the open door. We stared at each other in silence.

With every step I took, my heart pounded harder and harder. *When had Nate come outside?* What had he heard or seen? Inch by inch, my mind raced and my thoughts spun.

Finally I reached the landing and looked at him. He said nothing but stood aside and held the door open for me. Our arms brushed lightly as I walked past him.

He knows.

CHAPTER twenty-four

He knows.

We returned to the dance, to our table, and not long after-ward, left. While I drove, Haley and Brett giggled and kissed in the backseat. After dropping them at Haley's house, I took Nate home. I tried not to grip the wheel as I steered, tried to slow the pace of my beating heart, but it was impossible. The tension in the car was as thick as the fog outside it.

What are you waiting for? I wanted to shout at Nate. *Say something!*

It felt like a year from the time we left Haley's until I pulled up Nate's driveway. With every twist and turn in the road, I thought something would stir within him, jostle him to life, but he remained stoically silent.

The car rolled to a stop and Nate slowly eased himself out of the passenger side, one long leg at a time. I could tell he was in physical pain, tired from the long night, and he exhaled with a sigh as he stood up. I started to get out of the car, but he stopped me.

"I'm good," he said quietly. "I'll talk to you tomorrow."

But, but, but—

The words *I'm so sorry* were on the tip of my tongue, but I couldn't speak them aloud. I felt like something was stuck in my throat and I couldn't breathe. As Nate started up the steps of his house, I saw an image of him standing at the school, his eyes on me as I turned away from Lee. It burned itself into my brain, refusing to let go.

Even after I'd been home for hours, after I'd said good night to my parents, carefully hung up Allison's dress, and washed my makeup off, I still could not get that picture of Nate out of my head.

I lay in bed, curled up on my side and face buried in my pillow, cursing myself for what I'd done.

Tears soaked my pillowcase; I'd screwed everything up. Everything. I had the best guy in the world and I was throwing him away for what? For whom?

And what was worse, Nate had seen what an awful person I was, how deceitful I could be. I'd hurt him and I'd hurt us. I wouldn't blame him if he hated me forever.

* * *

For the rest of the weekend, I must have checked my phone about a hundred times every hour, but Nate never called or texted me. I ran the scenario in my mind over and over again, trying to imagine the timing of when Lee left, how close Nate was to us, how quickly he could have gotten outside, and how much of the conversation he might have heard. Each time I did, I came to a different conclusion. It was like living in purgatory.

So it was a tremendous shock when I got a call from him on Monday morning at our usual time. "Ready to go?" he asked, as if nothing had happened.

I hustled outside and met him on the road before he could get to my house.

I did the same thing on Tuesday and on Wednesday, and each time, Nate didn't speak a word about the dance. He talked about the speech he was going to give in a few weeks, about my grades, about my essay. We made jokes about Emma and her Brownie troop. We wondered how much longer she would idolize him.

Had I been in some alternate universe on Saturday night?

Each morning I felt like I was running on weak ice, as if I might slip at any moment and crack through to freezing water. Would today be the day Nate asked me about Lee?

How about today?

Or today?

And when would I have the guts to tell him?

Never.

I had to. But I couldn't. And it ate at me every single day. My stomach cinched up when my phone rang and didn't relax until long after I was in the shower, until I was on my way to school.

"Earth to Middie?" Haley called to me on Friday morning, knocking loudly on my locker door. "You awake yet?"

"Yeah, I'm awake," I said. I dove into my locker and searched for a clean pad of notebook paper and pens that didn't leak. I was a little tired, true, and certainly distracted. And so was she: a minute after she'd arrived at my locker, Brett appeared behind her.

She giggled as he put his hand over her eyes. "Um, is it Ryan Gosling?"

"Uh-uh."

"Justin Bieber?"

"Ugh, gross, no!" Brett said and released her. She tumbled backward into his arms and he landed a kiss on her lips.

I busied myself in my locker, humming to myself and tuning them out. I knew it was hypocritical of me, but their PDA irritated me. I just didn't want to watch another couple together.

A moment later, Haley knocked again on the metal door—alone. Brett was gone. "I had to deal with *your* smoochy-smoochy with Nate for years."

"You're right," I agreed. "I'm sorry. He's a nice guy."

"And he's a good kisser too. Just the right amount of tongue."

"Good. I'm glad. I think."

Haley laughed. "I don't know if he's, like, *the one*. Not like Nate is for you. But I like hanging with him."

I avoided my best friend's gaze. "Yeah, sure."

"I mean, no one's like Nate."

My heart and brain tugged as she said his name again, I wished I could tell her about Nate, but then I'd have to confess about Lee, and there was no way I would do that. I shut my locker and we headed down the hallway, arms locked at the elbow.

"The formal's over, Middie! It's just a few months until graduation."

I nodded, but my thoughts were still absorbed by Nate and Lee.

"Hey," Haley said, concern in her voice. "You okay? Something you want to talk about?"

I hoped she couldn't read everything on my face. I shook my head and tried to smile. "Crazy, you know? Just . . . crazy. Nate and graduation and—"

"Whoo-hoo!" Haley's eyes lit up. "Senior year!"

We arrived at homeroom and Haley and I jostled each other goofily as we tried to enter side by side. "I'm gonna miss you when you're off at school with Nate," she said in a voice that was quiet by Haley's standards. "I kind of feel like I was starting to see a new side of you."

I leaned into her. "Yeah, me too."

* * *

By Saturday night, I'd apologized to Nate in about a million ways, but only in my imagination. He picked me up in his truck without telling me where we were headed, except to say it was a nice restaurant. I chose one of Allison's pretty dresses; it had a floral skirt that swirled around my knees. I paired it with short black booties and wore my hair loose and in waves.

Tonight had to be the night to talk about Lee. I wasn't even sure I could eat if we didn't get this out in the open.

The restaurant was a seafood place that was known for serving huge amounts of fish and pasta that people took home in Styrofoam containers. Nate and I sat near one of the many fish tanks; the bubbling water was like a musical accompaniment to our meal.

Throughout dinner, I sensed something was coming, something horrible. The question was, should I wait for Nate to bring it up or should I suck it up, be a big girl, and do it myself?

"Middie, I want to talk to you."

Too late. This is it. He had a week to think about it; maybe he even talked to Lee. The knot in my stomach tightened.

He reached under his chair and pulled out a plastic bag. He handed it to me. "Go ahead, take it."

I unwrapped the bag and saw the beautiful wooden box I'd given him. The light in the restaurant hit the delicate curlicues and hand-cut metal hinges.

"I can't believe you had it all this time," I said with a

gasp. The wood was chipped in a few places and the bottom was slightly bowed, but otherwise it was in near-perfect condition.

"It was tough to hold on to. I almost left my backpack behind," he said, as if he too were amazed he still had it. "But I grabbed it when I ran out, and I guess that's how I was found . . . with it." He shook his head. "Crazy, huh?"

I ran my fingers over the design, feeling the swirls and ridges as if I were reading Braille.

"Open it."

"Hmm?"

"Open it." Nate's eyes shone.

I carefully flipped the clasp and used my fingernails to peel apart the top lid. The velvet lining was ripped, sadly, and the box itself was empty. I smiled, remembering all the items I'd placed inside. "Is everything gone?"

"Yeah, mostly."

I felt the loss of the items in the box as if they were my own. And then I recalled the secret hiding spot at the bottom of the box. "Did you find it?" I asked. If he had, he'd know exactly what I meant.

With a sly grin, he took his wallet out and opened it to show me. Nestled beside a couple of twenties and tens was a triangular-shaped paper, what everyone called "footballs": blue-lined notebook paper folded into a stiff triangle, ends tucked into one side. It was a "football" because one kid would hold his fingers up on the edge of a desk as if they were a goal post and another would try to flick the paper over with his finger.

But we also used them to pass notes. One person would write on the paper, fold it, flick it across a desk to someone else who would then write on it, fold it back up, and flick it to the next person. This was a note between me and Nate from when he was a sophomore and I was a freshman. There was something more exciting about an actual physical note than a text. It was more personal, more intimate to feel the paper in my hand, paper we had both touched. I'd tucked one into the bottom of the shade box for Nate to find.

I took it from his wallet and unfolded it. Almost instantly I began to tear up. The words, in black and blue ink and pencil, began to blur in front of my eyes.

> *You look supergood in that sweater.*
> *I was late to class because of you!*
> *What time's the movie tonight?*
> *I miss you!!!!*

"How long did we keep that one going?" he asked me. "Can you figure it out?"

I shook my head. "A week? Our handwriting got smaller and smaller to fit on the paper."

"And the triangle got softer and softer," he said.

I looked up from the note and held Nate's gentle gaze. "You kept it."

"Well, to be honest, I didn't actually find it until I was back in the city." Nate's smile was sheepish. "You hid it pretty well."

I felt absurdly proud of that. "Thank you."

"You're welcome. Now go ahead and look inside."

"I did. It's empty."

"Is it?"

The secret compartment. My eyes flew open when I saw what was inside.

A ring.

I stared at it, mouth agape.

"It's not what you think!" Nate held up his hand quickly. "It's a promise. Me to you. And, hopefully, you to me."

The ring wasn't fancy, just a simple band of white gold with a small diamond surrounded by a trio of emeralds. Nate's grandmother had given it to him before she'd passed away two years ago. I knew she intended the ring for me—she'd approved of me from our first meeting—but I doubted she knew it was coming to me before my eighteenth birthday.

I took the ring from him and held it up but couldn't bring myself to put it on my finger. *Winter formal.* My brain flashed to the school, to the Vespa's taillights in the fog, to Nate standing at the front door. I had to say something. I set the ring down on the table. "Nate, I have to tell you something."

He sat back in his chair and regarded me. "It's over, isn't it?"

"It's . . . what?" I felt panic grip my chest.

"You and Lee?"

"You knew?"

"Lee told me."

My whole body froze in place. "When did he . . . What did he tell you?"

Nate shook his head dismissively. "Look, you both thought I was a goner out there. I did too."

"But . . ." Did he know we'd texted? That I'd called Lee? That he was still on my mind?

"Lee told me it was over. He said he's seeing someone else now. A girl named Liza? I don't know. They work together or something."

My heart sank. "He . . . he said that? Yeah, good, that's good that he told you. When, um, when was this?"

"After the dance."

I saw something move out of the corner of my eye. Nate was holding the ring up again. "It's all right. I understand. You thought I was gone. Middie, I wasn't even sure I was alive myself. But I'm back now and . . . Please, Middie. Take it."

This was a second chance with Nate. I'd blown it, but now I could make it up to him. All I had to do was take the ring. That was what I should do, right?

"You and me," Nate said. "Just like we always planned."

I pulled back and met his gaze. "You're sure that's what you want?"

"It's what I've *always* wanted," he said. "Haven't you? Can't you see us together?"

I could. I had. But did I still?

Nate pointed to the wooden box on the table. "That proved it to me," he said. "That proved how perfect we are together."

Perfect. I felt the weight of expectation settle on my shoulders. I didn't want to disappoint Nate. How could I, after all he'd been through?

He still loved me. He still wanted to be with me. I would be a fool to turn him down.

And besides, Lee is with another girl. He doesn't love me. He never loved me.

My cheeks flushed and my lips trembled: Had I really just thought those words? Lee had nothing to do with this. It was about Nate and me.

"Middie?" Nate said quietly, his voice hopeful.

I took the ring from Nate and slipped it over the third finger of my right hand. "Yes," I said. "Yes, I promise."

CHAPTER *twenty-five*

Snap!

"I am so sending this out to the interwebs," Haley said as she clicked her iPhone over my ring. We were at a corner table at the Matchbox on Monday afternoon, drinking giant cups of frothy cappuccino.

"It's not really something to celebrate," I'd cautioned her when I showed her the ring at my locker that morning. "I'm not even wearing it on my left hand."

She aimed her phone on an angle and squinted at the image on the screen. "Don't move. This is perfect."

Snap! More typing. Another picture sent out into the ether.

She saw my worried look and waved me away. "It's just a few friends, not the world. Did you set a date?" she asked, settling back in her chair and crossing long, muscular legs in front of her as she sipped at her coffee.

"I told you it's not official. We are not actually *engaged*."

Haley's phone buzzed on the table and she grinned at it. "Hang on. Text. Corey. And another from Katrina. Oh, a third from Debra. Can I tell them we're here?" she asked even as she typed a response. "Katrina says don't say any-thing until she gets here. Okay?"

"But there's nothing—"

"Ah! Stop!" She held a palm up to me while she tapped her phone with the other hand. "They'll be over in, like, five. Let's just sit quietly."

"No more pictures?"

"No more pictures."

I splayed the fingers of my right hand on top of the table and adjusted the ring so the diamond and emeralds were perfectly centered. I felt incredibly lucky: Nate had forgiven me and Lee. Every single one of my friends would jump at the chance to be in my position. It was kind of insane that he wanted *me*.

"What are you getting Nate for Valentine's Day?" I heard Haley ask.

"Oh geez, I have no idea," I said.

"It better be something special after he gave you that blingy-bling."

I twisted the ring on my finger just as my phone buzzed with a text. Allison. *Omg! xoxoxox*

I smiled at the message. She sent another: *Best guy ever! Lucky!*

I was. Luckiest girl ever.

Then I wondered who else had seen Haley's photos.

Between final exams and taking the SATs for a second time, the rest of January passed in a blur. But I did manage to find the perfect Valentine's Day gift for Nate, and I couldn't wait to give it to him.

About an hour before Nate was coming to pick me up, Emma waltzed into my room with a wrapped box and crawled onto my bed. "It's not for you," she said. "It's for Nate. Can I give it to him tonight?"

"You want to go on our date?"

She rolled her eyes as if I were stupid. "He's coming here first. I want to give it to him then. *Before* you give him yours," she added.

I handed the present back with a grin and shooed her off the bed. "Sure, now go so I can get ready for my *date*."

"Okay, okay," she grumbled, dragging herself to the door. "You and Nate are getting married now, aren't you?"

I froze. "What makes you say that?"

"The ring. Allison said that's an engagement ring."

"Well, not really, but—"

"If you and Nate don't get married, can I marry him?"

"Can you . . . ?"

"Not *now*," she said. "I'm not old enough yet. Duh."

"Maybe you should ask Nate instead of me."

"Oh. Okay." She shrugged and left my room.

Nine years old, I thought. *Only nine and she has her whole life planned out. First she will conquer Brownies, then the Girl Scouts, and then Nate. If she were ten years older, she probably would make a good choice for him.* I laughed to myself.

The moment he arrived, before he could even set foot in the living room, Emma thrust her present at Nate. "Happy Valentine's Day! This is from me. Not Middie."

Nate accepted the gift graciously, of course, and even gave her a peck on the cheek as a thank-you. She'd made him an intricate friendship bracelet with very masculine colors of brown and navy blue, which he insisted on wearing right away.

"Okay, Middie, it's your turn," she said.

I glanced at Nate. "Well, I kind of thought I'd give you your present when we were out."

"You don't mind doing it now, do you?" he asked.

"Okay, sure." I pulled a flat box out from the dining room and handed it to him. "You first," I told him as I sat down on the couch beside him. I couldn't wait to see the look on his face when he saw what I'd gotten him.

Emma hung over Nate's shoulder as he carefully unwrapped the paper. "Rip it!" she shouted at him. "Don't be neat!"

He grinned at her and then up at me. "You sound just like your sister."

As usual, Nate took his sweet time. He even paused briefly to smooth the unwrapped paper with his fingers and place it in a neat pile. Finally, he opened the top of the box.

Under the tissue paper was a brand-new shade box to replace the one that had been damaged in the jungle. Nate's eyes lit up. "Middie! It's perfect."

I grinned, happy he liked it. "It's not as nice as the other one—"

"I love it."

"And it's not filled like the other one—"

"We'll fill it together." He leaned over and kissed me quickly on the lips. "Now open yours." He handed me a much larger box, also flat, wrapped expertly in red-and-white Valentine's Day paper.

With great care, I shook the box from side to side and then held it aloft as if I could see through the bottom of the wrapping. Then, unlike Nate, I tore off the ribbons and paper and threw them in the air like confetti. Emma clapped her hands. Inside, under a layer of white tissue paper, was a dress.

A blue dress.

A plain blue dress.

I stood and held it up to my body. It was conservatively styled, with cuffed sleeves and cloth-covered buttons, a thin belt around the waist, and a stiff pointed collar. The material was twill, smooth and satiny, and the hem fell to my knees.

It was ugly. It was boring.

It was . . . not me.

Not me *anymore*.

"I like it!" Emma said.

I felt Nate's eyes on me, waiting for my response. I . . .

I hate it.

I glanced up at him. "It's nice."

Nate let out a breath. "Allison helped me pick it out. I wanted to get you something new so you wouldn't have to wear her clothes anymore."

"Her clothes?"

"Yeah, they were nice, but they really weren't *you*." Nate's eyes lit up. "You can wear it next week on campus. Allison said it will look good with my suit."

"Ooh, can I come?" Emma asked. "I want to see you give your speech!"

And in that moment, I saw my life ahead as plain as the dress in my hands: no surprises, no challenges, no changes allowed. Our lives would be as neatly put together as the folded wrapping paper on the table. Our clothes would match. Our schools would match. Our schedules would match. Our lives would match.

Nate wanted to return to the security he'd had before his trip.

I wanted the messiness I'd had after he left.

He wanted comfort and simple colors.

I wanted lace and high-heeled boots and skirts that swirled.

I carefully folded the dress back into the box and replaced the lid. Then I put it down on the coffee table.

"Middie? Is it the wrong size?" Nate asked. "Do you want to exchange it?"

I stared at the box and said nothing. But there must have been something in my body language that told Emma that I wanted some privacy with Nate, because she scurried up the stairs to her room, leaving us alone. I walked over to the fireplace and picked up a photograph of all of us and Nate at a barbecue about seven years ago. Emma was just a toddler holding on to Nate's legs for support. Nate had been in our lives then, even when he was just a friend.

He was just a friend. *He's just a friend.*

I twisted the ring off my finger and, turning from the fireplace, held it out to Nate in the palm of my hand. "I can't take this."

"But why? I thought everything was back to normal."

"It . . . is. It is back to normal, and I guess . . . I guess I don't want normal." Objects in the room swam before my eyes—the couch, the coffee table, the gifts and wrapping paper—as if I were underwater. Nate gazed down at his lap, at his grandmother's ring.

"I don't understand. I love you. Don't you love me?"

"I do love you. I'll always love you, but . . . I'm sorry, Nate," I whispered.

Nate wouldn't yell. I knew that. He wouldn't throw anything or lose his temper. Although I wished he would. It would make it a lot easier to say good-bye.

"You're . . . sure?" he asked me quietly.

I nodded quickly before I completely lost it. "I really am. I'm horrible, a horrible person."

"You could never be horrible," he whispered.

I closed my eyes and felt tears fall down my cheeks.

He stood and tucked the ring into his pocket. His face was so long, so forlorn, I wanted to tell him, *Wait! I'm wrong, I'm so wrong, I didn't mean any of it. Please take me back—*

But I didn't. I watched him go, leaving the present I'd gotten him.

I held the box and felt the years of friendship, of love, of Nate and Middie together forever, stretch between us. We'd been each other's first everythings: date, kiss, make-out session. We'd been to proms and swim parties, to church potlucks and summer barbecues. We'd marched in parades down Main Street and attended CPR classes together. School and family and friends were all intertwined for years and years and years.

I loved Nate. I loved who he was in my life. But I wanted to have *more* experiences in my life.

Tell us about an experience that defines you.

I didn't want the definition of me to be Nate.

I wanted more *firsts* in my life, and even some seconds and thirds.

I let go of the box. I let go of Nate.

I arrived at Lee's house at dusk and the place looked closed up, doors locked, windows dark. I didn't see the Vespa anywhere, so I assumed Lee was out with Liza to celebrate Valentine's Day.

I didn't really want to see him. I only wanted to drop off his sweatshirt, the one he'd loaned me on our night in the tree house. With this, I was free of all . . . entanglements. I was finally just me, just Middie.

No. *Meredith.* I was Meredith Daniels.

Just as I placed a plastic bag with the hoodie on the front step of Lee's house, I heard the *crunch* of gravel behind me and turned to see Lee ride up on his Vespa, alone. He swung his leg off the seat and dropped the kickstand. "What are you doing?" he asked, his voice hard.

"Leaving."

"What's that?" He bobbed his head at the bag at my feet.

"Yours."

He crossed the space between us in several long strides and snatched the bag off the step. "My sweatshirt."

"What'd you think it was?" I felt my voice rise. I should have stepped back and away from him as he approached, but I held my ground. "I don't keep anything that isn't mine."

He stared down at me. "Neither do I."

"If it's not freely given to me, I don't want it."

"Neither do I," he said again.

We were inches apart but truly so far away from each other. A cool moist wind blew through us and between us. Snow was in the air.

"I should go," I said, trying to keep my tone firm but light. I didn't need Lee to see I was still nervous around him, that my skin still tingled when I was near him and my heart thumped in my ears. I started to walk around him, but he stopped me.

"Does Nate know you're here?" he asked. I shook my head and he snorted derisively. "Figures."

Anger bubbled up in me. I clenched my fingers into fists by my sides. "I never *cheated*. Nate was gone. You were here. Nate came back. You were gone." I leaned into him. "See how that works? No cheating."

He laughed once and took a step toward me. "Please. You still wanted me even when he was around."

I rolled my eyes. "You? Get over yourself."

"Still calling, still texting—"

"Still crashing parties you weren't invited to." Even as we argued, our bodies moved closer, as if we were magnetized to each other. The gap between us narrowed to centimeters, until we were separated by just the clothes we were wearing. I felt my fingers reaching toward him, felt his hips sway into mine and his breath blow the delicate hairs on my cheek. We were so close I could almost hear his heart beating through his chest.

His lips were nearly touching mine. "Why are you here? Go back to Nate and start planning your silly little wedding."

"You knew about that?" I asked.

"I'm not completely ignorant of social media." Lee's eyes blazed. "And I know I could never give something like *that* to you. Manicured lawns and perfection? Look at my crappy bullshit fucking life." He gestured a long arm at his house, at the peeling paint and bent window shades. "That's why I am your backup plan. The guy you keep in the wings in case anything happens. Like when someone *dies*. I will not be your backup plan."

I wanted to slap him across the face. "Tell me you don't love me," I said.

"I don't love you."

"I don't believe you."

"I *don't* love you."

He started to walk away.

"But I love you," I blurted. He spun back to face me, stared hard at me again.

I scoffed and shook my head at him. "You are a fucking idiot, you know that? Do you know what I did, Lee? Huh? I destroyed everything. I fucked it all up. I threw it all away. All that perfection, all that manicured crap? It's gone, all gone. The ideal guy, the perfect future, the having the world on a string?" I made a snipping gesture in the air. "I cut it loose. I cut *Nate* loose."

Lee stared. His mouth opened and closed.

"And I don't know what there was between us, but I know that it *felt right*. And that was enough. I had to be honest—with myself and with Nate."

Lee, his face pale, said nothing, so I kept going.

"Oh, and the ring?" I held up both hands, flipped them over, showed him they were empty. "I gave it back. And I don't want one from *you*. I don't want anything from you. All I wanted—all I cared about in the time we were together—was that *you saw me*." I lowered my voice to a whisper. "You saw me."

I waited for him to respond. His face was blank. He was utterly silent.

Seriously? I turned sharply and stalked away.

I got behind the wheel of my mom's car and tried to put the keys in the ignition. My fingers fumbled, dropping them on the floor, and when I picked my head back up, I saw Lee leaning his hands on the hood of the car.

We stared at each other through the windshield. Snowflakes fell like tears, kissing the glass. I watched as Lee came to the driver's-side door, opening it and lifting me to my feet. He wrapped his arms around me and pressed his lips to mine.

I felt myself melt under his touch. My hands slid around his back and under his jacket; I could feel the heat of his skin through his shirt. It warmed me from my spine to my toes.

"I see you," he said, his voice, raspy and coarse. "All I see is you."

Lee backed me up against the side of the car and pinned me in place. He pressed his hands on either side of me; I couldn't move even if I wanted to. He grinned slyly at me. "And now I have you where I want you."

I grinned back. "Who says I don't have *you* where I want *you*?"

"Touché, Meredith Daniels. Touché." He bent his head to my neck. "I love you," I heard him mumble.

"What was that?" I managed to unpin myself enough to gently push him away from me. "Did you say something?"

He shook his head. "Must have been the wind."

"Huh? Really? I would have sworn you said 'I lo—'"

He kissed me again, but I didn't mind the interruption. Finally, he paused and let out a long, slow exhale. He looked up at the sky and blinked. "Did you notice it's snowing?"

I tilted my head up; delicate flakes dotted my nose and cheeks. "Yeah, it is."

"What should we do now?"

I shrugged. "Maybe we should run away together."

Lee feigned astonishment. "That's awfully spontaneous. Next you'll tell me you want to join the circus." I felt him kiss the corner of my lips as I smiled.

"I've got a great magic act," I said. "I can make an entire future disappear."

He leaned into me. "Show me everything."

I laced my hands around the back of his neck and pulled him to me. "All right. I will."

Tell Us About an Experience That Defines You.

One? There is no one experience—no one person, no one event—that defines me. As Walt Whitman once wrote, "I contain multitudes." Life is messy. Plans are written and rewritten, tossed up and down and around. The only way to find out who you really are is to take a risk, a leap, a walk under a waterfall. When you stop worrying that you'll have nothing, then you know you're on the right path.

ACKNOWLEDGMENTS

This book is a work of fiction—except for the parts inspired by all the guys who broke my heart and the few whose hearts I broke. They know who they are, although some of the former might think they're the latter. Thank you.

This book is also a work of love. Extraspecial thanks go to my editor, Kristen Pettit (who never forgot me—thank you!), who didn't mind sharing her own stories of heartbreak and loss with me; to editorial director Jen Klonsky and editorial assistant Elizabeth Lynch, both of whom championed the book and provided much-appreciated support from day one; and to the sales and marketing team at HarperCollins, cover designer Michelle Taormina, and copy editor Janet

Robbins, whose combined professionalism, talent, and eye for the smallest detail make me so proud to be part of their world. Thank you.

I am grateful to Charlie Olsen at InkWell Management, and my manager and good friend, Adam Peck at Synchronicity Management, and all of my students and friends for their kindness and encouragement. Writer friends especially know the ups and downs and have just the right words to say: Carrie Watson, Carol Tanzman, Liane Bonin, and Sally Nemeth. Thank you.

My family and husband have always been the ones I can count on through the best and worst of it all, and there isn't enough time and space to let them know how much they mean to me. Thank you.

Born in Europe and raised in America, CAT JORDAN has spent her life in the visual and performing arts as a dancer, painter, and filmmaker. A nomad by nature, she's found inspiration for her stories and choreography around the world—from Venice, California, to Venice, Italy. You can visit her online at www.catjordanbooks.com.

JOIN THE Epic Reads COMMUNITY

THE ULTIMATE YA DESTINATION

◀ **DISCOVER** ▶
your next favorite read

◀ **MEET** ▶
new authors to love

◀ **WIN** ▶
free books

◀ **SHARE** ▶
infographics, playlists, quizzes, and more

◀ **WATCH** ▶
the latest videos

◀ **TUNE IN** ▶
to Tea Time with Team Epic Reads